PURSUIT

The driver of the Impreza didn't let that stop him, however. He sped down the street, heading for Riverside Street. If he got there, Kate would never catch him before he got on the highway.

"Yes," said Trepalli on the phone as she nudged the Forester to a little more speed. The Impreza slammed on the brakes as a car pulled out from a side street and Trepalli immediately rattled off, "CGB... damn."

The Impreza had shot around the other car and, ignoring the stop sign, pulled into traffic on Riverside. Horns blared and cars swerved but there were no accidents.

She reached the corner while the drivers were still screaming curses at the Impreza and turned right.

"Where is it?" she asked.

"I can't see it," said Marco. Then, "There!" He pointed with the cell phone and Kate caught a glimpse of a white car taking the on ramp onto the highway. She accelerated and passed two slower moving vehicles, but by the time she had taken the on ramp, the Impreza was long gone.

THE**UNTETHERED**WOMAN

by

MARCELLE DUBÉ

FALCON
RIDGE
PUBLISHING

*For Karen Abrahamson, who has talked
me off the ledge a few times.*

THEUNTETHEREDWOMAN

by

MARCELLE DUBÉ

CHAPTER 1

K ATE WALKED as fast as she could down the length of the empty Pierre Trudeau Airport terminal. At five feet three inches, she had been cursed with short legs and always felt she had to hurry so as not to be left behind. Nevertheless, she quickly outdistanced her fellow passengers, still slowly disembarking from the last flight from Winnipeg. She hadn't checked her brown leather tote bag and had refused to let the flight attendant take it from her, even though the flight was full. She had traveled all the way from Winnipeg to Montreal with the bag stuffed under the seat in front of her.

It was past midnight and all the magazine, coffee, and gift shops at this end of the terminal were shut behind metal screens, and the various embarkation gates were dark and empty. A faint smell of burnt coffee lingered in the air. The crowd of passengers shuffling behind her was curiously quiet, as if trying not to wake the airport.

At last she reached the staircase that led to the luggage pickup and exit area. She took the escalator, slinging her tote bag over her shoulder and running down the moving stairs, her sneaker soles slapping against the metal treads. Then she was past the baggy-eyed security guard and through the sliding glass door into the cavernous arrivals area, with its row of parallel conveyor belts standing still and mute, awaiting luggage.

The humidity hit her then and she immediately felt her scalp prickle with sweat. She always forgot just how humid Montreal got, even in September, unlike Manitoba where the same temperature was much more bearable in the dry air.

At the far end of the arrivals area, people milled around, obviously waiting for arriving passengers. Beyond them, a wall of glass interspersed with revolving doors led to the Montreal night, although all she could see right now was the reflection of the lights from the arrivals area. Already people were moving toward her as more and more passengers emerged through the glass doors behind her. She glanced from face to face and suddenly one face sprang into focus. John.

Kate's heart squeezed at seeing her brother-in-law's tall, lanky, jeans-clad figure striding toward her. She had been expecting Rose. Did that mean...?

Her running shoes squeaked on the floor as she hurried to meet John. He stooped to kiss her on the cheek, gave her a quick, fierce hug, then grabbed her bag with one hand and propelled her into movement with the other on the small of her back.

Before she could catch her breath to ask, he said, "She's still unconscious, but she's stable. There's no immediate danger."

Kate nodded even as she half ran to keep up with him. His hand left her back to grab her hand.

"Where's Rose?" In spite of her need to move fast, she suddenly found herself wondering why John was hurrying her along. Were things worse than he was saying?

"At the hospital." He held her close as he swept through the sliding glass doors into the Montreal night and its smell of moist earth and car exhaust. A string of at least a dozen taxis waited patiently at the curb for the attendant to call them up. Kate blinked at the concrete car park looming before her, and the car lanes, mostly empty, between her and the structure. Now they would wind their way through it, find the car, then pay at the toll booth before they were finally free to leave the airport grounds. Fatigue suddenly dropped on her shoulders like a heavy cloak.

Then John dropped her hand, fished through his jeans pocket, and pulled out a set of car keys. He pointed at a late model, dark blue—or was it black?—Subaru Forester, parked alone in an area clearly marked "AIRPORT PERSONNEL ONLY," and the car's lights sprang on.

Kate finally caught her breath when he popped the back of the Subaru and tossed her bag in.

"How did you manage this?" She waved at the forbidden parking spot.

John shrugged. "It's almost one in the morning." He closed the back of the car and grinned at her. "And the attendant is one of my students." He waved at the attendant, a tall young man with dark hair, who nodded back at him.

"Let's go," said John.

* * *

John and Rose lived in the old section of St. Lambert, a small town on the south shore of Montreal. It had been around nearly as long as Montreal itself and its core, the Village, always struck Kate as an odd mix of modern multi-story buildings and centuries-old heritage homes, most of which had been turned into museums or other public buildings.

But it had no hospital. Mom was in Armand-Cadieux Hospital in Greenfield Park, just past St. Lambert. John took the Champlain Bridge to cross the St. Lawrence River. This was Kate's favorite bridge, especially at night. Its wide open span left the view unimpeded, and she usually took a moment to admire the night lights on the approaching shore. It was more dramatic when they were driving into Montreal, of course, with its skyscrapers and fanciful light displays, but she liked both views.

This time, however, she spent the forty-five-minute drive grilling her brother-in-law about the accident. There'd been no time when Rose called. Kate had been meeting with her deputy chief—

was it only a few hours ago?—in his office when the call came.

They had been working on a proposal she wanted to bring to the upcoming meeting of southern Manitoba chiefs of police, who met twice a year to discuss issues of common interest.

This time, Kate wanted to bring forward an idea she and McKell had been batting around for a month or so, a kind of cop exchange that would see constables from smaller communities working in the bigger centers for a month or two, maybe even three, to give them the opportunity to experience policing in a bigger city. At the same time, constables in the bigger centers would take over their colleague's spot in the small towns, to learn about the restrictions of living and working in a small community.

Kate had read studies from Germany and England where this had been tried. Success had varied, of course, but when it worked, the exchange resulted in stronger networks between bigger centers and rural areas.

It would have been easier to travel in to Winnipeg together, but McKell hadn't wanted to stay at the meeting all day. After all, it was a chiefs' meeting.

"Besides," he added. "I'm scheduled to attend the parole board hearing at Red Hill on the same day. It could be tight." He leaned back in his old-fashioned wooden swivel chair. It creaked under his six-feet, solid frame but he didn't look worried. Not much worried Rob McKell, she'd come to realize in the year and a bit they had worked together.

"Are you a witness?" she asked him.

"Yes," said her DC with satisfaction. "I get to testify against that little pissant." McKell had short, graying brown hair and a receding hairline, which on him had the effect of highlighting his bone structure and very nice blue eyes. Blue eyes that almost danced in anticipation.

Kate suppressed a grin. "Anyone I know?"

He shook his head. "Before your time. Heck, before my time here. It's from my days as a military cop at Shilo." He sat up straight, and the chair protested loudly. "My car's still in the shop. I'll have to use a spare patrol car."

Kate nodded. That was fine. They didn't need it and he might only be gone for the morning, depending on the parole board hearing, while she would be home late that night. Ordinarily, she would spend the night at Bert's, but he was away at a forensics conference in Vancouver.

That was when Charlotte, the station's admin assistant, knocked on McKell's door jamb.

"Chief, you've got a call." Charlotte's pretty green eyes held a hint of concern. "It's your sister."

Kate glanced at DC McKell. "Excuse me, Rob," she said. "We'll finish this up later."

All thoughts of meetings and hearings disappeared when she got to her office and punched the button with the blinking light on her land line.

"Rose?" Her shoulders tightened a little. Rose never called her at work.

"Katie," said Rose. Her voice sounded thick, as if she'd been crying. "You need to come home. Mom's in the hospital. She was hit by a car."

Kate's legs gave way and she suddenly found herself sitting in the guest chair. She wanted to demand answers but she felt like she'd been punched in the gut and could only breathe in gasps.

"We don't know how bad it is," continued Rose. "I've bought you a ticket on the eight o'clock flight tonight. I emailed it to you. You're going to need to hurry."

Kate had automatically glanced at her watch. It was already almost four and it was a one-hour drive to the airport in Winnipeg. "All right," she had said. "Meet me in Montreal." And with that, she had hurried off to tell DC McKell and throw a few things into a bag.

Now, on the drive to the hospital, John patiently answered her questions.

"She's got a broken leg, but her hips are fine. She's got two cracked ribs and a concussion from her head hitting the pavement. A cut on her scalp." He glanced at Kate. "The whole side of her face is bruised, but that will heal. They're worried about the concussion."

Kate swallowed back the nausea that had accompanied her all the way from Mendenhall. Mom had been hit by a car. Dear God.

"How did it happen?" she asked.

In profile, John's chin jutted out in a familiar way. He was angry.

"A hit-and-run driver," said her brother-in-law. "Hetty was crossing the street in front of Madame Sophie's house when a car came out of nowhere and clipped her." He glanced at her. "He never even stopped and she never saw it coming."

Kate clasped her hands in her lap to still their trembling.

"Were there any witnesses?" she asked calmly. "How do you know the driver was male?"

John skillfully negotiated the bridge's off ramp and headed into St. Lambert. Instead of turning toward his house, however, he kept going toward Taschereau Boulevard. The highway was almost empty and the garages and car dealerships they passed stood dark and sleeping.

"A kid," said John. "He was skateboarding down the middle of the road and saw the whole thing. He said the car was a Kia Soul, dark green. He even caught part of the plate number. He saw that it was a man with dark hair and glasses, but that's all."

Kate's cop brain took over from the angry daughter. A Kia Soul. That was a fair-sized car. The vehicle couldn't have been going very fast, or it would have killed her mother.

"Are the police investigating?"

John shrugged and turned onto Taschereau. There were lots of cars on the multi-lane boulevard, even at that hour. Kate's stomach squeezed a little when she saw the big yellow bulk of Armand-Cadieux Hospital off to her right.

"I spoke to an Officer Claveau. I don't know how much effort they're going to put into it. It's not like it's a murder or anything."

The bitterness in John's voice belied his words and Kate clamped her mouth shut on the bad words that wanted to come out. First things first. She had to see Mom. Then she'd see about finding the driver.

* * *

"She's in intensive care?" Kate's voice rose on the last word as she turned an accusing look on John. He shook his head in bafflement.

"Madame," said the woman at the admissions desk quietly but firmly, "please keep your voice down."

"She was in Emergency the last time I saw her," he said. "Intensive Care must be better than that."

Kate bit the inside of her mouth and forced herself to calm down. It was the middle of the night, in spite of which the Emergency ward bustled with activity and noise. She glanced at the dozens of people seated in the waiting area. A few faces were turned her way. She blinked in an effort to get moisture into her sore eyes.

She turned back to the admissions clerk and reminded herself that the young woman was only doing her job.

"I'm sorry," said Kate sincerely. "Is my sister still with her?"

The young woman, whose name tag read "Antoinette," gave Kate a small smile and a shrug. She had lovely brown eyes and kept her thick, dark hair in a no-nonsense ponytail. "I do not know, madame," she said. Despite her heavy French-Canadian accent, her English was excellent. She glanced around, but there was no one waiting behind Kate and John. "I could call up and find out." She reached for the telephone.

"Mademoiselle," John leaned forward past Kate's shoulder and spoke into the round speaker embedded in the bullet-proof glass. "Perhaps we could go up and speak to the nurse in charge?" He had removed his Tilley hat when they entered the hospital and now he clutched it in the big, bony hand that rested on the counter. He stared intently into her eyes.

The young woman hesitated. Then she glanced at her watch. Finally she looked up at John. "Third floor. Follow the signs. If you cause a disturbance or disobey the nurse in charge, I'll come up there myself and throw you out."

John gave her a rakish grin and turned away. Kate glanced at the young woman and raised her eyebrows. The young woman rolled her eyes and shrugged, and Kate gave her a grateful smile before turning away to follow John to the elevators.

As soon as the elevator disgorged them onto the ward, John headed toward the horseshoe-shaped nursing station. In spite of the lateness of the hour, Intensive Care hummed with quiet purpose. The hallway lights were muted, with only the nursing station providing an island of light. Like the Intensive Care ward back home in Mendenhall, the nursing station was at the entrance to the ward. Kate glanced down the hallway. At least a dozen rooms, each with the door half open. As she watched, two nurses came out of two different rooms and converged in the hallway. They spoke for a few moments and one patted the other on the arm before turning around and reentering the room she had just left. The other nurse glanced at a clipboard she was carrying and headed for another room.

An older nurse sat at the nursing station, monitoring the various screens and telltales arrayed around her. She typed on a keyboard at intervals. She glanced up with a frown as John approached. The male nurse working next to her never took his eyes off the monitors.

"This floor is closed to visitors," said the older nurse in a low voice that nevertheless carried authority, "especially at this hour." Kate thought she detected a faint Scottish burr in her voice. The woman's name tag read "HATHAWAY."

Kate spoke before John could exercise his charm and possibly get them kicked out. By the look on this woman's face, she had seen too much to let a pair of intense brown eyes sway her.

"Ma'am," said Kate softly. "I've just flown in from Winnipeg. My mother was in a hit-and-run..." She stopped talking suddenly as her throat closed up and her eyes filled with tears. Damn. She had been doing so well.

But something in the nurse's world-weary eyes softened. Even the male nurse glanced up at them.

"Hesther Whibley?"

Kate blinked at the woman in incomprehension. Then John leaned over.

"Yes, that's right," he said.

Only then did Kate remember that in Quebec, hospitals used a woman's maiden name to identify her.

Nurse Hathaway nodded. "Your sister is with her," she said. "Why don't you wait in the family room and I'll fetch her."

Kate opened her mouth to ask which room was Mom's, but John took her by the arm and led her away. This habit of his was becoming irritating.

He stopped in front of a closed door labeled "FAMILY ROOM" and gently pushed it open. It was dark inside and Kate automatically reached for the switch. The lights came on to reveal a room the size of her living room in Mendenhall, with a flat-screen television perched in one corner high up on the wall, two easy chairs, a square, battered coffee table with a dozen magazines strewn over its surface, and two full-length couches facing each other across the coffee table.

On the one facing the door, her niece Amanda slept under a thin, blue, worn blanket.

Kate and John stood watching the young woman sleep. Kate found herself smiling. Amanda looked like Sleeping Beauty. Lord, she had missed the girl. Even as Kate considered reaching back to turn off the lights, Amanda bolted up and threw the blanket off.

"Grams?" she said. Then she sat, blinking up at them, as realization slowly seeped in behind her eyes. At last she looked at her watch, then looked up at her dad. "Any change?"

John shook his head and closed the door behind them so that

their conversation wouldn't disturb the quiet of the ward.

"No. The nurse has gone to get your mom. Maybe she can tell us something more."

Amanda stood up, the blanket pooling half on, half off the couch. She wore jeans and a heavy cotton sweater in yellow. Her hair floated around her face and shoulders in becoming disarray and her cheeks were flushed with sleep. Her blue eyes were bloodshot and there were dark circles beneath her eyes.

Kate found herself wondering how much of the tiredness came from the last fifteen hours, and how much had to do with her decision to break up with Marco Trepalli, the youngest—and handsomest—constable at the Mendenhall detachment.

At last, Amanda met Kate's gaze.

"Hi, Aunt Kate."

"Hello, Pumpkin," said Kate softly, and then Amanda was in Kate's arms and they were hugging tightly.

Amanda had left Mendenhall a month ago. She had packed up all her catering equipment and stored the boxes in Kate's shed, put her suitcases in her little Tercel, and returned to Montreal, six months after first arriving in Mendenhall. It was only after she was gone that Kate learned Marco Trepalli had asked the girl to marry him and that she had said no.

Kate missed her. She missed sharing her small house with her niece, missed their long, lingering dinners on the back deck, missed having young people come by the house to hang out. But Amanda was twenty-five. Maybe Mendenhall—and Marco—had been a passing fancy.

They disentangled themselves, but before Kate could ask any questions, the door opened again and Rose came in.

Kate caught her breath. Rose's short, artificially dark hair was disheveled. That in itself was to be expected, given the situation. But Rose wore no makeup, and that was completely unexpected. Her normally plump cheeks looked drawn and her dark eyes were lined with dozens of tiny wrinkles that Kate had never noticed before. Between her expertly plucked eyebrows lived a deep furrow. She looked much older than her forty-nine years.

Rose's gaze went automatically to her husband and then found Kate.

"You made it," she said with relief.

Kate walked around the coffee table to hug her sister.

"What about Charlie and Sean?" she remembered to ask.

"Charlie's in the Arctic still," said John from behind her. "And Sean is somewhere in the North Atlantic. We've left messages but who knows when they'll get them, and then make their way back."

Kate disentangled herself from her sister. Their brother Charlie and her nephew Sean were both marine biologists and spent a lot of time on scientific expeditions.

"How is she?" she finally asked, still holding her sister's shoulders.

Rose stepped back and ran her hands down her white linen shirt in an effort to smooth the wrinkles out. She, too, wore jeans, and a pair of flat, slip-on shoes in a buttery yellow leather. Kate couldn't remember ever seeing her sister dressed so casually.

"It could be worse," said Rose grimly. She sat down in one of the easy chairs and gestured at the others to sit, too. Kate sat down on the couch Amanda had been occupying and pulled the blanket up from the floor and onto the cushion next to her.

"The car couldn't have been going very fast," continued Rose, confirming Kate's suspicions, "or her injuries would have been much worse. According to the doctors, the car just bumped her hard enough to crack her tibia. Most of the injuries came from the fall." She took a deep, shaky breath. "She was carrying a parcel. She'd been to Madame Sophie's, just across the street." She looked at Kate, who nodded. Yes, she remembered Madame Sophie. The elderly woman was ten years older than Mom. The two had been friends for decades.

"She couldn't move her hands fast enough to break her fall," said John suddenly, startling Kate. She had been so focused on

Rose's words she had almost forgotten his presence. "She landed hard on her side and cracked a few ribs. Scraped her whole right side."

"The head injury is what's most worrisome," continued Rose. "Her head hit the pavement and caused a concussion." She faltered to a stop and clasped her hands in her lap. John went to sit on the arm of her chair and took one of her hands in his, and suddenly Kate desperately wished that Bert could be here.

"How bad?" she asked.

"If the brain swelling doesn't start going down," said Rose tremulously, "they're going to have to operate to relieve the pressure."

Kate's insides slowly turned to ice as the implications sank in. Mom was seventy-eight. Any operation at that age would be risky, but a brain operation…

"I want to see her," she said suddenly and stood up.

Rose nodded. "I know." She stood up, too. "They will only allow one of us in there at a time." She shrugged. "There's really no point to any of us being there. They're keeping her in an artificially induced coma until the brain swelling goes down."

Yes, Kate understood that. But she still needed to see her mother. Needed to see for herself that Hetty Williams was alive. Without a word, she stepped toward the door, then stopped. She looked at Rose over her shoulder.

"Room 3008," said Rose quietly. "Across the hall, to your left."

Kate nodded and opened the door, aware that the others were watching her leave and making no effort to follow. Had John seen Mom yet? Had Amanda?

Down the hallway, Nurse Hathaway glanced up when Kate emerged from the room. She watched as Kate closed the door behind her and softly crossed the hallway, heading for Room 3008. The male nurse had disappeared, but a young female nurse was seated at the console, keeping her eye on the monitors.

Kate reached her mother's room and gently pushed the door open. The room was dark except for two night lights plugged into the wall sockets, one by the door, and one by her bed. She paused a moment to let her eyes adjust then closed the door behind her. The room was small, with space enough for one bed. The remaining space was filled with equipment bolted to the wall at the head of the bed or standing free on either side. A variety of machines gave off faint greenish or reddish glows from their tiny screens and each one seemed to whoosh or whir faintly. The effect was that of white noise.

Finally her eye traced the various tubes and wires trailing from the machines to disappear under the sheets and blanket covering the small figure on the bed.

Kate's first impression was that someone had made a mistake. Her mother was much bigger than this woman.

Then she saw the long, white braid draped carefully over one shoulder and resting on top of the blankets, and in spite of all her efforts to avoid looking, her gaze pulled upward to find her mother's battered face. The entire right side of her face was scraped raw and starting to scab over. Her right eye, temple, and cheek were swollen to almost twice their normal size, distorting her already round face. A bandage wrapped around her head, tinged pink where blood had seeped through.

"Oh, Mom," she whispered. Her feet brought her closer though she wasn't really sure she wanted to be closer. Under the blankets, lying so still, Mom looked smaller. Diminished.

A sob caught in her throat and she swallowed hard, refusing to give in. The family didn't need her tears right now. They needed her strength. There would be time for tears later.

If Bert were here, she could borrow some of his strength. He would know the right things to say.

She realized suddenly that she was stroking Mom's left cheek. Mom had always had the most marvelous complexion. Even now, she barely had any wrinkles.

"That's because the fat plumps them up," she always joked.

Kate smiled and took a deep breath. For the first time, she

noticed the chair tucked in among the equipment, and the blanket tossed over the back. This was where Rose had been keeping watch. She glanced around the tiny, claustrophobic room and made her decision.

She kissed her mother's left cheek and a moment later she was back in the family room.

"Right," she said decisively. "Is she dying?"

Rose's head drew back as if she had been slapped and even Amanda gasped. But John just looked at her.

"No," he said. "There's no immediate danger."

"Then we're going home," said Kate. "In the morning, we'll take turns staying with her." Rose opened her mouth, an argument ready to spill out, and Kate shook her head.

"No, Rose. This is going to be long and drawn out. We're all going to need our rest and we won't be getting it here."

A small smile played around John's lips but it disappeared quickly when Rose turned to him. He nodded.

"She's right, you know. Hetty is in good hands. We won't be doing her any good by getting ourselves exhausted before the real work of recovery starts."

In the end, Rose grudgingly agreed, and Kate thought she saw relief flit over Amanda's features. They stopped at the nursing station and Kate spoke to Nurse Hathaway.

"We're going home for now," she said. "Will you...?"

Nurse Hathaway nodded. "We will call you if there is any serious change to your mother's condition."

"We'll be back in the morning," said Rose.

"Very well," said the nurse, with what Kate thought was a touch of resignation.

And with that, Kate ushered them to the elevator and out of the hospital.

CHAPTER 2

DESPITE her exhaustion, Kate woke up at seven o'clock, which was six o'clock by her internal clock. She sighed and rolled over to stare up at the ceiling. Pale daylight crept in all around the navy cotton curtains of Sean's room.

As sleep slowly receded, she studied the sailing ships printed in white on the curtains, then glanced at the bookshelves where, interspersed among the reference books on marine life, was a collection of tiny wooden sailing ships that Sean had built as a boy.

She always thought it was strange that he had chosen to follow in his Uncle Charlie's footsteps rather than become a geologist, like his dad.

The small desk he had used for his homework had been replaced by a loveseat and the single bed was now a double bed, to accommodate guests. The room was a hybrid of Sean's room and a guest room. Every time she stayed here, she always felt like the boy Sean was just waiting for her to leave so he could get his room back.

Finally she got up and rummaged through her bag on the loveseat to find a sweatshirt to put over her pajamas. Then she padded down the oak-floored hallway and down the stairs to the main floor, following the aroma of coffee all the way to the kitchen. She smiled when she saw Amanda there, chopping red peppers.

"Good morning, Aunt Kate," said the girl with a smile. She still had circles beneath her eyes but her smile was warm. Her hair was up in its customary ponytail and she wore jeans, sandals, and an oversized red sweatshirt emblazoned with U of T. University of Toronto?

Hmm. Amanda had hung on to some of Trepalli's clothes. Interesting.

"Morning, Pumpkin," said Kate, dropping a kiss on her niece's cheek. "Omelet?"

Amanda nodded. "I knew you'd be up soon, so this one is for us. I'll make one for Mom and Dad when they get up."

Kate glanced at the clock above the window over the fancy, underhung kitchen sink. Seven-thirty. She grinned. "I don't know how you got to be an early riser when they both like to sleep in."

Amanda grinned, too. "Are you sure I'm not really *your* daughter and Mom and Dad raised me for you?"

Kate laughed. "I'm sure that's the explanation. You're my secret daughter." It surprised her how much the thought warmed her.

"I don't think so," said Rose, walking into the kitchen and tying a pink robe over a white cotton nightie. "You didn't get that cooking gene from her," she told her daughter, pointing at Kate. Then she glared at Kate. "And if you weren't around for the dirty diapers, you don't get to claim her now."

Kate grinned unrepentantly and walked over to the kitchen sink to wash her hands. Rose wrapped an arm around Amanda's waist and studied the ingredients on the cutting board.

"Better add a few more eggs, sweetheart. Your dad is up, too."

"What is all the ruckus?" asked John plaintively as he entered the kitchen. His brown leather slippers slapped against the tile floor. He had thrown on jeans and a ratty grey sweatshirt with oil stains on the sleeves and holes at the collar and cuffs. His white hair was shaped like a snarled, lopsided bike helmet. He looked like the sole survivor of a bike apocalypse. They all stared at him until he ran his hands self-consciously through his hair.

"What?" he said.

"Omelet in ten minutes," said Amanda. "Dad, you can set the table. Mom, you can help with the mushrooms. Aunt Kate, you can pour everyone some coffee."

Oh yes, thought Kate smugly, *she could so be my daughter.*

When John helped Kate carry the cups to the table, she looked at him sideways.

"Did you call?" she asked softly.

Without looking at her, he nodded.

"No change," he replied, just as quietly.

Kate poured coffee into the mugs. No change in Mom's condition. She didn't know whether to be relieved or anxious.

"I'll take first shift," said Amanda when they were all seated. John had automatically set the small kitchen table, rather than the larger one in the dining room, and they all sat close to each other. "I promised Chef Brabant I would help with a catering job this afternoon." She paused with her fork halfway to her mouth and looked uncertainly at her mother. "Is that all right?"

"Of course it's all right," said Rose. She pushed a stubborn lock of hair out of her eyes. "We've agreed to take turns and there's no point in you sitting around the house. If there's a change, we'll call you."

Kate's gaze dropped to her plate as a silence descended, putting lie to their previous cheerfulness.

If there's a change. In other words, if Mom dies.

"So," she said when the silence threatened to linger. "Who's the officer investigating the case?"

"I have his card," said John, getting up and hurrying out of the kitchen.

Rose and Amanda turned to Kate, frowning.

"Kate," said Rose warningly, "what are you going to do?"

Kate blinked at the warning in her voice. "I'm just going to introduce myself," she said. "Ask if he has any leads."

Before either one could respond, John came back, brandishing a business card.

"Here," he said.

Kate took it and studied it. It read:

Agent Jean-Louis Claveau
Service de police
Agglomération de Longueuil

She stared at it in confusion. Longueuil? Why was the Longueuil police investigating a St. Lambert hit-and-run?

And then she remembered that Longueuil had recently amalgamated all the surrounding, smaller towns. Great. Now she'd be dealing with a cop whose loyalty might or might not be to the citizens of St. Lambert.

"All right," said Amanda, standing up. She took a final sip of her coffee. "I have to go." She glanced around at the kitchen mess. "You all can handle this, right?" And without waiting for their response, she left.

John finished the last bite of omelet. "I'm pretty sure that was a twinkle in her eye."

Kate laughed and started clearing the dishes.

* * *

Once the kitchen was clean and she had taken her shower, Kate escaped to the sun room. It had been added on to the original house about ten years ago and was easily the most used room in the house, accommodating Rose's mini-studio, a television, bookshelves, and comfy rattan furniture. The windows all around the room displayed the view of the large, lush backyard, with its cypress trees bordering the edges, a vegetable garden in the sunny spot by the garage, and a wild garden just below the windows. Kate peered a little more closely. A hint of yellow in the rose bushes on the corner heralded fall. Wouldn't be long now.

She used Rose's land line to call the number on Constable Claveau's card.

"*Service de police*," said a young woman.

"*Bonjour*," said Kate in her rusty French, "I would like to speak with *Agent* Jean-Louis Claveau, please."

"His line is call-forwarded to Reception," replied the young woman in flawless English. "Can someone else help you?"

Kate thought for a moment. The constable's notes might not even be on file yet. The accident only happened yesterday.

"No, I think I'd best speak to him directly," she said finally. "Do you know if he is off duty?" If he was, she would have to finagle his home phone number out of someone. She didn't want to waste time waiting for him to get back. And what if he was on days off? No. She needed to talk to the man.

"I'm sorry, *madame*," said the woman at the other end. Her tone had gone from professionally polite to guarded. "I'm not at liberty to say."

Of course not. Kate sighed silently. All right, then. The hard way.

"I understand," she said. "In that case, may I speak with the duty officer?"

"*Certainement*," said the woman, and Kate thought she detected a hint of relief in her voice. "That would be Sergeant Paul Tremblay. One moment, please."

The line went quiet for long seconds and Kate spent the time imagining the conversation between the young woman and the duty officer. The sun had finally crested the cypress trees in the backyard and shafts of sunlight shot into the room, burnishing the bamboo back of the settee and warming the room by several degrees. A desk stood in the corner, with two large computer screens side by side. In the other corner, where the light would fall on it, was an old-fashioned drafting table, where Rose did the illuminated certificates she specialized in. Kate noted with admiration and no small degree of bemusement that there wasn't a single speck of dust to be seen on any of the surfaces.

"Sergeant Tremblay," said a male voice suddenly in her ear and she jumped. "How can I help you?"

Kate's heart still thudded in residual alarm but she forced her voice to be calm.

"*Bonjour*, Sergeant Tremblay," she said, "thank you for taking my call. My name is Kate Williams. I'm the chief of police of Mendenhall, Manitoba."

There was a silence at the other end as the man assimilated the information. She knew he would be studying the display on his phone to see where the call originated from, and she wondered what his reaction would be when he saw that it was a local number.

"Welcome to Quebec, Chief Williams," said Tremblay politely. And waited.

Kate found herself grinning. She liked this guy.

"Actually, Sergeant, Quebec is home. I grew up in St. Lambert." She pronounced it the French way.

There was a hint of warmth in his voice when next he spoke. "In that case, welcome home, Chief. How can I help you?"

"Thank you," said Kate, recognizing the hint for what it was. "I'm calling for personal reasons. My mother was in a hit-and-run yesterday afternoon here in St. Lambert, and I was hoping to talk to the constable assigned to the investigation."

"I am very sorry to hear about your mother," said Tremblay, his accent suddenly more noticeable. "How is she?"

Tears pricked her eyes suddenly and she swallowed hard. "She's in a coma," she said. "We're hoping for the best, but she's seventy-eight." Her throat closed up and she stopped talking. Dammit.

There was a sigh at the other end. "It will take me a few minutes to discover the name of the officer—"

"I have his card," said Kate quickly. "Jean-Louis Claveau."

"*Un moment*," said Tremblay. She heard keys clacking at the other end as he searched. Finally he came back to her.

"Claveau should be coming on duty at noon. I don't see... ah, here we are. Is your mother's name Hesther Whibley?"

Kate nodded. "Yes, that's her maiden name. Her married name is Williams."

The background noise suddenly rose as a door opened. She heard his muted voice talking to someone else and realized he had placed his hand over the receiver. Finally he spoke again.

"Very few details, I'm afraid," he said. "Only a preliminary report for now. He shows the location of the accident and a brief interview with the person who called it in."

Kate already knew that. Madame Sophie had heard the sound of the car hitting Mom and looked out to see Mom lying on the pavement. She had called nine-one-one before calling Rose. Kate swallowed hard as her breakfast tried to crawl back up. She couldn't stop imagining the sound of the car hitting her mother.

"Madame Sophie," she said softly. "She's eighty-seven and still sharp, though she has a bad heart."

Sergeant Tremblay remained silent, giving her time to compose herself. Finally she gathered her wits.

"What about the witness?" she asked.

"Witness?" repeated the sergeant. He paused, clearly looking the preliminary report. "Only Madame Sophie Bernier."

Kate sat up. "There was a boy, playing in the street," she said. "He gave a description of the driver."

"It's not here." She could hear the shrug in his voice. "But it *is* only a preliminary report. Why don't I ask him to call you when he comes on duty? That way he can fill you in himself."

"Thank you, Sergeant Tremblay," said Kate, recognizing that she'd gone as far as she could with the duty officer. "I appreciate your help." She gave him her cell phone number and hung up.

As frustrating as it was, there was nothing to do now but wait. It might not be surprising that the constable had only filed a preliminary report, depending on how busy he had been yesterday. But his notebook would contain more information, and Kate wanted that information.

She glanced at her watch. Nine-fifteen. Still too early to call Mendenhall—McKell wouldn't be in for another forty-five minutes, or nine o'clock Manitoba time—but Bert would be up. Wait—what time was it in Vancouver? Bert had flown there for a conference, leaving yesterday. No, day before yesterday. Kate had seriously considered sending her DC to the same conference, but she just didn't have the budget for it. Winnipeg's police training budget was much richer than hers. She had pointed out that it was overkill to send a deputy chief to a forensics conference, but Bert had only grinned and promised to share anything he learned with her and McKell.

So, nine-fifteen in Montreal made it six-fifteen in Vancouver. He'd be up. She pulled out her cell phone from her back pocket, looked up her contacts, and hit the "Bert cell" number. After three rings, a gruff male voice answered.

"Langdon."

"Hey," she said.

"Hey yourself," he replied, his voice suddenly gentle. "How's your mom?"

Kate ignored the prickling behind her eyelids and cleared her throat. "Still in a coma. If the swelling of her brain doesn't subside soon, they'll have to operate."

"I'll take the next available flight out."

Kate shook her head. "No. Really."

"Katie," said Bert in his most reasonable tone. "We should be together."

Again, she shook her head. "My family is here and we're all focused on her. If you were here, I'd be grateful, but I'd feel guilty and selfish. And I'd be worrying about keeping you away from your duties."

There was a long silence. Finally, Bert said, "You know when we promised we'd always be honest with each other? I'd kind of like to qualify that now."

Kate laughed. "Oh, Bert—"

"I know, I know," he said grumpily. "But you have to promise to keep me posted. And to let me know if you change your mind."

"I promise."

"I feel pretty useless over here."

She smiled, knowing he would hear it in her voice. "Not useless. I already feel better for talking to you."

"Now you're just buttering me up."

She laughed again, just as Rose appeared at the glass door separating the sun room from the stairs leading to the kitchen. She carried a tray on which sat coffee cups and a French press full of coffee, but before Kate could jump up to help her, she used her elbow to expertly release the catch and pushed the door open with her hip. Kate and Bert signed off and Kate cleared the home decorating magazines off the glass-top coffee table to make space for the tray.

John walked in behind Rose. He still wore jeans, but these were clean. He'd switched out the ratty sweatshirt for a clean white shirt and a tweed jacket. His white hair was brushed straight back, emphasizing his high forehead and piercing dark eyes.

"I have a class at ten-thirty," he said. "After that, I'll relieve Amanda at the hospital." With a nod to them, he grabbed his cream-colored Tilley hat from the coat rack by the door before heading back to give Rose a kiss on the cheek.

"See you later, sweetheart," said Rose absently as she poured coffee into the mugs.

Kate smiled to herself. They'd been married almost thirty years and she suspected they loved each other more than ever.

The door closed firmly behind John and he walked around the side of the house to the gate. A flicker of yellow in the cypress trees reminded her again that fall was just around the corner.

A sudden pang almost doubled her over. Would Mom see another fall?

She stood up suddenly, startling Rose, and grabbed her phone from the coffee table.

"I just have to make a quick call to the station," she told her sister. "Back in a minute." She escaped to the backyard before Rose could see the tears in her eyes.

She hated feeling like this. It wasn't as if Mom were dead. They would run tests and they would fix her.

They would.

She walked around on the grass for a minute, letting the tension ease out through her bare feet. It really was a lovely backyard. There were still a few tiger lilies by the side of the cedar-shingled shed. John had built a patio a few years back and now two lawn chairs sat on it in front of the sun room, beyond the wild garden. When Amanda and Sean were little, there had been an above-ground pool in the yard. She had spent a lot of time in that pool, goofing around with her niece and nephew while Mom and Dad looked on and Rose and John worked the barbecue.

Kate moved to the warm paving stone, feeling the heat seep up through her bare soles while the tops of her feet felt chilled by the breeze. She shivered. She should have put a sweatshirt over her tee-shirt.

Finally she called the station.

"Mendenhall police," came Albertson's voice. "Oh, hey, Chief."

"Hi Stan," said Kate. "How're things at the station?"

"Most of the farmers are bringing in their crops," he said. "Everyone's too busy to cause much trouble. Saturday might be different."

Yes, indeed. On Saturday, the young men and women who had worked so hard all week would want to blow off a little steam.

"So the weather's holding?"

"For now," said Albertson. "They're calling for rain in a couple of days."

So. There wouldn't be too much celebrating on Saturday, then. Everyone would be back in the fields on Sunday. Until the crops were in, everyone worked like fiends to get ahead of the fall rains.

"How are things at your end?" asked Albertson softly.

The damned tears caught her by surprise and she pressed the phone against her chest to cough them out. Finally she brought the phone back to her ear.

"It's too early to tell," she said. She could hear the tightness in her voice. "Some broken bones, but there's brain swelling."

There was a silence at the other end while Albertson absorbed the information. He was an older man, inching ever closer to retirement even though he was only a few years older than her. She would miss his steadying influence on the younger members of her force and his dry sense of humor.

"I'm sorry, Chief," he said finally. "Is there anything we can do at this end?" There was a hint of frustration in his voice, and in spite of everything, she smiled.

"Nothing I can think of, Stan, but thanks. Is the DC around?"

"Yes, ma'am. Transferring."

A moment later, there was a click on the line followed by, "So, how is she?"

McKell was never one for small talk.

"Broken leg, broken ribs. Brain swelling. She's in a coma. We'll find out today if they need to operate to relieve the swelling."

Just like Albertson, McKell paused to assimilate the news.

"Shit," he said finally.

Kate smiled even as the damned tears started leaking out again. Rob McKell never swore or used bad language. This was his odd way of expressing sympathy.

She took a deep breath. "Yes," she agreed. "How's everything there?"

"Nothing to worry about, Chief," he said firmly. "Everything is normal."

"Well, you're understaffed right now," Kate pointed out. Marco Trepalli had left a few days ago for two weeks' leave and

Tourmeline was finally on that forensic fingerprinting course in Ottawa. And now she was away.

"It's nothing we can't handle," said McKell. "But while I have you on the line, want me to give your excuses to the chiefs?"

Oh. She had completely forgotten about the meeting tomorrow.

"I'd like you to go," she said slowly. "You can give the presentation. Otherwise, it'll be another six months before we can talk to all of them in one room. Do you think you can swing it?"

"Sure." She heard the shrug in his voice. "We've been working on it long enough. It's time to float it by them. Besides, it turns out I'm only testifying at the parole board after lunch. Plenty of time."

"Good. Call me after the meeting," she said.

"Will do. And you keep us posted, too."

He hung up without giving her a chance to respond, as though afraid he had already said too much. Kate sighed. A year she'd been working with the man. Would she ever get used to his abrupt ways?

She wanted to go to the hospital and sit by her mother's side and will her to health, but her shift was at six o'clock tonight, after Rose's.

Right. Enough moping. It was going on eleven. She would start interviewing the neighbors right away. No real reason to wait until she spoke with Constable Claveau.

She returned to the sun room where Rose was still sitting, slowly sipping her coffee. A sunbeam had found her lap, turning her soft gray slacks almost white. She wore a pale pink front-buttoned sweater that was probably cashmere, knowing Rose. No earrings—she had never gotten her ears pierced—but she wore a heavy silver bracelet with a bunch of different baubles. She even wore dark gray flats on her feet. Light makeup, short hair brushed until it gleamed darkly... She looked like she was ready to attend a board meeting at some volunteer organization or meet her friends downtown for lunch.

Kate glanced down at her black tee-shirt, jeans, and bare feet, and sighed.

"Any word from Amanda?" she asked as her sister rose to pour Kate a fresh cup of coffee.

Rose shrugged. "She called about half an hour ago. No change. They were going to take Mom for more tests. All right," she said determinedly, sitting back down in the chair next to Kate's. "What are you up to?"

"Up to?" asked Kate. She reached for her cup and then hesitated. Rose had put cream in the coffee. Oh, well. She would just have to force herself.

"Yes, up to," said Rose, leaning back and sipping her coffee. "I know that look, Katie Williams. You're planning something."

Kate sipped her coffee to give herself time to think. Rose had added sugar, too. Cream and sugar. She was trying to avoid both. She glanced sideways at her sister and wasn't surprised to find her staring back knowingly. Kate was the eldest, at fifty four, followed by Charlie at fifty two and, finally, Rose. So why did she always feel like Rose was the older sister?

She sighed.

"I want to talk to Madame Sophie," she said. "And to any other neighbors who might have been around at the time. And I want to talk to the kid who saw what happened."

Rose frowned. "You would just be going over the same ground as the police."

Kate shrugged. "Maybe. But I spoke to the duty officer and he saw no mention of the witness in the officer's preliminary report. Maybe he already spoke to the kid and dismissed his account, but I need to know for sure. Besides, those people know me. They're more likely to talk to me than to the police."

Rose's frown deepened. "You *are* the police. And they're not all the same people you knew as a kid. Those who are still around haven't seen you since you went off to the academy. That's what? Thirty years ago? Thirty-five?" Kate tried to object but Rose just kept talking. "Why not try being a daughter, for once, instead of a cop?"

Kate's mouth opened in shock and heat rose in her cheeks. Of all...

"If you mean that I should sit around wringing my hands and wailing, I'd rather work on finding the bastard who hit her. If it's all the same to you."

The minute she said it, she wished she could cram the words back in her mouth.

Rose's face flushed and her lips tightened.

Crap. Why was it so easy to fall back into the patterns of their childhood?

"That's right, Kate," Rose said stiffly, but before she could finish, the front doorbell rang. Both of them jumped up and coffee sloshed over Kate's jeans.

"Dammit!" The hot liquid seeped through the heavy denim and onto her leg, burning her. While Rose hurried to answer the front door, Kate went to the kitchen and used cold water on the coffee stain. She tried to remember if she had packed another pair of pants in her hurry yesterday.

Out in the hallway, Rose opened the door.

"Hello," she said in a polite tone reserved for strangers.

"Ma'am," said a familiar voice.

Kate stopped scrubbing and raised her head. A wall separated her from the hallway and, damp dishcloth still in hand, she walked over to the doorway and peered down the hallway to the front door.

There, silhouetted against the bright day, stood Marco Trepalli.

CHAPTER 3

TREPALLI stared back at Kate.

"Chief?"

Rose glanced from Kate to Trepalli and back again. "You know each other?" she asked in confusion.

"Trepalli, what the hell—" began Kate, and then the light bulb went off and she closed her eyes. "Oh."

"I have no idea what is going on here," said Rose finally, "but come in."

No, thought Kate, *don't let him in. We really don't need this right now.* But she moved back and made room in the hallway, which suddenly got darker when Trepalli stepped in and Rose closed the door.

"Come to the sun room," said Rose in a tone that presumed obedience. "I'll bring another cup."

Kate silently handed Rose the wet dishcloth and turned to lead the way back down the five steps that led to the sun room. She opened the glass door and went through, holding it open for the constable. She waved him to the settee and let the door close behind her.

His long legs bridged the distance to the settee in two strides and he turned to face her uncertainly. For the first time, she noticed that he was carrying a small bouquet of white freesias. As though the sight triggered her other senses, she realized that she'd been smelling the light, peppery scent for a while. He wore jeans and a light leather jacket, black, and a blue polo shirt that brought out the navy in his eyes. His thick black hair was freshly trimmed and he was freshly shaven.

Gorgeous, of course, but he was still too thin, and the self-confidence—all right, the brashness—was gone. No more swagger for Marco Trepalli. He had been brought down by Amanda's refusal to marry him, and now he was *here*. Here, in her sister's home.

For crying out loud. Amanda had left Manitoba to get away from him. What was he doing?

"Constable, are you stalking my niece?" she asked fiercely, aware that Rose would come in at any moment.

His face turned white, then blotchy. For a moment, she thought he was going to pass out.

"Sit down," she ordered.

He sat down on the couch, his back to the window. She stepped closer and lowered her voice.

"What are you doing here? How did you even know that Amanda is staying here?"

Trepalli looked down at the flowers, then back up at Kate. His color was still high, but there was determination in his eyes.

"I didn't, ma'am," he said. "I came to meet her parents."

Oh, for Pete's sake. The flowers weren't for Amanda. They were for Rose. Kate wanted to roll her eyes but she couldn't help but feel sorry for the boy. He had fallen for Amanda while she was living in Mendenhall and Kate had thought Amanda was in love with him, too. But last month, after an admittedly traumatic experience with an escaped convict, Amanda had moved back to Montreal.

Her decision had shocked Kate, but it had devastated Marco. Kate had watched the youngest member of the Mendenhall Police force grow thin and haggard looking. Even McKell had begun to worry about the boy. So when Trepalli asked for a couple of weeks off to visit his family in Toronto, Kate had agreed with relief, with McKell's support.

They should have known better.

"Chief?"

She blinked. He was looking at her with curiosity.

"I would never have come if I'd known..." he trailed off, obviously realizing he wasn't helping his case.

Kate sighed.

"You couldn't have picked a worse time," she said, her anger suddenly deserting her. She sat down in the wicker chair across from Trepalli and reached for her cup, only to remember it was on the kitchen counter, where she had left it.

"My mother was in an accident yesterday," she said, and proceeded to tell him what had happened.

As she finished, Rose entered with another tray with cups and a small plate of cookies that looked suspiciously like Amanda's chocolate chip cookies. Trepalli sprang up to take the tray from her. There was a moment of awkwardness when he realized he was still holding the flowers, but he managed to bring the tray back to the coffee table without dropping anything. When he straightened, he stood looking down at Rose from his six-foot-one height.

"Ma'am," he said politely. "My name is Marco Trepalli. These are for you." He handed her the flowers.

Rose accepted the flowers with a gracious nod and sat down. Only then did Trepalli resume his seat. Rose slid a sideways glance at Kate, but Kate was too busy biting the inside of her mouth to keep from smiling. This wasn't funny.

Well, maybe a little bit funny.

"Marco is a constable with the Mendenhall police," said Kate carefully.

Rose smiled politely, still confused. "Thank you for the lovely flowers," she said. She leaned forward and put the small bouquet on the table, then picked up the French press and poured coffee into a cup, which she handed to Trepalli.

"Do you have family in the area?" she asked.

"In Toronto. Thank you, ma'am," he said. "I'm very sorry to intrude at a time like this." Almost against his will, his gaze traveled back to Kate. "Do we know anything about the driver? Anybody get plate numbers?"

Out of the corner of her eye, Kate saw Rose's eyebrow lift.

That's right, baby sister, she thought with satisfaction. *That's how cops think.*

"I was about to go interview potential witnesses," said Kate. "And I'm waiting on a phone call from the investigating officer."

"Excuse me?" said Rose, turning to Kate. "Did you send for Mr. Trepalli to help you with this?"

Kate recognized the building anger in Rose's eyes and mentally replayed the last few minutes. She could see how Rose could have misinterpreted Trepalli's arrival.

"Oh," said Trepalli, drawing their attention. He was looking at Rose. "Then I guess Amanda never mentioned me?" There was such disappointment in his voice that Kate's heart went out to the boy. She had told Rose and John that Amanda was seeing someone, but only once she was sure Amanda had mentioned him. After all, the girl was entitled to her privacy. Kate couldn't remember if she'd ever mentioned Trepalli's name, however.

Rose frowned and her eyes got an unfocused look. Then she stood up.

"Are you the boy who broke my daughter's heart?" she demanded.

Uh oh.

"Ma'am?" said Trepalli, nonplussed. As far as he was concerned, Amanda had broken *his* heart.

"Trepalli," said Kate, standing up. "Do you have a car?"

"Yes, ma'am." He rose, too.

"You may as well come with me."

"Yes, ma'am," he said and she was sure she detected a note of relief in his voice. He set the cup down on the table. "Where are we going?"

Kate turned toward the glass door.

"To interview witnesses," she said, and abandoned him to Rose while she fetched her shoes and jacket.

CHAPTER 4

KATE HAD expected a rental car, but the gray Accord was an older model with a small dent in the rear fender. Probably belonged to one of Trepalli's numerous brothers and sisters.

They didn't need the car. Mom's house was only a few blocks away from where Rose and John lived. But it was the only excuse she could think of to get the boy out of Rose's clutches intact.

"What the hell were you thinking?" she asked as she put her seat belt on. She turned to face him but he was staring at the house, where Rose stood in the living room window, staring back at them with her arms crossed. Kate could feel her sister's irritation like a wave of heat on a cold day. She sighed.

"She hates me, doesn't she?" said Trepalli morosely. "Great first impression." He started the car and put his seat belt on.

Kate's first impulse was to reassure him that of course Rose didn't hate him, but she had seen the look on her sister's face when she accused him of breaking Amanda's heart.

"Look," she said carefully, "you don't have to drive me anywhere. The hit-and-run happened just a few streets over. I can walk. Go home."

With a last glance at Rose's house, Trepalli put the Accord in gear and pulled into the street.

"I'm here," he said. "I may as well help. Besides, I haven't met her dad yet." He glanced at her. "Where are we going?"

Kate took a deep breath and clamped her lips shut over the arguments that wanted to tumble out. He wanted to meet John. Of course he wanted to meet John. He probably wanted to declare his intentions about Amanda. Profess his undying love.

She gave him directions past the quiet, well-kept, single-family homes on Rose's street, to where the street ended in a tee intersection at a park that took up most of two blocks. A few young mothers and the odd young father stood around talking while their children played in the playground in the center of the park. When she and Rose were growing up here, the park had been a field, and beyond it, forest. They had played every day in the trees, pretending they were pirates or spies, building forts in winter, playing hide and seek.

Now this area of St. Lambert was built up and filled with older people, most of them retired. But younger families were starting to move back in, attracted by the larger lot sizes and lower prices on the older homes.

"Chief?"

Kate blinked and glanced at the boy. He'd been patiently waiting for her to tell him which way to turn.

"Right," she said, waving in the direction she wanted him to go. "Third street down, turn right again."

There was a *dépanneur* on the corner of Mom's street, where she had bought popsicles when she was a child, and at the other end was the busier Riverside Street that led into the downtown core.

"There," she said, pointing at the two-story brick house in which she had grown up. She had always liked the sand-colored bricks and the decorative stone work where the front met the sides. The white, covered porch was a recent addition. Only fifteen years old. "Park behind the sedan." Mom still drove Dad's old silver Lincoln Continental, even though the thing was a gas guzzler. Of course, she rarely took it out, since she walked everywhere.

She closed her eyes against the sudden pain. Mom wouldn't be walking anytime soon.

Trepalli pulled in and turned the engine off. "Big house."

Kate opened her eyes and peered through windshield at the house. It *was* big, but so were all the houses in this area. It was just the house where she'd grown up. But it had four bedrooms and a study, plus an attic and a low-ceilinged basement where the hot water tank and the furnace lived. Way too big for Mom, but she loved it.

For the first time, she remembered that Mom was supposed to have a—a what? A boyfriend? A beau? Rose had mentioned last month that Mom was seeing a retired colonel. Was she still seeing him? Should someone call him?

"Chief?" said Trepalli again. This time there was worry in his voice.

She smiled and shook her head. "All right, let's do this." She got out of the car and let the door close behind her. The wind ruffled her hair and she realized she had forgotten to put it up. Oh well. She wasn't in uniform, after all.

Trepalli got out of the car, too, and she saw that he had a note-pad with him. Another thing she had forgotten. "You always carry one with you?" she asked, half in amusement, half in curiosity.

He grinned. "You never know when you might need to take notes."

Kate shook her head. "Constable Trepalli, you never cease to amaze me."

He smiled again, but there was a hint of sadness behind it.

"Right," she said firmly. She pointed across and down the street to a two-story house with white clapboard on the front half, and red brick on the back half. There were two front doors, each reached by a separate staircase with wrought iron railings. The doors were separated by a large picture window, which was mir-rored on the second floor. It was seven houses down, almost to the

corner of Riverside. Sophie Bernier had owned the place for as long
as Kate could remember, and rented out the upstairs for a modest
amount so that she could have stability in her renters.

"That's where Madame Sophie lives," she said. "My mother left
her place at about one-thirty yesterday afternoon." Dear Lord—was
it only *yesterday*? "Madame Sophie phoned nine-one-one."

They set out toward Madame Sophie's house, walking pur-
posefully.

"So," said Trepalli casually.

Kate glanced at him, aware that he was shortening his step to
accommodate her shorter legs. The sun gleamed on his head, turning his black hair almost blue. His face was tanned and his eyes
clear and direct. Really, how could Amanda resist him?

"Yes?" replied Kate, steeling herself.

"Did Amanda move back in with her folks?"

Kate looked away. Would Amanda be mad at her if Kate gave
him information? This was why she had disapproved of the relationship in the first place. Even back in February, she had known,
known, that she would end up in the middle of a muddle.

But Amanda had seemed so happy with him…

She sighed. She seemed to be doing an awful lot of sighing
lately. "Yes, Constable. Until she can find her own place."

Trepalli nodded and didn't ask any more questions, thank-
fully.

They reached Madame Sophie's house and Kate paused at the
walk, looking up at the door on the right, at the top of the short
flight of stairs. She was suddenly unsure of herself. Maybe Rose
was right and this wasn't a good idea. When was the last time
she had seen the old lady? Seven years ago? Maybe the woman
wouldn't remember her.

The door suddenly opened and Madame Sophie stepped out.

"Katie Williams, is that you?"

The old woman's voice was still the same: querulous, and with
a thick French accent. She was eighty-seven and lived alone. Al-

ways had. She had never married, had never had children. Every time Kate spent time with the woman, it reaffirmed for her that the universe did indeed unfold as it should.

"Madame Sophie," said Kate, forcing a smile. "It's good to see you."

"*Vraiment?*" said the old woman. "It's unfortunate that it takes your mother getting injured for you to come see me."

Kate swallowed a sigh. Madame Sophie had never liked her. Kate didn't know why. Surely the old woman couldn't still hold a grudge about the baseball through her window?

"Well, don't stand there like a ninny," said Madame Sophie. "Come inside." She turned on her heel and walked back in. She wore a pair of black woolen slacks and a sweater set in a riot of pink and green flowers. She had always been thin, but now she looked angular. She still wore her clothes like she was a fashion model. Even her hair, white but still thick, was up in a fancy bun.

"Looks like she was going out," whispered Trepalli as he climbed the wooden steps behind her.

Kate shook her head. "No. She always dresses up." Probably because she has nothing else to do with her days, she thought, and then was immediately ashamed of herself.

Kate could sense Trepalli's interest but she didn't look at him. Instead, reluctantly, she followed Madame Sophie inside.

"Close the door, young man," came the old woman's voice from inside—*the kitchen*, Kate thought. "You're letting in the flies."

Trepalli quickly followed Kate inside and closed the heavy wooden door behind him. A trio of narrow windows staggered across the top part of the door, letting in enough light to make out a long, dark hallway and a narrow staircase to their right.

Upstairs would be the bedrooms, of course. Kate couldn't remember ever going up there. And if she recalled correctly, the kitchen was at the far end of the hallway, with the sitting room, or salon, as Madame Sophie called it, through the doorway to their left and the dining room beyond it, next to the kitchen.

"Well?" said Madame Sophie. She stood in the doorway to the kitchen, limned by the light coming through.

"Coming," said Kate. She was very careful to wipe her shoes on the door mat before heading down the hallway.

The kitchen immediately brought Kate back to her childhood. Linoleum tiles in a black-and-white checkerboard pattern looked brand new. A large, harvest table with a bench on one side and two chairs on the other took pride of place in the large room. Turquoise Arborite counters, cotton curtains in bright yellow with white flowers, a single door, with a window, leading to the backyard. The only modern things in the room were the stainless steel double-wide refrigerator and gas stove. Only then did Kate remember that Madame Sophie liked to cook.

"Sit," said Madame Sophie as she busied herself with filling a teapot. From the steam emerging from the kettle, Kate guessed the woman had just boiled some water for herself.

She waved Trepalli to the bench and sat down next to him, keeping an eye on the old woman.

Predictably, Trepalli jumped up when Madame Sophie turned with a tray in her hands.

"Allow me, Madame," he said with a smile.

Madame Sophie's eyebrow raised slightly, causing a ripple effect among the tiny wrinkles under her eyebrow. But she allowed Trepalli to take the tray and sat down across from Kate.

"Rose tells me your mother is still in a coma," she said without preamble.

Kate's heart squeezed in pain and she had to look down at the table for a moment. Fortunately, Trepalli covered her reaction by setting the tray down with a clatter.

"Sorry," he apologized, then proceeded to place a china cup and saucer in front of each of their spots. He removed the small milk dispenser, a honey pot, and the spoons, and returned the tray to the counter.

Kate took a deep breath and finally locked up at Madame Sophie.

"She is," she said. "They were going to take her for tests today. After that, we'll know more."

Madame Sophie looked down at her empty cup and said nothing.

She and Mom had been friends for over fifty years. This must be incredibly hard on the old woman.

"Would you like to see her?" Kate asked impulsively and then wished she could retract the invitation. She and Rose had barely been allowed to see Mom. She wasn't at all sure she could convince the nurses to let Madame Sophie in.

But Madame Sophie shook her head. "*Non. Merci.* I have been in too many hospitals lately. I will wait until she is back home."

The faith in the woman's voice was almost Kate's undoing. She swallowed hard, refusing to let the tears come.

"Madame Bernier," said Trepalli suddenly, "I'm sorry. I should have introduced myself. I'm Marco Trepalli. I work with Chief Williams in Mendenhall."

Madame Sophie blinked in confusion, then turned to Kate. "You brought one of your officers with you?"

A bubble of hysterical laughter threatened to escape and Kate coughed.

"Not exactly," she said. "It's a coincidence that Constable Trepalli is here, but since he is here, he's agreed to help me investigate my mother's accident."

"Young man," said Madame Sophie, "please pour the tea."

"Yes, ma'am," said Trepalli, immediately rising to do her bidding.

"You do know that we have very fine policemen here, do you not?" asked Madame Sophie sternly, turning to Kate.

"Yes," agreed Kate. "In fact, I've already been in touch with them." She tried a smile but only got Madame Sophie's frown in return. "I thought I'd check with you to see if you remember anything more. The details we got were very sketchy."

Trepalli finished filling the cups and the old woman thanked him with a nod, then wrapped her thin fingers around the cup as if she were cold.

"Hetty came for lunch." She looked up at Kate. "She always comes for lunch on Wednesdays. On Saturdays, I go to her place."

Kate nodded, but in truth, she hadn't known.

"I made veal scaloppine and a fresh green salad," continued Madame Sophie. Her watery blue eyes unfocused as she remembered. "We had gelato for dessert." She smiled a little. "She has a sweet tooth, your mother."

Kate smiled, too. Yes, Mom did, and as a consequence, she constantly struggled to keep her weight down.

"We had a visit," continued Madame Sophie, "and we decided to go to the new yarn shop, the one on Berthelet." She took a sip of the tea.

Out of the corner of her eye, Kate saw Trepalli add honey to his tea and stir. A breeze had picked up, ruffling the bright curtains in the window. A few leaves dropped from the maple tree shading the backyard. A smell of freshly mown grass wafted in, mingling with the aroma of the Earl Grey tea.

"So Hetty left to get the car. She was carrying a box with a tea set in it. She had broken her teapot and was going to buy another one, but I had a spare set. I expect it's destroyed."

Kate nodded but she didn't know. Rose had mentioned that Mom had been carrying a parcel, but not what had happened to it.

"I decided to change, but I wasn't halfway up the stairs when I heard a sound from the street." She closed her eyes, her papery eyelids fluttering slightly. "I had left all the windows open on the main floor," she explained, her eyes still closed. "Because it was so nice out." She opened her eyes and looked at Kate. "I didn't know what the sound was but I decided to go check. Then I heard a woman scream."

Kate's throat closed on the questions she needed to ask, and she swallowed hard, but they still wouldn't come.

"Was it Mrs. Williams?" asked Trepalli matter of factly.

His tone seemed to snap Madame Sophie out of her distress. She shook her head.

"I think it was Alice Munson. She lives across the way and is home with a new baby. By the time I got outside, she was kneeling next to Hetty on the pavement."

Kate took a tremulous breath. "So you didn't actually see the accident?"

Madame Sophie shook her head. "Non. I didn't know what had happened, only that Hetty was on the pavement." She hesitated. "There was blood. A few more people were coming out of their houses, but most people on this street work during the day. I couldn't be sure that anyone had called for help, so I went back inside and called nine-one-one."

"Then did you go outside?" asked Trepalli. He had pulled out a short pencil and was jotting down notes in his notebook. Madame Sophie seemed nonplussed at his actions, but when he looked up at her, she answered readily.

"Yes, I did. I brought my first aid kit."

Kate and Trepalli looked at her and she shrugged. "I didn't know what else to do."

Kate controlled an impulse to place a hand over the old lady's, knowing it would offend her. Instead, she nodded carefully.

"You couldn't know how severe her injuries were."

Madame Sophie pushed her cup and saucer away and clasped her thin hands together. They were veined and mottled but still retained a hint of the elegance of the woman she had once been.

"The ambulance came soon after," she said with finality.

"Thank you, Madame Sophie," said Kate, recognizing that the woman had reached the end of her willingness to discuss the matter. But Trepalli apparently hadn't.

"Who were the others who showed up?" he asked. "Anybody you didn't know?"

The old lady frowned at him but he just smiled pleasantly and waited.

"Alice. The old fool who lives in the house next to hers, Eli Jacobsen. Étienne Laroche. He's been home sick."

When she lapsed into silence, Kate frowned.

"What about the boy?"

"What boy?" asked Madame Sophie.

"John told me that there was a boy on a skateboard. That he'd seen the driver."

But Madame Sophie's eyebrows both rose in surprise.

"I saw no boy there," she said. "It was a school day, after all."

Kate sat back against the hard wooden chair. Had she misunderstood John? Or was Madame Sophie wrong?

CHAPTER 5

K ATE STOOD staring down at the dark spots on the pavement. She could almost see Mom lying there, covered in scrapes and blood, unconscious, with her brain already swelling dangerously in her skull.

"Chief."

Had she had time to realize what was happening?

"Chief?"

She looked up at Trepalli's touch on her bare arm. The day was warming up and she had removed her jacket. Now the breeze played on the pale hairs on her arms and she shivered a little.

"What is it, Constable?"

He pointed to the slight gutter by the sidewalk. The blue-and-white lid of a teapot lay broken in two amid the leaves and debris. There was no sign of the rest of the teapot, or the box it had been in. Someone must have picked up the pieces and missed these two.

She cleared her throat. "All right," she said. "This is the spot, then."

Trepalli scanned the street on both sides. They stood in the middle, as there was no traffic. Madame Sophie was right. Everyone was at work. A few cars were parked on the street, but most driveways were empty. The houses were a mixture of single-family homes and duplexes, all built in the 1960s of brick and stone. She was aware of the old woman's gaze on her but pretended she didn't know that Madame Sophie was watching them.

"I don't see any skid marks," said Trepalli slowly, still eyeing the street. "This guy didn't even try to brake."

"That's what the kid said."

Trepalli looked down at her. He had taken off his leather jacket, too, and now it hung over his shoulder, hooked by one finger. In his blue polo shirt and jeans, he looked like the picture of virility. Except, of course, for the shadows lurking in his eyes.

"How did you find out about the kid?" he asked.

Kate blinked, thinking back. "My brother-in-law told me. On the way in from the airport."

He nodded. "Then we need to find out who told *him*."

Yes, of course. She pulled out her cell phone and glanced at the time. Almost one o'clock. John would be at the hospital, having replaced Amanda. She looked up his number in her contacts list and called him. As the phone rang, Trepalli took her elbow and gently nudged her out of the center of the street. Only then did she become aware that a car was coming. They stood on the sidewalk as it drove by. After four rings, John answered.

"Kate? What's the matter?"

"Nothing," she hurriedly assured him. "How's Mom?"

"They just wheeled her out. I think they're doing an MRI. Or maybe it's a CT scan—I can't remember. Her color is better today, but the bruising is pretty horrible."

"When will they have the results?"

"Later this afternoon, I hope." He hesitated and she could imagine him standing in the hospital room, a big man more accustomed to roaming the wilderness in search of rock formations than sitting in a hospital room, waiting.

Trepalli cleared his throat and Kate nodded.

"John, on the way from the airport, you told me that a kid on a skateboard had seen the driver of the car. Who told you?"

There was a long silence at the other end. Finally Kate said, "John?"

"I'm trying," he said impatiently. "A lot was happening at the same time."

Kate nodded, even though he couldn't see her. "Does Constable Claveau know about the kid?"

"Not from me," said John and she could hear the shrug in his voice. "He barely spoke to me, once he found out I hadn't seen anything."

She could sympathize with John's frustration, but she also understood the investigating officer's point of view. It was crucial to talk to people who had witnessed the accident or its aftermath while their memories were still fresh. If John hadn't seen anything, then Claveau wouldn't want to waste any time on him.

"All right," said Kate. "I'll see you later then."

"I'll be home as soon as Rose relieves me," said John. "Who knows? I may even have news."

They signed off and Kate sighed.

"No luck," she said. "He can't remember who told him."

"Well, someone saw the kid," said Trepalli. "Let's knock on some doors."

Kate couldn't help but smile. Trepalli was always willing to put in the work, even the grunt work. Canvassing was never a cop's favorite job, but it was often crucial to an investigation. Sometimes people didn't realize what they knew until the right question was asked.

They spent the next hour knocking on doors on both sides of the street. There was no answer at most of them, but at six, the homeowners were home.

They spoke to Alice Munson and Eli Jacobsen, neither of whom had actually seen the accident or the car. Étienne Laroche was not home. Presumably he felt better today. Neither Alice, nor Eli, nor any of the other people they spoke to had seen a kid on a skateboard.

"For Pete's sake," said Kate when they ended up back at Trepalli's car. "Someone must have seen *something*."

Trepalli had flung his jacket into the back seat and now he leaned back against the Accord's dusty trunk, one foot resting on the bumper.

"It's gotta be Laroche," he said. "He's the only one we haven't interviewed. We can come back later, when he's home."

Kate shook her head. "I'll be at the hospital until late tonight."

Trepalli studied her face for a moment. "All right," he said. "I'll ask Ms. Munson if she knows where he works. Or maybe Jacobsen or Madame Bernier know."

Before she could say anything, he took off at a lope down the sidewalk. He bounded up the steps of the duplex where Alice Munson lived and rang the doorbell. When she answered, they spoke for a few minutes, then Trepalli turned and ran back down the stairs only to head for Jacobsen's house.

Her phone suddenly rang, startling her, and she fished it out of her back pocket.

"Williams," she said automatically, forgetting that she wasn't on duty.

"Chief Williams, this is *Agent* Claveau of the Longueuil Police," said a no-nonsense voice. "I'm returning your call."

* * *

"What kid?" said Claveau, and Kate's heart sank.

They had agreed to meet at a diner in St. Hubert, on Chambly Road. It was quite a ways from St. Lambert, but Kate wasn't about to quibble. Besides, there wasn't much traffic at this time of day. Comparatively speaking.

Claveau was a stocky young man, about Trepalli's age. He had brown curly hair and piercing brown eyes under forbidding brows. He stood up when Kate walked in and shook hands with her, and with Trepalli. The two young men eyed each other cautiously before sitting down across from each other.

The smells in the diner reminded Kate that she was due for

some food, so she and Trepalli ordered lunch while Claveau shook his head and claimed it was too early in his shift to eat. The lunchtime crowd had cleared out, leaving only a few other patrons in the diner. Red booths with cracked vinyl seats lined three of the walls, and a long counter with stools faced the fourth wall. In the middle of the room, small, square tables on metal pedestal legs filled the space. She could smell French fries and onions.

"Someone told my brother-in-law that a kid saw the accident, and the driver," said Kate. She took a deep breath. "He even got a partial plate."

Claveau shook his head. "None of the witnesses told me that."

"Who did you interview?" asked Trepalli.

Claveau turned his attention to Trepalli. "All the ones I needed to."

"Well, you must have missed one," said Trepalli coolly.

Claveau's fierce eyes narrowed. "You're a little out of your jurisdiction, don't you think?"

Before Trepalli could open his mouth and take them down a path of no return, Kate spoke.

"Yes, we are," she said. "And normally, I would never stick my nose where it doesn't belong. But this is my mother." She paused to let that sink in. Claveau's shoulders relaxed a little and Kate gave Trepalli a warning glance. He had the grace to look abashed.

"My brother-in-law can't remember who told him," she continued. "But he didn't make it up, so someone out there knows who this kid is. Constable Trepalli asked everyone in the neighborhood if they had seen this kid, but no one had."

"The only one I missed is Étienne Laroche. He was home sick yesterday but seems to have gone to work today."

Claveau nodded. "He's a schoolteacher in Greenfield Park. I can swing by at dinner time and speak to him again." He shrugged. "But like I said, he never mentioned a kid yesterday."

"It's important," said Kate. She pulled out the scrap of paper John had given her that morning. It read BA, the only part of the license plate the kid had gotten. A Quebec license plate. She read it out to him. "According to my brother-in-law, it was a dark green Kia Soul. Newer model."

Claveau jotted down the information in his notebook. "I'll check it out," he said, "but it means nothing without a witness."

Kate nodded. She knew. At that moment, the waitress arrived with their lunch and while she and Trepalli dug in, Claveau stepped outside to make a call. He came back a couple of minutes later and the waitress immediately walked over with a fresh pot of coffee.

"*Merci*, Martine," he said as she refilled his cup. She dimpled at him, a pretty little thing who should still be in school, Kate suspected.

Claveau watched the girl walk away before turning back to Kate and Trepalli.

"My office is doing a motor vehicles search, but it may take a while," he said. He took a sip of his coffee. "My partner is coming to pick me up," he said. "I will keep you informed of our progress."

Kate chafed, but there was nothing they could do until they found the car or the kid. Preferably both. She took a bite of her club sandwich and chewed absently. It was almost two. Rose would be heading out to the hospital in time for her three o'clock shift. Thank goodness. She didn't think she could handle Rose *and* Trepalli at the same time.

Trepalli. She glanced sideways at him but he was concentrating on his cheeseburger. Oh, dear Lord, what was she going to do about Trepalli?

And how was she going to convince Rose that she hadn't asked him to come?

"There's my ride," said Claveau suddenly. He pushed his cup away and stood up.

Kate scrambled to her feet, too, as the young constable reached down to pick up his cap from the empty chair next to him.

"Thank you, *Agent* Claveau," she said formally, shaking his hand. "I really appreciate this."

He nodded noncommittally and reached into his pocket.

"No, please," said Kate quickly. "The least I can do is buy you a coffee."

He grinned suddenly and Kate was amazed at the transformation from a stern, cynical police officer to an attractive, charming young man. No wonder young Martine dimpled for him.

"I am curious about one thing," he said, glancing at Trepalli, who had come to stand next to Kate. "I can understand why Chief Williams is here, but what brought *you* here?"

Kate almost winced, but Marco took the question in stride.

"A girl," he said. He looked his counterpart in the eye. "The chief was just as surprised to see me as I was to see her."

Well. Didn't that say nothing at all. Kate watched Claveau's face and saw the moment he decided to let Trepalli's statement lie.

"*Bon*," he said, placing his cap on his head. "I'll be in touch."

"See you," said Kate. She noticed that neither man offered to shake hands with the other.

When he'd left, Trepalli slid his plate across the table and sat down to face Kate.

"I've been thinking," he said, leaning forward. "Yesterday was a school day, wasn't it?"

Kate nodded slowly. "Wednesday. As far as I know it was."

"A kid old enough to recognize the make and model of a car should be in school, but this one was skateboarding down the street."

Kate's eyebrows rose. He was right. This kid—if he existed—should have been in school at around one-thirty in the afternoon, even if he came home for lunch.

"He was playing hooky," said Kate.

"That's what I think," said Trepalli, popping the last bite of hamburger into his mouth. He chewed in silence for a moment, then added. "Any schools near your mom's place?"

Kate gave her young constable a lopsided smile. There was hope for him yet.

* * *

Well. She hadn't thought this one out, had she?

Kate sat in Trepalli's car, staring at École Gustave Bolton morosely. The school yard was empty but she could see people moving around behind the open windows on all three stories of the red brick building. It had been built in the seventies and it depressed her to realize how outdated it looked. It was newer than the primary school she had attended, which was long gone now.

They had left the diner, filled with renewed optimism until they parked in front of the school and realized there was no way they could obtain the information they wanted. No school administrator would release the name of a student to a stranger, no matter how many badges she flashed at them. Heck, they might not even let her in the door. She was wearing jeans and a tee-shirt, for Pete's sake.

Next to her, Trepalli sighed. "Sorry, Chief. Not such a good idea, after all."

She nodded absently, still staring at the school. The school day was winding down. Pretty soon the school buses would arrive, blocking her view of the school yard through the chain-link fence.

"The kid must really like skateboarding if he's willing to risk getting caught playing hooky," she said. The passenger-side window was open, letting in the breeze and the smell of mulch and growing things. She turned to look at Trepalli, who was frowning at her.

"If it was me," he said slowly, "I wouldn't risk it on my street. Too many people know me. Know my mom."

Kate's eyebrows rose. "So you would pick a street far enough from home that there'd be little risk of getting caught. How would you get out of your house without being seen?"

Trepalli shrugged. "The backyard. Most people work during the day, and those who work at night sleep during the day. If his backyard connects to a neighbor's backyard and they're not home, then presto, he's on the next street over without anyone on his street being the wiser."

Kate thought about it. "To be safe, I'd want to go one or two streets farther."

"Yes. Still, that's a lot of streets to cover."

Kate nodded. "Chances are pretty slim."

Trepalli reached for the ignition and started the Accord.

* * *

At five-thirty, John called, startling Kate so badly she jumped. They'd been traveling up and down the streets adjoining Mom's street for two hours, sometimes parking for fifteen minutes at a time, watching for kids skateboarding, with no luck.

She fished the phone out of her back pocket and pressed the talk button.

"Where are you?" asked John. "Rose said you left hours ago."

"Is she still there?" asked Kate. "I thought she went to the hospital a while ago." Then she turned her head sharply to look at the clock in the dashboard.

Five-thirty. Holy cow. She had to be at the hospital at six o'clock.

"She did," said John. "Are you still relieving her?"

"Of course," said Kate.

"Who's the young man you brought with you?" His voice was carefully neutral.

Kate glanced at Trepalli, only to find him watching her with interest.

"I didn't bring him with me," she corrected. "But he is a constable from Mendenhall."

"Amanda's constable from Mendenhall?"

Kate nodded. "Yes."

"I think you'd better bring him around."

Kate thought quickly. She really, really didn't want to bring Trepalli around to meet John. There was no telling what John's reaction would be. On the other hand, she could drop by, quickly introduce the boy, then beg off with the excuse that Trepalli had to drive her to the hospital.

"All right," she said. "We'll be there in a few minutes."

She hung up and turned to her constable.

"John wants to meet you."

"Is Amanda there?"

Probably not, thought Kate, *not if she knows you're going to be there*. She shrugged.

"I don't know."

* * *

Amanda wasn't there. Neither was Rose—of course not, she was at the hospital watching over Mom.

Trepalli had remained silent for the all-too-short trip back to Rose's house. He parked on the street, so as not to block John's Forester. There was no reluctance in his step when he followed her up the driveway, through the gate, and around the back of the house to the sun room door. Kate glanced through the windows. The sun was low in the sky, behind the tall cypress trees so that long shadows rested across the sun room. It was empty.

She looked over her shoulder. "Ready?"

Trepalli looked down at her. "Yes."

A small part of her admired him for his courage, but most of her wished he had stayed in Toronto. With a sigh, she opened the door and went in.

"John?" she called. The glass door between the sun room and the kitchen had been propped open with a potted geranium.

Trepalli came in behind her and closed the door.

"Right here," called John, and he came down the steps from the kitchen to emerge into the sun room. He still wore his tweed jacket, as if he'd just arrived from the university. His white hair was disheveled, and in the fading light, it gleamed like a lion's mane. He was even taller than Trepalli, and still carried the muscles of almost forty years of tromping through the bush and hammering at rocks.

The two men stood staring at each other. John's face was as hard as stone and his normally kind eyes looked hard and cold.

Kate swallowed hard, wishing she didn't feel so nervous. It wasn't as if John would hurt Trepalli.

Would he?

Then Trepalli did something so brave, it sent a little shiver up Kate's scalp. He stepped forward and offered his hand.

"Mr. Coburn. My name is Marco Trepalli."

John let the long, slow seconds trickle by and Kate could feel the temperature in the room drop. Then he put his hand out and shook Trepalli's.

"Have you eaten?" he said, still unsmiling. "I'm reheating stew."

Kate jumped in before Trepalli could open his mouth. "Sorry, John, but he has to drive me to the hospital."

A small smile flitted across John's face so quickly that Kate could have imagined it.

"Take my car," he said without looking at her. "This young man and I are going to get acquainted."

CHAPTER 6

DEAR LORD, she had thrown him to the wolves.

Kate stuck the parking stub in her jeans pocket and strode through the parking lot to the entrance of the Armand-Cadieux Hospital, trying not to feel guilty.

This is what he wants, she told herself firmly. *He came here specifically to meet Amanda's parents.*

She just hoped he survived the experience.

The moment she stepped inside the hospital, a sense of *déjà vu* swept over her. How many times had she done this? Gone to a hospital to check on someone who had been injured, or to speak to the medical examiner about someone who'd died? No matter where she was, all hospitals smelled the same: antiseptic and a little sour.

She made her way to the elevator and up to the intensive care ward. She took advantage of the fact that there was no one at the nurses' station and hurried to Mom's room, pushing the door open and slipping inside before a nurse could emerge from one of the other rooms.

"I was starting to think you'd forgotten," said Rose tartly.

Oh, give it a rest, thought Kate. She forced herself to smile.

"Well, I didn't. How is she?"

The room faced east so that it was now gloomy as the light

faded outside. Telltale lights on the equipment around Mom's bed blinked or shone steadily. One machine whirred a little. A window was cracked open, letting in some fresh air. Rose was nothing but a shadowy outline, standing in front of the window.

"The swelling is going down." There was a quavery quality to Rose's voice and all of Kate's irritation dissipated. She stepped closer to the bed. "Tomorrow they're going to stop the drugs keeping her in a coma."

A weight she hadn't known she was carrying slipped off Kate's shoulders.

"She's going to be all right?"

Rose shrugged.

"They won't say yes or no. They're just saying that the swelling is going down."'

"We'll take that as a good sign," said Kate firmly. "Now, go home. I'll call if there's any change."

Rose stretched stiffly and turned to put something down on her chair.

"Have you eaten?" she asked, sidling past a machine.

Kate shook her head. "No. I'll eat after." She hesitated a moment, then said, "Trepalli's at the house."

Rose stopped next to her. "Is Amanda there?"

"No. I don't know where she is. Maybe still working."

"Honestly, Kate," said Rose, her voice heavy with disapproval. "What were you thinking, bringing him with you?"

"I didn't bring him with me!" Kate took hold of her temper and lowered her voice. "I had no idea he was planning this, or I would have stopped him." Somehow.

"Sure," said Rose, walking over to the door. She slipped on her linen jacket and tucked her purse under her arm. Without another word, she opened the door and left.

Dammitall! Did Rose seriously think she would have brought the boy with her? To do what? Investigate the hit-and-run? Or to pursue Amanda?

Frankly, either one was insulting. What? She got the call from Rose about the accident and immediately told Trepalli to pack his bags, this was his chance to meet the parents?

For crying out loud.

At last she stopped fuming and turned toward her mother. There was a light fixture on the wall above the bed and Kate carefully made her way to it and flicked it on. The sudden light chased the shadows away and drew her gaze down to the figure under the blankets.

The braid was exactly where it had been last night, but everything else looked worse. The right side of her face was purple and red and still swollen. The bandage around her head had been replaced but it still looked grey against the snowy whiteness of Mom's hair. Her arms were on top of the blankets, and intravenous needles were inserted at her elbows. Her right hand and forearm were scraped and purple where they emerged from the short-sleeved hospital gown. Beneath the blanket, her left leg was elevated on a pillow and distorted by a cast.

Even in the yellow light, she looked pale.

The door opened suddenly and a nurse bustled in. She stopped and blinked in surprise when she caught sight of Kate. She carried a clipboard.

"You must be the sister," she said cheerfully, advancing on the bed once again.

The woman was in her thirties, tall and thin, with curly brown hair pulled up in a frizzy bun. She wore the ubiquitous hospital scrubs but her top was punchy with flowers. She carried herself with the self-confidence of competence.

"Kate," said Kate. "How is she?"

"I'm Stephanie," said the nurse. She flipped through the pages on the clipboard and began noting down the various machines' readings. Just when Kate was about to repeat herself, the nurse continued. "Your mother is doing remarkably well," she said.

"For a woman her age?" Kate finished the unspoken thought.

Stephanie looked up from her writing.

"For someone who's smashed her head against the pavement," she corrected. "A brain injury is a serious thing, no matter the age." She reached for her patient's arm and squeezed it gently. "She's getting a little cold. Let's cover her arms."

Together they tucked Mom's arms under the blankets and pulled the blankets up to her chin.

"Should I close the window?" asked Kate.

"No," said Stephanie. She crossed her arms over the clipboard. "It's good to have fresh air and outside noises. I'll close the window in a few hours." She eyed the chair that Rose had vacated. "Why don't you read to her for a while?" she suggested. "It might help bring her back to hear a familiar voice."

Kate didn't know what to say to that and she didn't have the courage to ask the nurse what she meant—that Mom might not make her way back at all or that hearing a familiar voice might hurry along the healing process.

"I'll be back in an hour," said Stephanie, and she left.

Kate stood staring at the door for long seconds. Finally she turned back to the bed and went over to kiss her mother's un-marred cheek.

"I hope you like Louis L'Amour," she said, glancing at the book Rose had left behind, "because that's what we've got."

She sat down and began to read to the accompaniment of the various machines' whirs and clicks.

* * *

"He's *where*?" asked Kate.

"I put him up at your mother's place," said John equably.

Kate glanced from him to Rose's angry face in confusion. They were standing in the middle of the kitchen, where Kate had gone to find something to eat when she returned from the hospital. The kitchen still smelled of stew. She had been reluctant to ask about Trepalli, but she had to make sure the boy was all right.

"Without asking me," said Rose. She brought a bowl down on

the counter with a clatter.

Kate turned back to John. The house was cool now, and she was cold in her tee-shirt.

"Why on Earth are you letting him use Mom's house?"

John shrugged slightly. He had changed back into his grubby jeans and wore a grey sweater over top of a white tee-shirt.

"It was late. I wasn't going to let him drive all the way back to Toronto tonight. And the house is sitting empty."

Kate looked at Rose, but her sister was ladling stew from a plastic container into the bowl in preparation for microwaving it and didn't look at Kate. But Kate didn't need to see Rose's face to know she was angry.

Furious.

Was John suicidal?

Finally she put her arms out in a helpless gesture.

"I have no idea what I'm supposed to do now."

Rose whirled on her, ladle up and dripping.

"I think you've done quite enough, don't you?"

"For crying out loud, Rose, how many times do I have—"

"What's all the yelling about?" interrupted Amanda, standing in the doorway to the kitchen.

They all turned to look at her. She still wore her chef's jacket and a pair of black slacks, and her blond hair was up in a flawless bun.

She looked from face to face.

"What are you guys arguing about?" Her shoulders drooped tiredly after spending the day working, but she smiled tentatively at them.

Oh, Lord.

Kate glanced at her watch. Nine-thirty. It wasn't too late to go see that schoolteacher.

"I have to go," she said before anyone else could speak. "Interview. I'll be back in a bit."

Ignoring John's amused look and Rose's outrage, she squeezed past Amanda, ran down the steps to the sun room, and escaped.

* * *

Despite the bite to the wind through the thin shell of her jacket, Kate was grateful to be away from the impending explosion. What had John been thinking? And if he thought Rose was mad, just how did he think Amanda was going to react when she found out Trepalli had come to her house and was now staying a few streets over?

She walked toward the park at the end of the street, stretching her legs and letting her arms swing loosely. It felt good to be moving after the last couple of days. She almost wished she were going for a run, but though she'd worn her running shoes, she hadn't packed her track pants. And running in jeans was a nonstarter.

The wind smelled fresh and clean and sighed through trees in the yards she passed. This was an older section of town, with some of the houses barely set back from the street, most of their land in the backyards. The streetlights were set far apart and were on the other side of the street so that she traveled in gloom. When she found herself peering into living room windows, she turned her attention back to the street. She could hear the distant sound of cars passing on Riverside Street behind her, but otherwise, there was no traffic, no one else on the sidewalk. Ahead of her, the park loomed darkly, with only the children's playground lit up with a floodlight. The swings, with their light rubber seats, swayed in the wind, as if guided by invisible children.

She turned at the corner and stepped up her pace. Nine-thirty was not too outrageously late to call on someone, but ten o'clock at night definitely was. Three streets over, she turned right and eyed the homes across the street. Most still had lights on, but again, no one was outside. She lengthened her stride. The schoolteacher's house was across from Madame Sophie's, and over by a few. So, about ten houses past Mom's.

She noticed the lights on in her mother's house, but ducked her head so she wouldn't see inside. She couldn't believe her constable was staying at her mother's house. Oh, Lord—what if McKell found out? How could he ever believ—

"Chief."

Kate jumped and whirled, her hands out, her heat beating like a jackhammer in her chest.

Trepalli sat on the front steps of her mother's house, his upper body reared back as if in alarm, an expression of horror on his face.

"Sorry!" he said. "I didn't mean to scare you."

Kate breathed deeply, trying to force her heart back where it belonged. "Of course not," she said at last. "That's why you didn't sit out in the dark waiting to waylay me as I walked by."

He grinned tentatively and stood up before coming down the steps to join her.

"I didn't exactly waylay you," he said.

Tell that to my heart, thought Kate.

"Besides, I was pretty sure you would want to talk to the schoolteacher and I wanted to catch you before you did."

She looked up at him, not sure if she should be upset or comforted that he knew her so well. Maybe it meant she was predictable.

"All right," she said. "What about him?"

He locked his hands behind his back and looked down at his feet.

"I, uh... I already spoke to him." He looked at her and his hands sprang away from behind his back to wave eloquently as he spoke. "I wasn't sure when you'd leave the hospital, and I knew it was important, and Claveau never called..." He stopped suddenly. In the dimness of the light standards, he looked suddenly uncertain. "Did he?"

Kate sighed and sat down on one of the cold wooden steps. Trepalli hesitated a moment, then sat down next to her.

"No, he didn't call me," she said. Maybe he got too busy to interview the teacher, but Kate wondered if it was something else. Sergeant Tremblay had seemed sympathetic and had actually gotten Claveau to call, and Claveau had met with her, but maybe that was out of curiosity more than a desire to help.

"What did you find out?" she asked. She envied Trepalli his leather jacket. Surely it was warmer than her light cotton one.

He pulled his notepad out of his back pocket and flipped through it until he found the right page.

"Mr. Étienne Laroche, forty six. He's been a teacher at Holy Trinity Elementary School—a private school in Greenfield Park," he added, "for the last ten years."

Kate controlled an impulse to sigh. Couldn't he just get to the important part?

"He was home yesterday, nursing a cold. He lives alone."

Yes, yes, yes, thought Kate. *But did he see the kid?*

As though sensing her impatience, Trepalli looked at her. "He heard the accident and went outside to see what was happening. He saw a dark car speeding off but couldn't say what kind it was. He didn't catch the plate number."

"In other words," she said, "we have nothing."

Trepalli shook his head. "He saw a kid standing in the middle of the street, staring after the car. He thinks the kid may have seen the driver."

Kate's heart leapt in hope. "Does he know the kid?"

Trepalli shook his head and flipped the notebook closed. "No. He knows most of the kids in the neighborhood, and he says this kid isn't one of them. He figures the kid was playing hooky from École Gustave Bolton."

"Did he speak to the boy?" she asked. It was fine to get confirmation that the kid existed, but they still didn't have much to go on to help identify him.

"No." Trepalli sighed. "The kid took off on his skateboard, heading east down a side street."

Kate opened her mouth to ask another question and closed it. If the teacher hadn't spoken to the kid, then who had told John that the kid had seen the driver? And part of the plate?

"Why didn't he tell the cops?" asked Kate in frustration. Surely Claveau would have tracked the kid down if he knew what the teacher had seen.

"He didn't think of it," said Trepalli. His expression was carefully neutral.

Kate sighed. She suspected the local cops would pin their hopes on finding the car through body shops. A car involved in a hit-and-run always had body damage—a dented bumper, blood, maybe a dented hood. Sometimes a damaged windshield. The owner would want to get the car fixed as soon as possible and hide the evidence.

Well, she didn't have Claveau's resources. Not here. She would have to follow the harder leads.

For a moment, she forgot to be a cop as the horror of the accident swept over her again. Some maniac had hit an old woman while she was crossing the street and just left her there.

"I don't suppose your teacher got a description of the boy?" She had to squeeze the words out past her tight throat. Trepalli acted as if he didn't notice.

"Well, Mr. Laroche may not know sh— uh, anything about cars," he said, "but he does know kids. He says this one is about eleven years old, white, with dark hair cut short in the back and sides, longer on top. Laroche couldn't tell what color the kid's eyes were. He was about five feet tall, skinny, wearing black jeans with a droopy seat, a sweatshirt with a Colorful Dead logo on the front."

"That describes just about any eleven-year-old boy," said Kate morosely.

Trepalli grinned. "I saved the best for last. His skateboard was an Air Grabz."

Kate stared at him. "And that means...?"

Trepalli's grin widened. "They're top of the line and very expensive. Not many eleven-year-old kids will have one."

Kate really wanted to ask him how he knew, but she just didn't think she could handle learning that he owned one.

"Good work, Constable," she said finally. She looked at him. In the light spilling from her mother's living room window, he looked mysterious. Dashing, even. She couldn't help but admire his courage. She didn't know if she could have done what he had done today—bearding the lion in his den, as it were. She wondered what Bert would have to say.

"How's your mom?" asked Trepalli gently.

Kate sighed. "They're taking her off the drugs tomorrow and are hoping she'll come out of the coma soon. The swelling is going down. Now we have to wait and see if there's been any damage."

Trepalli's forearms rested on his knees and his clasped hands hung loosely between them. He stared at the houses across the street.

"Ma'am, I'm sorry I came when I did," he said softly. "If I'd known about the accident, I would have stayed away."

A car drove by slowly—white Impreza—and Kate watched its progress for a few seconds before replying.

"I know, Constable." She wanted to add so much more, like, what the hell was he thinking? How could he think it was a good idea to follow his ex-girlfriend halfway across the country? And did he think it would endear him to Amanda to go behind her back to meet her parents?

But she kept her mouth shut.

"I'm very grateful that you're letting me stay at your mother's house."

Kate gave him a sideways glance. "Hardly my idea, Constable."

"Do you think Amanda—"

Kate stood up abruptly.

"I should get back," she said, not looking at him. "They'll be wondering where I've gone."

Trepalli stood up, too. "Ma'am?"

Oh, for Pete's sake. Didn't he know when to leave well enough alone?

"Yes, Constable?"

"I've been invited to breakfast."

She turned then to look up at him, but couldn't for the life of her read his expression.

Breakfast. Holy cow.

At a loss for words, she settled for a nod, then headed back the way she had come.

* * *

The backyard light had been left on for her and the sun room door had been left unlocked. She locked the door behind her and turned off the outside lights.

A faint odor of beef stew lingered, reminding Kate that she still hadn't eaten, and she resigned herself to waking up starved in the morning, if not in the middle of the night. She knew better than to eat now. The food would land in a lump in her stomach and keep her from sleeping.

She sighed. Apparently there would be a good breakfast.

She removed her jacket and hung it up on the coatrack, then took off her running shoes and set them on the mat by the door before padding up the steps to the kitchen. Someone had left the light on for her and she pulled a glass out of the cupboard and filled it with water. She stood drinking and staring out the window at her reflection and the side of the house next door.

She glanced up at the clock above the window. Ten fifteen. Maybe she could get up early and avoid the whole breakfast event. Go to the hospital and see how Mom was doing.

It was only seven fifteen in Vancouver. Time enough to call Bert before she went to bed.

A movement in the reflection caused her to turn around slowly. Amanda stood in the doorway to the hall.

"Hi," she said softly. Her honey blond hair was loose around her shoulders and she wore the red University of Toronto sweatshirt over top of cotton pajama pants.

"Hi," said Kate. She smiled at her niece and gestured toward the sun room. Amanda nodded and they both headed downstairs, where they could talk without disturbing Rose and John.

Amanda turned on one of the side lamps and they settled in their seats. She looked at Kate for a long moment, and Kate waited.

"Did you know he was coming?" asked Amanda. Her bottom lip trembled slightly and she pressed her lips together.

Kate shook her head. "No. He didn't tell me his plans. I thought he went home to Toronto. I would never have guessed he would do this."

A smile flitted across Amanda's face.

"You never know what he's going to do next," she agreed.

Like ask you to marry him, thought Kate. Suddenly, she wanted to be back in Mendenhall, at her station, listening to the routine sounds of her constables coming and going. In fact, she wanted to be anywhere but here, stuck in the middle of this relationship drama.

But she *was* here, and until she knew what was happening with Mom, she was going to stay here.

She sighed. Like it or not, she was part of this little drama—or maybe comedy—now.

"Did you know he's coming for breakfast?" she asked her niece.

Amanda nodded. "Mom told me. She's really mad at Dad."

And rightly so, thought Kate. What the hell was John playing at?

"So, your dad's the one who invited Tre— Marco for breakfast?"

Amanda nodded. "Apparently."

Kate studied Amanda's face for a moment. "And how do you feel about it?" she asked finally.

Amanda shrugged. "It's their house. They can invite whoever they want." She gave Kate a small smile. "I don't have to be there, however."

Kate nodded. "I was planning to avoid breakfast, too. I'll take the first shift."

"Oh no, you don't," said Amanda in alarm. "I was planning to take the first shift."

Kate grinned at her. "We'll both go," she said. "Give your mom even more reason to be mad."

Amanda smiled, too, but it was a sad smile. "I just don't want to see him," she said. "It's better this way." She stood up. "I'm going to bed. See you in the morning."

Kate nodded. "Sleep tight, Pumpkin."

Amanda left, closing the glass door behind her, and Kate pulled out her phone and called Bert.

"Hey," he said, picking up on the first ring. At the sound of his voice, her shoulders immediately relaxed. She hadn't realized how tense she was. She heard voices in the background but a moment later they were gone. He had muted the television.

"Hey yourself," she said.

"How's your mom?"

Kate sighed. "We'll know more tomorrow. The swelling's going down. They're stopping the drugs. They want to see if she'll wake up on her own."

"Katie, I know you're worried," he said, his voice like a warm blanket all around her, "but this is good news. They wouldn't be taking her off the drugs if they felt she was still in danger."

It was true. Of course it was true. But just thinking of her mom lying so still in the hospital bed, hooked up to all those tubes and the equipment... This was the first time Kate had ever seen her mother looking anything but vital and strong.

Her throat tightened and the tears threatened. She coughed slightly and forced a smile on her face. "You'll never guess who showed up at Rose's door this morning."

There was a pause, and she could picture the puzzled expression on his face.

"You're right," he said finally. "I'll never guess. Who was it?"

"Trepalli."

This time the pause was so long that she started laughing, in spite of everything. "I know, eh?" She told him the events of the day, regaling him with Rose's reaction at meeting the boy and later, John's reaction. Then she filled him in on her meeting with Claveau, and what she and Trepalli had learned from the school-teacher.

"You've been busy," said Bert. "What's your next move?"

At that moment, she felt a fierce surge of affection for him. Not once did he mention that she was out of her jurisdiction or that she should leave it to the local cops. This was one of the reasons she loved the guy. He got it.

"I'm going to throw myself on the mercy of the school principal," said Kate. In her experience, principals were always torn between helping the police and protecting their students. If she explained that she just wanted to talk to the kid, maybe the principal would relent.

Apparently, Bert had his doubts.

"And if that doesn't work?"

Kate sighed. "Then I'll wait until after school and check out the streets in the neighborhood. Again. According to Trepalli, the kid's got a fancy skateboard that should be easy to spot."

"And in the meantime, I'm sure the locals are searching the body shops for vehicles with suspicious damage. Although the owner might be keeping it hidden in their garage."

Yes, that was what was worrying her. The owner would be stupid to take the car to a repair shop. Surely they'd guess that the police would be keeping an eye on exactly that. No, a smart man— or woman—would wait a month or even two before taking it in. And in the meantime, he would keep the vehicle hidden.

The thought depressed her. Finding a hit-and-run driver was notoriously difficult.

"Katie?"

"Still here," she assured him.

"Go easy on Trepalli," said Bert gently. "The guy's got it bad for Amanda. And you know, I thought it was mutual."

"Maybe," said Kate. "But if she doesn't want to see him, he's just going to have to accept it."

"I know," said Bert sadly. "But I kind of hope they work it out."

Kate said nothing. She didn't know how she felt about the whole thing.

CHAPTER 7

BY THE TIME Kate and Amanda arrived at Mom's hospital room the next morning, she was awake. Or almost awake.

"But her eyes are open," said Amanda after the nurse informed them that Hetty wasn't completely conscious.

"Yes," agreed Jérome, the nurse on duty. He was busy entering information on an electronic tablet as he spoke to them. "Now her brain has to catch up to her body."

Kate's ears had to catch up to his words. She was a little rusty with the French-Canadian accent. It was still very early—barely six o'clock. It had still been dark when she and Amanda arrived. The nurses at the duty station had been surprised to see them, but had allowed them in.

"But is she all right?" asked Amanda, looking at her grandmother's wandering eyes with dismay.

The male nurse stopped for a moment and looked down at Amanda. He was a tall one, at least six feet one, with broad shoulders and strong arms emerging from his short-sleeved uniform. A stethoscope hung from his thick neck and disappeared into the breast pocket of the plain green top. His dark hair was cut short in a skull-hugging brush cut. There were pouches under his green eyes and stubble shaded his chin.

"Your *grand-mère* is doing very well." He looked from Amanda to Kate and smiled. "In fact, we are very pleased with her progress."

Kate glanced down. Mom's gaze was wandering all over the place: to the window, the door, even, several times, to Kate and Amanda. But Kate could tell Mom wasn't really there. This was progress?

"We will take her for more tests in a few hours," continued Jérome. "But you can sit and talk to her for now. Give her something to follow back from wherever she is." And with that, he left them alone in the room.

Amanda glanced at Kate, alarm plain on her face. "What is *that* supposed to mean?"

Kate shrugged. "Maybe it suffered in translation." But she did know what he meant. Mom's mind was wandering somewhere out of reach, unable to home in, just as her eyes were unable to focus on anything. She wanted to be reassuring for Amanda, but honestly, it was kind of spooky to think about.

"Let's sit," she finally suggested, and shrugged out of her jacket. They had slipped out of the house before John and Rose were up, foregoing showers in an effort to get while the getting was good. Kate left a note on the kitchen counter and turned her phone off. Rose was going to be mad.

Then again, Rose was going to be mad no matter what Kate did.

Amanda unzipped her hoodie and slipped out of it, hanging it across the back of the second chair they had dragged in. Kate was surprised the staff had allowed both of them in. She suspected it was because they felt Mom was close to waking up. The thought cheered her immeasurably.

Amanda sat down and reached across to hold her grandmother's hand.

"Hi, Grams," she said softly. "It's me, your favorite granddaughter."

Kate smiled. "Amanda, you're her *only* granddaughter."

"A minor detail," said Amada. Then she jumped. "She just squeezed my hand!"

Kate leaned in and they both stared intently at Mom's face, but her gaze wandered with no more direction than before. Still, hope grew a few more tendrils inside Kate's heart and she grinned at her niece.

"Maybe we should sing the sailor song."

Amanda laughed and patted her grandmother's hand.

"What can you do with a drunken sailor," she sang.

"What can you do with a drunken sailor," Kate repeated.

"What can you with a drunken sailor," sang Amanda.

"Early in the morning!" They finished together and burst out laughing.

There was no change in Mom, but Jérome stuck his head in and looked enquiringly at them.

Kate cleared her throat. "Her favorite song," she explained.

"Good idea," he said, and withdrew.

The next few hours passed with them singing bits of various songs they knew Mom liked, reading from the Louis L'Amour novel, and telling her what was happening in the greater world.

There was no change in Hetty until Kate mentioned that Marco Trepalli had come to the house. For a moment, Mom's gaze caught hers and Kate sucked in a breath. Then her gaze wandered off again.

She's in there, thought Kate, suddenly awash in relief. *She's trying to get back to us.*

"Don't tell her that," objected Amanda. She had missed the eye contact and now frowned at Kate. "I don't want her getting ideas."

"Did you hear that, Mom?" asked Kate. "She doesn't want me to tell you that a boy has followed her halfway across the country to meet her parents, in spite of her breaking up with him."

Mom's eyes turned toward her and remained fixed on her face for a few seconds, then her gaze wandered off again.

This time, Amanda had seen it. She gasped softly.

"In fact," continued Kate, "while Amanda and I are sitting here with you, he's having breakfast with Rose and John. I wonder what he's telling them." She glanced slyly at Amanda, but her niece was looking at her grandmother.

"She smiled," she said with wonder. Her eyes suddenly filled with tears. "Oh Grams, hurry up and come back."

The door opened and an orderly came in, followed by Jérome. He studied the telltales on the machines and then turned to look at Hetty. "Good," he said with satisfaction.

"She squeezed my hand," said Amanda.

"And looked at me a couple of times," added Kate. For a moment, she felt like a student seeking approval from a teacher.

"Oh, yes," murmured Jérome, "she's on her way back." He looked at them. "We need to take her away for tests now," he said. "It'll take a few hours."

Kate's stomach growled as if in response and his eyebrows rose in amusement.

"Time enough for breakfast, certainly," he said.

* * *

They decided to leave the hospital grounds entirely and drove up Taschereau Boulevard to a diner tucked between a carpet store and a used car dealership. The cars in the lot were covered with a fine mist of dew that the morning sun was rapidly drying off.

The morning rush had eased and they were able to pick a table by the window, in the sunshine.

Once they were seated, Kate pulled out her phone. Five missed calls—all from Rose—and one message waiting. With a sigh, she tapped the icon. The message consisted of one word:

COWARD.

"What's so funny?" asked Amanda.

The waitress, an older woman with lively brown eyes and a ready smile, arrived then with the coffeepot and they both turned their mugs over. The woman filled the mugs and handed them each a laminated menu.

Kate sipped her coffee gingerly, and then with pleasure.

"Your mom is calling me a coward," she said.

Amanda brought her mug to her face and breathed deeply. "Well, you are," she said, before taking a sip.

Kate allowed one eyebrow to rise. "Said the pot to the kettle."

Amanda laughed and picked up the menu. "I'm starving."

"Me, too," said Kate with satisfaction. She hadn't realized how worried she'd been until they saw Mom this morning. "Let's order, and then I'll call your folks." What she really wanted to do was call Bert, but it was five-thirty in the morning in Vancouver. She could wait.

Two minutes later, orders placed, Kate called the house. After three rings, John answered.

"Hey," said Kate. "I thought you'd be at the university by now."

"I don't teach on Fridays," said John. "Perks of tenure. You missed a good breakfast."

"I'm sure," agreed Kate. "Is the boy still there?" She felt Amanda's attention zeroing in on her like a laser, but she didn't look at her.

"Nope," said John. "He just left. Said something about going to the school to try and find out who the kid with the skateboard is."

Alarm spiked through her at the thought of Trepalli going to the school without her until she remembered that he was much better with secretaries and kids than she was. Heck, just about anybody was better with kids than she was. But still. He should have talked to her first.

"You still there?" asked John.

"Still here," said Kate. The waitress arrived with their orange juice and Amanda thanked her. "I have news," continued Kate and she proceeded to tell him about Mom's progress. When she was done, John gave a heartfelt sigh.

"That's wonderful news," he said. "Rose is on her way there now. I think she was hoping you'd still be there."

Ha. No doubt she was.

"I'm going to try to catch up with Trep— with Marco," said Kate. "And maybe call Constable Claveau."

"He's good people, you know," said John.

Kate blinked. "I thought you didn't know him."

"Not the cop," said John patiently. "Marco."

Kate stared down at the table top and the glass of orange juice sparkling in a shaft of morning sun.

"Yes."

John allowed the silence to stretch. Then he said, "But you don't approve?"

She knew he wanted her to tell him if there was a reason he should disapprove, too, but there wasn't. Not really. Marco Trepalli was a fine young man. He was a good cop, with good moral judgment and great instincts. Sure, he was a womanizer, or at least, he had been until he met Amanda, but was only twenty-six, for Pete's sake. Why not have fun while he was young and single?

Except that it looked like he didn't want to be single any more. Oh, no. It now looked like Marco Trepalli had set his cap for Amanda Coburn and was determined to win her back.

And how was this any of her business? It wasn't. Except that Amanda was her niece. Family. The daughter she would never have. Did she really want Amanda to marry a cop?

Last February, Amanda had been shot by that crazy woman, Alexandra Kowalski. Then just last month, she had been taken by an escaped convict and almost *drowned*. Kate still shuddered every time she thought about reaching down into the dark water to catch Amanda's long hair and haul her to the surface.

None of that would have happened if Amanda hadn't been living with Kate. A cop.

"Hello?" said John, and she realized he had been repeating her name.

"Sorry, John," said Kate, shaking herself out of her bad memories. "Our food is here. I'll talk to you when I get back." She broke the connection and tucked the phone into her jacket pocket.

Amanda was watching her.

"What's the matter?" she asked quietly.

Mercifully, the waitress chose that moment to bring Amanda's fruit cup and yogurt and Kate's cheese omelet, and they set upon the food like starving women. Which they were.

* * *

An hour later, they returned to the house. John came down the stairs from the kitchen to greet them in the sun room with a sardonic smile.

"If it isn't the gutless wonders," he said.

Before Kate could say a word, Amanda turned on her dad. Her face was bleached of color and, all of a sudden, her eyes looked several shades darker.

"Don't even try," she said, and for the first time, Kate realized that her niece was furious.

Holy cow. How had she spent the morning with her without realizing this? She stepped sideways to avoid getting between them. Unfortunately, John blocked the stairs up to the kitchen and Amanda the door to the backyard, or Kate would have made her escape.

"You've got some nerve," continued Amanda without skipping a beat. She stood staring at her father, her arms crossed.

John blinked in surprise and opened his mouth but Amanda shot a hand out to stop him.

"No, Dad. This is your home, and you can invite whoever you want. But this is *my* personal life you're messing around with. *Mine*. And I broke up with him. Now I need to know if you're going to keep inviting him over, because if you are, I'm going to move out."

Kate finally remembered to close her mouth and dragged her gaze away from her niece's face. She risked a glance at John but his face gave away nothing. Finally he gave his daughter a wry smile.

"All right, sweetheart," he said gently. "You've made your point.

I like him, but I won't invite him back until you say so."

Kate caught the semantic sleight of hand but Amanda only nodded.

"Good. I'm going to take a shower now."

John turned sideways and she brushed past him to take the steps up to the main level. He turned back to Kate, laughter in his eyes.

What the heck was he up to?

"Coffee?" he asked innocently, then turned to go upstairs to the kitchen without waiting for an answer.

At that moment, Kate's phone rang and she fished it out of her jacket pocket. Bert. She thumbed it on.

"Hey," she said.

"Hey, yourself," he replied. "How's your mom?"

So Kate filled him in and was still talking when John arrived with her cup. She thanked him with a nod and he went back upstairs. Kate sat down in the chair she had come to think of as hers. The sun had yet to spill into the backyard and it was still cool in the sun room, but it was peaceful to sit and stare at the sunflowers and tiger lilies in the garden while talking to Bert.

Finally she glanced at her watch. Almost ten. "I should go," she said. "I need to catch up to Trepalli before he pisses someone off and gets us thrown out of the province."

"Right," said Bert. "As long as he's talking to a woman, you should be all right."

Kate rolled her eyes. "Don't tell me you're envious."

"Hey!" objected Bert. "I'll have you know that at his age, I was a going concern, too."

She couldn't help it. She laughed.

"Now that hurt," said Bert reproachfully.

"I'll make it up to you," she promised.

Bert's voice dropped to a low growl. "I'll hold you to that."

* * *

She called Jean-Louis Claveau's number, but wasn't surprised to be told the constable wasn't on shift yet. She asked to be transferred to his voice mail and left him a message telling him she had an update for him and to please call her.

Then she took a shower and borrowed John's Forester.

She had pulled a clean pair of jeans and a long-sleeved white tee-shirt out of her bag, and with her light navy jacket, she looked halfway presentable; but once she arrived at École Gustave Bolton and parked on the street, she sat staring at the low-slung building and the empty playground with its monkey bars, swing sets, and climbing puzzle for long minutes. Nothing had changed since yesterday morning. She still couldn't just waltz up to the front doors and ask to speak to the kid who had an Air Grabz skateboard. Neither could Trepalli, and she didn't care how charming he was.

What the hell had she been thinking?

A rap on the passenger-side window startled her and she turned to see Trepalli looking in at her. She unlocked the door and he slipped in, bringing with him a faint smell of cedar-scented aftershave. He was in jeans again, and a plain gray sweatshirt with the sleeves pushed up.

"Good morning, Chief."

Kate studied his face for a moment. He didn't look like a man who had set out to wreak havoc.

"Good morning, Constable," she said finally. "Did you go in?"

He shook his head, looking a little sheepish. "I ran out of nerve," he said. "I couldn't think of a way of approaching this that didn't sound like I was a pervert."

Kate grinned in spite of herself. "Hard without a badge," she agreed.

He sighed and sat back glumly. "So now what?"

But Kate's attention had caught on another car, a white Impreza, parked facing them on the other side of the street in front of a stone and glass duplex. She could see a shadow behind the steering wheel, but the car was in the shade and it was impossible to see clearly through the windshield.

"Chief?" Trepalli's gaze followed hers. "That car looks familiar..."

Kate nodded. "Last night. It drove by when we were talking on the stairs."

Trepalli made as if to get out of the car and her hand shot out to clamp on his forearm.

"Don't," she said. "He would have seen us last night. If he sees you coming toward him, he'll take off. Let's just wait and see what he does."

Trepalli nodded. "He?"

She shrugged. "An assumption." *But a good one,* she thought. This driver might be the same one who had hit her mother. She struggled to keep her breathing under control and finally remembered to let go of Trepalli.

He squinted, then shook his head. "I can't make out the plate."

"There's only one," she said. "At the rear."

He turned to look at her. "Do you think he saw me get in?"

"Where's your car?" she asked, glancing in the rearview.

"On the side street," said Trepalli, pointing it out.

"Well, if he hasn't left, the chances are he didn't see you."

They both stared at the car parked a few blocks away.

"It could be someone who lives in the neighborhood," said Trepalli, clearly unconvinced. "Come to pick up a kid for an appointment or something."

Kate was already shaking her head. "A parent would go inside to fetch the kid. No school would allow the kid to leave otherwise. Besides, why even let the kid go to school if they have an appointment this early in the day?" She glanced at the dashboard clock. "It's ten-thirty. School's been in for what, an hour and a half?"

Trepalli nodded but frowned. She couldn't blame him. This was a dumb idea. She couldn't go into the school and ask about a kid by describing his skateboard. And she couldn't go knocking on the Impreza's window and demand to see the driver's identification based on the fact that she had seen his car—or maybe *her* car—

drive by on her mother's street last night.

She was being ridiculous.

"Ma'am...?"

"Yes?" she replied absently, still absorbed by her conundrum. She felt like an amateur.

"Do you think the kid is in danger?"

Kate turned away from the Impreza and stared at him. Holy cow. She had been so obsessed with what the kid had seen that it hadn't even occurred to her he might be in danger. If he had seen the driver, then the driver had seen *him*. She swallowed.

"We can't wait for Claveau to get back on shift," she said slowly. "We have to call the duty officer and let him know."

Trepalli nodded.

Kate fished out her phone. "Keep an eye on him," she said. "We need that plate number."

She dialed Claveau's number again, knowing it was call forwarded to the switchboard. From there she was transferred to the duty officer's number.

"Sergeant Tremblay."

"Sergeant, this is Kate Williams." When he didn't respond right away, she added, "from Mendenhall."

"Ah," said the sergeant in recognition. "Chief Williams. How can I help you?" His voice was professionally friendly, but she could hear the note of caution in it.

A loud buzzer sounded from the school and almost immediately the doors opened to disgorge dozens of children who ran to the playground or separated out into small groups to play tag. The sound of their voices reminded her of screeching seagulls, fighting over a shell on the beach. She eyed them carefully as she answered the duty officer.

"Sorry to disturb you again, Sergeant," she said. "*Agent* Claveau is off duty and this couldn't wait." She quickly filled him in on what they had learned so far. She could hear the clicking of a keyboard as he typed in the information she was giving him.

She watched carefully, but saw no kids with skateboards. In fact, these kids seemed really young—no more than eight or nine, she guessed. She saw half a dozen kids, boys and girls, waiting their turn to jump rope. Two kids hung from the monkey bars, ignoring the yells of their schoolmates who were waiting to get on. At the slide, a steady stream of children clambered up only to shriek with laughter as they slid down to land in the sand pit at the base of the slide.

Maybe they took turns on the playground? She couldn't imagine an eleven-year-old wanting to use that slide, or the monkey bars. Wouldn't those be considered too babyish?

"Chief," said the sergeant, startling her. "I don't want to seem unsympathetic, but don't you think you're taking this a bit too far?"

Her attention telescoped back to the car and she frowned at the steering wheel.

"In what way, exactly?" she asked coolly. Next to her, Trepalli shifted in his seat, obviously catching the change in tone.

"*Madame*," Tremblay replied, his tone matching hers in coolness. "I understand that you wish to find the driver who hit your mother. The process is hardly ever fast enough for the victim or the family's satisfaction. However, the process is in place for a reason. Let us do our job."

In other words, her judgment was impaired.

Frustration boiled up. "I would," she responded tartly, "but you aren't *doing* your job. Your constable didn't even know about the kid and his skateboard. And now that this kid might be in danger, the best you can do is tell me to mind my own business. How are you going to feel if there's another hit-and-run, only this time it's a kid on a skateboard?"

There was a long silence at the other end, and for a moment, Kate thought he had hung up. Maybe she had gone too far. She still needed the local constabulary. Or did she? It wasn't like they were being of much help.

Next to her, Trepalli was staring at her with wide eyes. Then she caught a movement and looked around to see the Impreza backing up into a driveway. What the hell was he doing? Then the driver drove forward out of the driveway and sped away from them.

"Shit!" she said and flung the phone into Trepalli's lap. She heard Tremblay's voice faintly saying, "Hello? Hello?" but she was too busy starting the car and peeling away to pay much attention.

Trepalli hurriedly buckled up and then picked up the phone.

"This is Constable Trepalli of the Mendenhall Police Department," he said. "We are in pursuit of a late model white Impreza, four doors, no visible markings."

He squinted through the windshield and Kate could almost hear his thoughts urging her to go faster. She didn't dare. This was a school zone and there were cars parked along both sides of the street. All it took was one kid running out from between parked cars.

The driver of the Impreza didn't let that stop him, however. He sped down the street, heading for Riverside Street. If he got there, she would never catch him before he got on the highway.

"Yes," said Trepalli as she nudged the Forester to a little more speed. The Impreza slammed on the brakes as a car pulled out from a side street and Trepalli immediately rattled off, "CGB... damn."

The Impreza had shot around the other car and, ignoring the stop sign, pulled into traffic on Riverside. Horns blared and cars swerved but there were no accidents.

She reached the corner while the drivers were still screaming curses at the Impreza and turned right.

"Where is it?" she asked.

"I can't see it," said Marco. Then, "There!" He pointed with the cell phone and Kate caught a glimpse of a white car taking the on ramp onto the highway. She accelerated and passed two slower moving vehicles, but by the time she had taken the on ramp, the Impreza was long gone.

CHAPTER 8

KATE SAT in one of the hard oak chairs in front of Sergeant Tremblay's desk. The sergeant was talking to someone just outside his door, behind her. He had told Trepalli in very clear terms that they were to report to the Longueuil police station on Curé Poirier right *now* or he would send two squad cars to escort them in.

Fury had flamed through her at being called in like a misbehaving student to the principal's office, but she had made her way off the highway and to the long, low, two-story building that housed the Longueuil police station.

They had been met at the entrance by a young female constable with a stern expression. Trepalli hadn't even tried to charm her. The young woman had walked them through a large room bigger than Kate's entire detachment, with a linoleum-tiled floor and high dividers hiding desks. Except for the half dozen uniformed officers walking about and the pervasive smell of old coffee, it could have been an insurance office. From behind the dividers came the sounds of voices, telephones ringing, and the clicking of keyboard keys. The young woman walked them through the large room to the back, where Sergeant Tremblay's office was, and asked them to wait inside.

The moment she left, Kate turned to Trepalli. "You wait outside," she said grimly. "You don't need to be involved in this."

With a relieved nod, he stepped back out.

She saw no point in involving him with the Longueuil constabulary. The boy was on holiday. He certainly hadn't planned to be dragged into an investigation by the boss he thought he had left behind in Manitoba. Of course, she hadn't exactly planned on this, either, and if he hadn't come knocking on Rose's door, he wouldn't be in this position right now.

The rationalization didn't help.

She had been waiting ten minutes, and the longer she waited, the colder her anger grew. Did Tremblay think he was dealing with a rookie? She tamped down the anger, refusing to let his little game goad her. But one more minute and she was out of there. She forced herself to lean back in the hard wooden chair, and rested her arms on the curved arms.

The office held a battered, dark wood desk that didn't match the chairs, a two-tier beige plastic tray for files on the corner, and an older model computer monitor, with the tower tucked away under the desk. A four-drawer vertical filing cabinet stood in one corner. There was a Quebec flag in a stand in another corner, and a window between the two, looking out on the station's parking lot. The window was open, and the sound of traffic from Curé Poirier seeped into the room.

On the wall opposite the desk were two photos, one of Hélène Arseneault, the premier of the province, and the other of Lionel Boursier, the Chief Superintendent. Otherwise there were no personal photos or mementos, not even a plant. The door plate read "Duty Officer," not "Sergeant Paul Tremblay." This was a shared office, then, for the use of whoever was the duty officer at any given time. Must be nice to have that kind of space.

The door opened and a man she presumed was Tremblay walked in holding a file folder. His hair was just about shorn off, but the half inch he allowed to survive was the color of iron wool. His eyes were hazel, set in a stern, thin-lipped face that gave nothing away.

He reminded her of McKell, with ten years and twenty pounds added on.

"Chief Williams," he said with a faint French-Canadian accent as he came around the desk. She wouldn't have been surprised if he'd remained standing in order to emphasize his psychological advantage, but he sat down.

Then he dropped the file folder on top of his empty desk and rubbed his hands tiredly over his face. "Chief Williams," he began again, then stopped. He looked at her. "*Madame*, you have all my sympathy. You do. But I cannot allow you to conduct your own investigation in my jurisdiction, and I cannot allow a car chase." His voice rose on the last two words before he clamped his mouth shut.

In spite of herself, Kate felt a twinge of empathy for the guy.

But still.

She raised an eyebrow at him. "Is it safe to presume that you are Sergeant Tremblay?" she asked coolly.

His face slowly turned bright red.

"I beg your pardon, *Madame*," he said stiffly. "Yes, of course. My name is Paul Tremblay."

Kate allowed herself a gracious nod but no smile. She studied him for a moment, struggling to hang on to her anger. "I can appreciate your position," she said carefully. She did *not* want to sound apologetic, but at the same time, she needed this guy to do his job. "I would like to point out that I did not endanger civilians in my pursuit, and I broke it off the moment the car was no longer in view." Damn. That sounded like an excuse. "And if we hadn't followed the car, you wouldn't have a partial plate number now." She eyed him but didn't see any softening of his expression. "As for conducting an investigation..." She shrugged. "All I did was talk to a few people, neighbors of my mother's. Hardly an investigation."

Tremblay's expression told her she wasn't fooling him.

"Chief Williams, you brought a constable from your force with you."

The breeze from the window fluttered the corner of the flag and floated the sounds of voices and a faint trail of exhaust fumes.

"Believe me, the constable's reasons for being here have nothing to do with me." Tremblay's eyebrows rose in disbelief and she leaned forward. "Sergeant, I'm sure I would feel the same way you do if you had come to my jurisdiction and were talking to witnesses." She took a deep breath, surprised to find her hands were shaking. "But no one was looking for the boy who could identify the driver." She shrugged. "And the same car that was trolling down my mother's street last night was parked in front of the school where we think the boy goes. What would you have done?"

The sergeant placed his hands on the edge of his desk and stared at her. She couldn't read his expression. He might have been trying not to smile, or he might have been figuring out what to charge her with.

"I do not think it is unusual to see the same car twice in the same neighborhood," he pointed out. His accent seemed more pronounced.

"Then why did he run?"

Tremblay shrugged. "Because you were chasing him? Which brings me to my next question. What were you doing at the school in the first place?"

Kate breathed in and out a few times.

He could still be useful, she reminded herself. *Be nice.*

"I was hoping to see an eleven-year-old boy with an Air Grabz skateboard and find out his name." She shrugged. "If I could have figured out a way of going in and asking about the kid, I would have," she said honestly. "Back home, not only would the principal have refused to help, she would have called the police if a stranger came in off the street with that kind of request."

A little smile crossed the sergeant's face, and Kate realized with a shock that he was handsome.

"Here also, *Madame*."

"Sergeant," she said slowly. "You know why we were there, but why was the other driver there? And why take off like that if the reason was innocent? He was there for the same reason we were. He was hoping to spot the kid."

"Perhaps," said Tremblay, and now there was no smile. "But you will do us the courtesy of letting us do our job without telling us how to do it." He raised a quelling hand when Kate tried to object. "*Non, Madame.* This is not your jurisdiction. You have no authority here. And yet you feel you can come here and criticize our methods with impunity. How would you feel if I went to Mendenhall and did that to you?"

Kate refused to look away. She knew damned well how she'd feel. But none of her constables would run a slipshod investigation the way young Claveau had. She would have fired anyone who was that bad at their job. Tremblay had to know that Claveau had failed, yet he was defending him.

Of course, he's defending him, she suddenly realized. *He's not about to air personnel issues to an outsider.*

How the hell was she going to enlist this guy's help without implying—or stating baldly—that his guy was incompetent? And as far as Tremblay was concerned, she wasn't a cop right now. She was an emotionally-compromised family member.

And maybe she was, but there was something here, she could feel it. And so could Trepalli. Tremblay hadn't seen the Impreza take off. They had. You developed a feeling for a case when you were on it long enough. And dammitall, she had a feeling.

"Sergeant Tremblay," she said, looking him in the eye, trying to impress the seriousness of the situation, "if nothing else, please look into the kid. He may be in danger."

"Chief Williams," began Tremblay, but before he could finish, Kate's phone rang, the ring tone cutting through the ambient noise of the building.

"Excuse me." She fished the phone out of her jacket pocket and glanced at the screen. It was Mendenhall. She swiped the screen to decline the call. She would call the station back later. She tucked the phone back in her pocket.

"*Madame*," the sergeant tried again. "Out of courtesy for your rank, and for your situation, I will tell you this. A white, four-door Impreza was reported stolen this morning in Greenfield Park. The same first three letters as the one your officer reported. The owner went to take his car to work and found it missing. It had been in the driveway the night before when he went to bed."

Huh. She shifted on the hard chair, working it out. According to John, the driver who hit her mother had been driving a dark green Kia Soul. He wouldn't want to drive the same car around the neighborhood. But to steal a car? That was a whole other order of business. You had to have nerve to steal a car out of someone's driveway, then drive it around the neighborhood where you'd hit an old woman, and then park by a school, hoping to catch a glimpse of the kid who could identify you.

None of this felt right. She looked up at the sergeant and found Tremblay staring back at her, his mouth in a straight line. She saw the same realization in his eyes.

They weren't dealing with John Q. Public here. They were dealing with a professional.

The door opened suddenly and Kate turned around to see Trepalli standing in the doorway, his cell phone in hand. He was looking at her, his normally tanned face pale. She straightened her back, suddenly alarmed.

"What is it?" she asked.

"It's Mendenhall, ma'am," he said, his expression grim. "The DC's been shot."

CHAPTER 9

ACCORDING to Albertson," said Trepalli, once they were back in John's car, "the DC was on his way to Winnipeg when it happened."

The shock hadn't worn off yet and Trepalli's words sounded like they came from the bottom of a well. She knew it would wear off once she started moving, but she couldn't drive right now. She turned in the driver's seat to face her constable. They had parked on the street in front of the police station, and pedestrians walked by them on one side and cars drove past on the other. The sun beat through the windshield but she still couldn't seem to get warm. The lingering new car smell of the Forester was making her feel queasy.

"Tell me."

Trepalli swallowed. He still looked sickly white and his hands were clenched into fists on his lap.

"He was caught up in the morning rush hour," he said. "On Portage." His blue, blue eyes looked shocky to her, but there was nothing she could do for him right now. "By the new overpass they're building near the golf course. Nobody saw the shooter, but Winnipeg cops think he was on the overpass. Whoever it was shot DC McKell as he approached. The shooter got away."

Dear God Almighty.

"Is he...?" She couldn't even bring herself to ask.

Trepalli shook his head. "Not dead. In serious condition at Grace Hospital."

She blinked at him, trying to assimilate it all. McKell shot and in serious condition. Shot by a sniper. Holy cow.

"I have to get back," she said to herself.

"Ma'am?" said Trepalli uncertainly.

She started the car, then looked at him. "I have to get back to Mendenhall."

Trepalli focused his entire attention on her. "What about your mother?"

Shock hit her in the pit of the stomach like a blow. Mom. How had she forgotten about Mom? She took a deep, shaky breath and thought it through. Finally she shook her head.

"My mother is doing better, and she's surrounded by family. She doesn't need me. My detachment needs me."

Trepalli remained silent for long seconds, studying her face. Finally he nodded agreement.

"Your family's not going to understand," he warned.

Kate put the car in drive and pulled out into the street. No, her family was definitely not going to understand.

* * *

Trepalli walked her to the hospital elevator.

"I'll wait for you in the cafeteria," he said as the doors opened. Kate nodded and rode up the double-door elevator alone. On the second floor, an orderly got in with an empty gurney and she moved over to allow him easy access. She got off on the third floor and made her way noiselessly toward Mom's room. There was no one at the nursing station, but a soft beeping noise from one of the computers told her they were probably responding to a patient in distress.

Her heart squeezed a little as she passed by the empty family lounge with its easy chairs and overstuffed couches. Was it really less than thirty-six hours ago that she had stood there and hugged

Rose and Amanda while she was filled in on Mom's accident?

The door to Mom's room was open a crack and she opened it wider to enter. A strange man sat by Mom's bedside, hands resting on the edge of the bed next to her arm. Her eyes were closed now and she looked asleep. Kate looked from Mom's face to the man and frowned.

"Who are you?" she asked abruptly, startling him.

He turned to face her. He was a thin man, older, Mom's age. He had a strong jaw and a narrow, barely hooked nose, with fierce white eyebrows over deep brown eyes that shone with intelligence and curiosity. He stood up, revealing himself to be tall, with wide shoulders and a straight back. He wore a pair of casual grey slacks, a white shirt open at the neck, and a tweed sports coat. He looked like he belonged at the yacht club.

"You must be Kate," he said in a low voice, making his way out of the tangle of machines and chairs toward her. He placed a hand under her elbow and gently turned her toward the door. "Hetty is asleep. I think I saw a waiting room along the hallway. Let's talk there."

As he talked, he guided her out the door, closing it behind them. Kate considered resisting, just to see what he would do, but there was something so genteel about his manner that she couldn't bring herself to be contrary.

He led her down the hallway to the family lounge and closed the door behind them. Kate caught a glimpse of Nurse Hathaway, walking toward the nursing station, before the door fully closed, then the man turned toward her with a smile.

"Alfred Stilwell," he said, putting his hand out. "I'm a friend of your mother's."

Kate shook his hand, unsurprised to find his grip strong and warm. This had to be Mom's beau. How else would he have been allowed in her room?

"Mr. Stilwell," she said formally. "I'm Kate Williams. Hetty's oldest daughter."

He released her hand with a smile and gestured her to one of the easy chairs. Kate sat down. The last time she had been in this room, it had been dark outside and she hadn't noticed that the windows faced a small park. Now the sun reached into the room, casting the back of one of the sofas in light while leaving the seat in shade. Stilwell sat down on the couch in the corner nearest her and leaned forward, elbows on his knees and big, bony hands linked together.

"You're a police chief, Hetty tells me."

Kate blinked. She didn't have time for this. The flight was at five o'clock and she still had to get back to the house and pack.

"Mr. Stilwell," she began.

"Please," he interrupted. "Call me Fred."

That gave her pause. She had never met anyone who seemed less like a Fred.

"Fred," she began again. "Where's Rose?"

"She's getting a bite to eat in the cafeteria," he said equably. The smile faded from his face. "It was a bit of a shock to return only to learn about the accident."

Only it wasn't an accident, was it? Kate tried to shake the idea out of her head, but she couldn't. Too many things didn't add up. The guy in the Impreza, waiting at the school... the Impreza itself being stolen... Maybe it was an accident, but it didn't feel right to her.

"When did you find out?" she asked gently.

"I got home last night." He shrugged. "I was visiting my children and grandchildren in Regina. Hetty wasn't answering her phone, then or this morning. Finally I called Sophie to see if Hetty was there." His gaze darkened and dropped to the floor. "I came as soon as I heard, and Rose rescued me when the nurses wouldn't let me see her."

His hands clenched into fists, then relaxed. He looked back up at her. "But all is well," he said with a smile. "She's being transferred out of intensive care this afternoon."

Kate sighed with relief. Well, that was good news. She wished she could talk to Mom before she left, but she didn't want to wake her.

The door to the lounge opened and Kate twisted around to see who it was. Rose stood framed in the doorway, one hand holding the door open, the other fluttering around her waist as if it couldn't figure out what to do with itself. It looked a little funny until Kate saw the red splotches on Rose's cheeks.

She knew that look.

"You're leaving?" Rose asked.

Fred rose. "Come inside," he said firmly. "And close the door."

At that moment, Kate remembered that he had been a colonel in the army. She could believe it.

Rose obediently stepped inside and released the wide door to close behind her. She didn't take her gaze off Kate. "How can you even consider leaving at a time like this?"

Kate stood up, too. She suddenly felt incredibly weary, as if she hadn't slept in a week. She really hadn't thought through how she would approach... Her thoughts trailed off as she replayed Rose's words.

"How did you know I was planning to leave?"

She caught the colonel's sharp turn of head toward her but kept her gaze on her sister.

"That *boy* told me," said Rose, almost spitting the word out.

Kate forced herself to be calm. She was too warm in the enclosed space and wanted to take her jacket off, but Rose would consider it stalling. She took a deep breath and warned herself to stay calm.

"Then you know that my deputy chief has been shot," she said carefully. Out of the corner of her eye, she saw the colonel start with surprise.

"And your mother's been hit by a car!" said Rose tartly. "Don't you think she should be your priority right now?"

Kate stared at her sister across the gulf of their experience.

Rose had chosen the path of hearth and home. She had stayed home to raise Amanda and Sean and only gone back to work part time once they were both in university. She had kept her hand in with graphic design and now had a thriving career, but even that work kept her at home. She knew nothing of the kind of life Kate had lived. The kind of responsibilities she faced.

"How bad is it?" asked the colonel, startling them both.

Kate's throat tightened and she had to clear it before she could speak. "He was shot by a sniper, and crashed the car. He's in serious condition."

Fred turned to Rose with a raised eyebrow. "Forgive me for intruding into what is clearly a family matter," he said, "but your sister's duty is with her detachment." He raised a hand when Rose glared at him. "Your mother is recovering. She does not need an operation. She is being transferred to the general ward this afternoon. Hetty does not need your sister right now, but her men do."

Kate wanted to kiss him, but by the look on Rose's face, she was the only one who felt like that.

"Thank you for your opinion, Fred," said Rose stiffly. "I disagree. Family should be together at a time like this. Kate has a detachment full of police officers who can handle things until she gets back."

"Excuse me," said Kate, recapturing their attention. "This isn't a debate. Rose, I'm sorry you feel that way, but I'm going. I don't have time to stand here and argue with you." She nodded at Fred. "Nice to meet you."

"Likewise." The colonel nodded and went over to the door to open it for her.

Kate paused next to her sister, but Rose didn't even look at her. With a sigh, she left.

As the door closed behind her, she heard Rose start in on the colonel. Then her glance fell on Mom's door and she decided she could spare thirty seconds to give her mother a kiss. But when she entered the room, she found Mom awake and alert.

"Katie!" she said with a smile.

"Mom," said Kate, grinning from ear to ear. She approached the bed and reached for Mom's free hand. It felt smaller and more fragile than she remembered. "You look like hell."

Mom's smile widened and she winced as the movement reached the scrapes and bruises on the right side of her face.

"Don't be shy, sweetheart," she said. "Tell me what you really think."

Kate laughed, and to her shock, started to cry. All the fears that she had held so tightly contained exploded out of her in a river of unstoppable grief and relief.

"Oh, sweetheart," murmured Mom, pulling Kate to her. They stayed like that for a long minute while Kate wept out her fears and Mom hugged her to her battered body. Finally, Kate pulled back.

"I'm supposed to be comforting you," she said with a hiccup. She released Mom's hand and fished through her pockets for a tissue. Finally she grabbed a few from the box on the nightstand and blew her nose.

Mom watched with a smile. "It's never easy to see your mother incapacitated," she said gently. "But the doctor tells me I'm doing well."

Kate finished wiping her face and tossed the sodden mess of tissues into the waste basket beyond a tangle of wires.

"How do you feel?" she finally asked, glancing at her mother's left leg. It was still elevated on pillows under the blanket.

Mom blinked and Kate could see her considering how she would answer. Then Hetty Williams looked at her daughter and smiled.

"Honestly? A little like something the cat dragged in and didn't have the heart to eat."

Kate laughed again, feeling better by the minute. Mom always said that as long as you had your sense of humor, you would be fine.

"Do you remember any of it?" she asked.

Mom shook her head. "I never saw the car coming. I remember flying through the air and then I woke up here." She glanced around the tiny room. "Freddy was just here, wasn't he?"

Kate nodded. "He's in the lounge with Rose." She took a deep breath and plunged ahead. "Mom, I hate to do this, but I have to go back to Manitoba."

Mom blinked up at her in silence. Then her gaze sharpened and she frowned.

"What's happened? Is it Bert?"

Kate wanted to smile. Mom hadn't even met Bert, though she'd spoken to him a few times on the phone. But she was bound and determined that Kate would "hang on to this one."

"No. Rob McKell, my deputy chief. He's been hurt." She didn't need to give her injured mother the gory details of exactly what had happened to McKell. Mom had her own issues to deal with.

But Mom was having none of it.

"There's more to it, isn't there?" she asked sharply. "What aren't you telling me?"

Kate sighed. She should have known better.

After she finished telling her mother as much as she knew, Hetty nodded, and winced again. Kate suspected she had a hell of a headache.

"Of course you have to go," said Hetty finally. "Your people need you." She took Kate's hand in hers and squeezed. "And you need to find whoever did this to him."

* * *

"I'm so sorry, Chief," said Trepalli. Again.

Oh God. Please stop apologizing, Kate begged him silently.

"Constable, don't worry about it," she said firmly. Trepalli handled the congested streets like a lifelong urbanite, but the traffic, the red lights, the drivers going too fast were all starting to wear on Kate's nerves. "Rose doesn't handle stress well, and she's been under quite a bit of stress recently. She'll calm down." One day.

"I'm sure I haven't helped," said Trepalli glumly. Kate glanced at him, noting again the shadows under his eyes. She felt... she didn't know how she felt. Guilty, maybe. He had come all this way with some sort of cockeyed plan to win Amanda back, and he had yet to even *see* the girl. Part of her was still angry. What the *hell* had he been thinking? But he hadn't been thinking, had he? No, he had followed his heart, and it had led him right into the middle of a Williams family drama.

And now, out of left field, McKell was down, too. But unlike Mom, he might not make it.

"Here we are," said Trepalli, pulling into the driveway of Rose's house. Amanda's Tercel was in the driveway, too. Kate glanced sideways at the boy, but he was busy taking his seatbelt off and opening the door. Had he noticed?

Not sure what he was planning to do, Kate hurriedly got out, too. The afternoon was already waning. She glanced at her watch. Almost three. She had to hurry, or she'd miss the flight.

"Are you sure you don't mind driving me?" she asked, striding up the driveway. When he didn't answer, she turned to see he had stopped walking and was staring at her.

"I'm going with you," he said, as if surprised she had thought otherwise.

"There's no need—"

"Ma'am," he said abruptly. "We're all going to be there."

Kate shut up. Of course they were. One of theirs was down. With a nod, she turned and opened the gate to the backyard, the boy right behind her. They would have to get Trepalli's car from where they had left it, on the side street by École Gustave Bolton.

Through the window in the sun room door, she could see Amanda curled up in a chair, ignoring the magazine on her lap, staring out the window to the back garden. At the sound of the door opening, she turned. The smile that lit up her face at the sight of her aunt quickly faded when she saw Trepalli behind Kate.

"I'll be back in five," said Kate, abandoning them to each other. She didn't have time to mediate, or energy to deal with their drama right now. Let them figure it out.

"Hey," said John, coming out of the dining room with an empty plate and a cup just as she entered the kitchen. "Rose called."

Kate nodded but kept going into Sean's room. "I'm sorry, John, but I don't have time to argue. I have a plane to catch in less than two hours."

John followed her into the bedroom, still holding the plate and cup. "No argument, Kate. You're doing what you need to do. Rose will eventually realize that."

The tears sprang up so quickly, Kate didn't have a chance to stop them. She turned to John and gave him a fierce hug, almost making him drop the plate.

Five minutes later, she had stuffed everything into her tote bag and was headed back toward the sun room when John suddenly caught her by the jacket in the hallway and stopped her.

She turned toward him in surprise but he put his finger up against his lip and pulled her into the kitchen. Only then did she hear them.

"...and to show up here!"

That was Amanda and she sounded angry. Kate glanced at John but he was staring intently at the corner cupboard that hid the doorway into the sun room.

"You left!" said Trepalli. "You just packed up your car and left. You never gave me a chance—"

"To do what?" interrupted Amanda more quietly. "To change my mind? I gave you my answer back in Mendenhall. What made you think it would be all right to just show up at my parents' house?"

"I had to do something!" Frustration had crept into Trepalli's voice and he forgot to keep his voice down. "When something is important to you, you have to go after it with everything you've got. And you're important to me, Amanda Coburn. You know that."

The silence that followed stretched on and Kate found herself leaning forward in anticipation. Had Amanda softened? Were they kissing?

"Really," said Amanda scornfully. "I'm so important to you that you're leaving."

Holy cow. If Kate hadn't left Rose behind in the hospital, she could have sworn that it was her sister talking. Where was the sweet Amanda she had always known? This Amanda had a little too much drama queen in her. She glanced at John, but now he was staring at the tile floor.

Apparently Trepalli agreed with her, though.

He laughed humorlessly.

"Amanda, I love you, but sometimes what's going on isn't about you. Right now I need to be back in Mendenhall. If you can't understand that, then maybe you're right, and you shouldn't be a cop's wife."

A moment later, the door to the backyard opened and closed softly. Before Kate and John could move, Amanda ran up the steps to the kitchen, only to stop when she saw her father and her aunt. Her eyes brimmed with tears and her cheeks were red. She stared at them for a second, then kept going through the kitchen and into the hallway that led to the bedrooms.

Kate finally remembered to breathe. After a moment, she risked a glance at her brother-in-law. To her surprise, John looked cheerful. He smiled down at her.

"Well, that went well," he said, giving her a one-armed hug. "Here, let me take that for you." He took the tote bag out of her hand and headed for the sun room, leaving a bemused Kate to follow behind.

CHAPTER 10

THE FLIGHT was full and Kate and Trepalli weren't seated together, which was just as well, judging by his silence all the way to the airport. In the end, John had driven them. Trepalli had left the keys to his cousin's car with John, promising that someone would be by in the next few days to drive it back to Toronto. He made no mention of coming back to Montreal.

There was a layover in Toronto and Kate offered to buy the boy dinner, but like her, he had very little appetite. She called the station only to be told that there was no change to McKell's condition and no word on the shooter. O'Hara was on the duty desk, unfortunately. He was a good cop, but taciturn at the best of times, and the more stressful the situation, the quieter he became. After a while, she gave up trying to get more than yes or no answers and hung up. They'd be there soon enough.

She tried calling Bert, but there was no answer. She left him a voice message, telling him what had happened, though he would already know. The entire Manitoba police community would know, no matter where they happened to be.

Then their flight was called and she and Trepalli lined up to board. When she noticed the slump in her constable's shoulders, she made an effort to straighten her own. This flight wasn't full but neither one suggested sitting together.

At last they landed. O'Hara had assured her that someone would be at the airport to pick them up but when they got to the arrivals gate, she saw no sign of the navy blue uniform of the Mendenhall Police Department. People streamed around them, hurrying to grab a cab or meet friends and family. She and Trepalli stood like trees in the middle of a river and tried to pick out a familiar face.

Then Trepalli touched her elbow and she looked up at him only to see him nodding toward an approaching figure. Kate blinked and then sagged with relief.

"Hey, Katie," said Bert with a gentle smile. He was dressed in jeans and a light blue windbreaker over a white polo shirt. He studied her carefully. "You look beat."

And then her bag was on the floor and she was in his arms and he was in hers. He felt solid and strong, and his big hands held her securely as she pressed her cheek against his, taking in the warm, musky smell of him and the fading scent of his spicy aftershave. His cheek bristled with stubble that would leave whisker burns on hers. It felt wonderful. Finally she swallowed hard and forced herself to pull away.

"When did you get back?"

"A few hours ago. Just long enough to drop off the suitcase at home and come back. I called Mendenhall and told them I'd pick you up." He finally pulled his gaze away from hers and nodded to Trepalli. "Marco. How're you holding up?"

"Fine, sir."

He was clearly far from fine, but when Bert glanced at her, she shook her head minutely. Not now.

"I want to see McKell," she said.

The stream of bodies had ebbed and Bert bent to pick up her bag. With an arm around her shoulders, he turned her toward the exit, looking back over his shoulder to make sure Trepalli was following.

"I called my office," he said. "They're keeping tabs on him."

Kate felt the blood drain from her face. Trepalli had moved up next to her and now they exchanged a look. Cops kept tabs on victims of violence because if they died, the charges were upped to murder. She swallowed hard.

"How bad...?"

Bert didn't look at her but kept forging past stragglers toward the glass sliding doors through which she could see the golden light of late afternoon. They were heading for the parking lot.

"He still hasn't regained consciousness," he said grimly. "They're operating on him now."

Operating!

She and Trepalli both stopped and stared at Bert. He nodded.

"The shot hit metal before going through the windshield. It fragmented. One fragment grazed his shoulder, but another one lodged close to his spine." His normally ruddy face looked pale, making his reddish stubble stand out. "Then he lost control of the car and it rolled. Thank God for seatbelts and airbags, or he'd be dead. As it is, he's got a broken arm and a dislocated knee."

Dear Lord. McKell. Kate swallowed hard and tried to ask what she was too afraid to ask. Trepalli beat her to it.

"His spine?"

Bert sighed heavily and stared at the large, pale gray tiles of the arrivals floor. Only a few people were left in the area, stragglers waiting for their lifts, likely. The air smelled of exhaust and, faintly, wet pavement. It had rained recently.

"He'll probably survive the operation. They don't know if he'll walk again."

Bert's words hit her like blows and she took a step back, bumping into Trepalli. He put a hand on her back to steady her, but she could feel his hand shaking. She looked up at him and saw the same horror on his face. Then his attention caught on something beyond her and his eyes narrowed.

"Ma'am, I believe we're being watched."

Kate controlled an impulse to look around. Instead she looked at Bert, who nodded.

"They're my men," he said grimly.

"Why are they watching us?" asked Kate, baffled.

"They're not watching you," said Bert carefully. "They're watching everyone else."

Trepalli looked as baffled as she felt. "Why?" he asked before Kate could.

Kate turned to Bert expectantly. Why, indeed?

Bert's face was a study in grim determination. Whatever he was about to say, he knew she wouldn't like it.

"Because McKell was driving Kate's Explorer."

* * *

They drove to Grace Hospital in Bert's green Honda CRV, accompanied by two unmarked cars. Once they reached the hospital, however, Bert sent the undercover officers away. They parked and walked quickly toward the entrance, Bert watching rooflines and doorways. The hospital loomed like an enormous tombstone in front of them. The sounds of the city seemed muted to her, as though the fading daylight also faded the noise of cars and sirens.

With the setting of the sun, a cool breeze sprang up and Kate shivered in her light jacket. Bert wrapped an arm around her waist, warming her. Trepalli walked on her other side, tall and silent, his blue eyes filled with dread.

As they walked into the lobby, Kate was almost overcome by nausea. She knew it came from having spent so much of the past forty-eight hours in the hospital where her mother was. All hospitals were essentially laid out the same. The young woman at the admissions desk looked up as they walked by and silently followed them with her gaze. Once they rounded her desk, Kate saw why.

The lobby's waiting area was filled with serious-looking men and women, some in police uniforms—both Mendenhall and Winnipeg, and a few from Brandon—and some in civilian clothes. Some officers sat silently, in the chairs. Others stood a little apart, talking in low tones. Beyond the waiting area, at the far end of the long, wide hall, was the emergency room waiting area. It was suppertime and only a few people were sitting in the waiting room. As though the thought triggered the realization, she became aware of the faint smell of cooking—something like cabbage, or maybe turnips. Whatever it was, it was nauseating.

Bert had removed his arm from her waist when they entered and now she was grateful. She had to pull herself together and be a cop again.

From the milling bodies, one peeled away and it was only when she approached that Kate realized it was Charlotte, the station's only administrative assistant.

"Chief," she said, stopping a few feet from Kate. Her pretty green eyes were bloodshot and her normally glossy, shoulder-length brown hair was disheveled, as if she had been running her hands through it repeatedly. She was in a pair of linen pants and matching sleeveless top, with a brightly patterned scarf looped casually around her neck.

"Charlotte," said Kate, then she stopped. She had no idea what she was supposed to say next.

Then Charlotte saw Trepalli and her face crumpled up. Without a word, Trepalli took her in his arms and held her while she cried, and Kate suddenly remembered that he and Charlotte had dated for a while. Before Amanda. In the waiting area, familiar and unfamiliar faces watched them and Kate felt on display. What should she do now?

Suddenly Bert's big hand was on the small of her back.

"Stendel's here," he murmured in her ear.

Whether it was Bert's touch or the mention of the Winnipeg chief of police's name, Kate found herself straightening and squaring her shoulders. It was time to behave like a chief of police. She had come back for this, to be there for her people. For McKell. They needed to see her strong and in charge.

And she was damned if she was going to show Stendel any weakness.

Stendel was talking to a man in surgical greens near a bank of elevators. The man had a clipboard under one arm.

Taking a deep breath, she headed toward them, aware of at least a dozen pairs of eyes following her movements. Stendel saw her first and turned toward her.

"Chief Williams," he said formally. They had never warmed to each other, despite the fact that they sat at the same tables during provincial meetings and that she and Bert, his deputy chief, had been seeing each other for six months.

"Chief Stendel," said Kate crisply. "What news?" She glanced at the man in surgical greens. He was not much taller than her and probably around forty-five, with thinning brown hair that was going grey at the temples. The arms emerging from his short-sleeved top were corded with lean muscles and he held himself lightly, as if he could spring into movement at any moment.

"This is Dr. Sturgess," said Stendel. "Doc, this is Kate Williams, chief of police in Mendenhall. McKell is her deputy chief." He looked at Kate. "The doc here operated on McKell."

The surgeon looked at Kate. He had warm brown eyes with laugh lines at the corner. Right now, however, it was the two deep grooves on either side of his mouth that dominated her attention.

"Chief Williams," said Sturgess, nodding in acknowledgement. "I was just telling Chief Stendel that the operation went well." Before Kate's hopes could surge, he raised a cautioning hand. "It's too early to tell if it was successful, however. We're going to keep him asleep for the next little while, so it may be a few days before we know. One way or the other." He glanced over her shoulder at the waiting room. "Tell them to go home," he added. "We'll call you when we know."

Kate nodded while privately deciding that she was damned if she was going to wait around for a phone call. She wanted to be there when McKell woke up. She wanted to be able to tell him they had found the person who had shot him.

An orderly with a cart rattled by and the doctor turned to follow him toward the emergency room. Stendel stared down at her. For once, his habitual smirk was gone.

"Anything I can do, Kate," he said softly. "Just ask."

Kate nodded again. "Thanks, John," she said. "I want in on the investigation."

Stendel blinked in surprise. "Of course," he said carefully, glancing over the top of her head. "We'll keep you informed every step—"

Kate shook her head sharply. "No, John. I don't want to know after the fact. I want to find the bastard who shot my DC."

Stendel looked suddenly very uncomfortable. "Chief Williams, you know as well as I do that you are too close to this case."

For Pete's sake! What was it these by-the-book cops didn't get? First Tremblay in Longueuil and now Stendel, treating her like she was too mentally fragile to know what she was asking. She took a deep breath and tried control her shaking.

Okay, fine. He was right. Technically.

She opened her mouth to say so but suddenly there was a hand on her arm and she looked around to find Bert standing next to her.

"Chief, your people are waiting to hear about McKell." There was a clear warning in his eyes and she felt a sudden rush of resentment. Him, too?

Then she looked past him and saw Boychuk and Tourmeline, and next to them, Friesen, Trepalli's usual partner, and Samantha Paterson, all in uniform. They must have come straight from the station after the end of their shift. Then she spotted Olinchuk and Oppenheimer in civilian clothes, all standing close together, all looking at her with the same expression.

She sighed softly. Bert was right. She glanced up at Stendel. "You'll post a guard on him?"

"Twenty-four hour," promised Stendel.

She nodded her acknowledgement and went to her people. They wouldn't have overheard the doctor. Bert stayed with Stendel, and she appreciated the courtesy.

She stopped a few feet from Oppenheimer. He was one of her younger constables, about Trepalli's age. But where Trepalli was tall and slim, Russ Oppenheimer was barely five feet nine, and stocky. He wasn't the smartest among her constables, but he made up for it by being observant and careful. His normally cheerful face was now somber and she realized with a shock that he was bracing himself. They all were.

"We won't know for a few days," she said bluntly. "The operation went well, but they won't know if there's any damage to his spine until he wakes up, and they plan to keep him asleep for at least another day."

She saw nods and if not exactly relief, then a slight relaxing of shoulders. It wasn't the news they were hoping for, but it could have been much worse.

Out of the corner of her eye, she saw Stendel and Bert approach the remaining officers and start talking in low voices. She looked around, suddenly wondering where Trepalli was, and saw him and Charlotte standing side by side, barely touching. She was struck by how handsome a couple they made, and how they clearly derived comfort from each other. Marco's gaze met hers, his blue eyes dark with a pain that was reflected in Charlotte's gaze.

Charlotte understood. She understood in a way that Amanda might never understand.

"Go home," said Kate suddenly. She jerked her gaze away from Marco and Charlotte and looked at the rest of her constables. "Go home. I'll stay here until we know more."

She saw uncertainty in some of their faces, but really, there wasn't anything they could do. "Go," she said softly. "I promise I'll call as soon as I have news."

* * *

"No."

Kate looked up at Trepalli and controlled an urge to shake him. They stood just outside the front doors of Grace Hospital. Bert would be upset to see her standing in full view like this, but she couldn't take his concerns seriously.

Night had arrived and with it, the warmth had gone. Kate's light jacket did little to protect her against the cool wind. Trepalli, on the other hand, seemed perfectly comfortable in his leather jacket. He stood facing her, arms crossed over his broad chest, a mulish cast to his normally handsome face.

"There's no reason to stay," Kate pointed out reasonably. "Catch a ride before it's too late." Bert had gone to get the car from the parking lot and it seemed to be taking him an awful long time, the coward.

"I'm still on leave," said the boy. "I have friends I can stay with in Winnipeg. And," he uncrossed his arms and pointed a finger at her, "you need me."

Kate bit the inside of her cheek against a sudden urge to smile. Well, wasn't he feeling all cocky and confident. Then she saw the pain in his eyes and the urge faded.

"Face it, Chief," he continued seriously, "Stendel will never allow you to investigate. He'll pull the same crap as the sarge did in Longueuil. And you can't even sneak around here because everyone knows you're the chief in Mendenhall." He stopped to take a shaky breath and his arms went out in a sweeping gesture. "My face hasn't been plastered all over the news, and I have friends in the WPS. I can get into places you can't."

Kate stared at him but she wasn't really seeing him. Crap. He made a good argument. In the last year, her face had indeed been plastered in the local papers—Mendenhall, Brandon, and Winnipeg, not to mention the dozens of small community papers throughout the province. First it had been an article when she arrived in Mendenhall. Then the Cop Games, which she had organized, the shooting in Riding Mountain Park, the emergency services exercise last February where they had found a real body... and he had a point about the Winnipeg Police Services resisting her involvement.

Stendel would shut her out. She knew he would.

But Bert wouldn't.

And Marco did know a lot of people in the WPS... many of them women. Still, between the two of them, they might be able to get to the bottom of McKell's shooting.

"All right, fine," she said ungraciously. "I'll be staying at Bert's. Where will you be?"

He shrugged. "I'll find somewhere."

As Bert finally pulled up and Trepalli walked over to pull his bag out of the back, Kate found herself staring at the young constable's back and wondering if he'd be staying with a woman.

And how Amanda would feel if she knew.

CHAPTER 11

A T SEVEN thirty the next morning, Kate found herself sitting alone at Bert's kitchen table, a massive thing made of maple, with clunky, square legs. It weighed a ton and had seen better days, judging by the number of rings and dents on its pale surface. Four chairs surrounded the table, none of which matched. There was even one that could have come from her mother's kitchen back in the sixties, ripped vinyl seat and all.

The chairs, the table... they matched the rest of the kitchen, with its old-fashioned wooden cupboards and round, metal pulls, the drawers that never snugged up properly, the battered porcelain sink with its rust stains that just wouldn't come out.

Kate, who was definitely no kitchen snob, had felt sorry for the kitchen the first time she saw it. Now she understood its understated charm much better. It had a big window over the sink, a window graced with fresh, yellow curtains. A door with another window in it led to a back deck of more recent vintage. In the summer, if Bert was home, that door was always open because he was always in the back yard, puttering with the lawnmower, weeding his vegetable garden.

It was a well-lived-in kitchen, one that had seen many generations and would welcome many more. Friendly. It was her favorite room in the house.

Now she sat with her feet up on the ripped vinyl seat of the neighboring chair, waiting patiently for Bert to call her. He'd headed for the office half an hour ago, even though it was Saturday. He wanted to read the reports for himself. Kate had bitten her tongue to keep from asking why he didn't have a laptop connected to his work files.

It wasn't that Bert was a Luddite when it came to technology. It was more that he believed in separation of home and office. He'd told her once that he'd seen his dad work himself to death at the age of fifty-six, and he didn't want that happening to him.

So he stayed at work until he was done, then he came home and didn't think about work again until he went back. He had his cell phone if his people needed him, and he went back in if necessary. But otherwise, home was home.

Must be nice.

She stopped toying with her cell phone and picked up the mug of coffee. He would call when he was ready. Her staring at the phone wasn't going to make it ring any faster.

Maybe she should call and see how Mom was doing. But her heart sank at the thought of talking to Rose. Or worse, Amanda. She had no idea what she could say to Amanda. She thought back to last night and seeing Charlotte in Trepalli's arms. It didn't have to mean anything. They had remained friends after they had stopped seeing each other. And friends comforted each other.

She could call the hospital directly. No need to talk to Rose only to be at the receiving end of another lecture. She pulled the cell phone toward her and stared at it. There was a way of getting on the internet with this thing, she was sure of it. She would go on, look up the hospital's phone number, and call.

She swiped the screen with her thumb, the cup held aloft in her other hand. Wasn't there an icon...?

The phone rang and she jerked back, sloshing hot coffee over her lap.

"Dammitall!" She jumped up and shook her leg, as if that

would cool her flesh. The phone rang again and she finally put the cup down and picked up the phone.

"Williams," she said.

"Hey," said Bert. "Everything okay?"

She sighed. No, of course everything was not okay. Her deputy chief had been shot, her station was in turmoil, and her mother was in hospital. Add to that the facts that her sister was mad at her and her niece might or might not have made a serious mistake, and things were just peachy.

"Fine," she said. "Just spilled some coffee. What'd you find out?"

"Not much," he said glumly. "There's not been much headway. If there were any witnesses, they aren't coming forward. Stendel's planning to put out an appeal for witnesses if he doesn't find someone soon."

Kate pursed her lips, thinking. She knew the area where the shooting had taken place. The shooter had been on an overpass under construction, on the Trans-Canada Highway as it entered Winnipeg proper and became Portage Avenue. The speed limit there was sixty kilometers an hour, still fast, but a man with a scope could easily shoot a driver.

Only if the shooter wanted to shoot a *specific* driver did it become a hell of a shot.

"Why now?" she asked. "Why there?"

"I've been asking myself the same questions," said Bert. "Why shoot at a speeding car, in broad daylight, with witnesses all over the highway?"

Kate shook her head. It didn't really make sense. It would be so much easier to pick off a victim while he was going about his business on foot. Why not shoot McKell—or her, if Bert's current theory was right—in Mendenhall? It would be easier to find them, easier to lie in wait in a smaller town.

And easier to get caught, she realized. Mendenhall *was* a small town. Strangers were noticed. The Trans-Canada didn't go through town, but passed by on the outskirts. There would be no quick getaway.

She told Bert her theory and he was silent for a few minutes, mulling it over.

"Could be," he said finally. "Especially the getaway part. Too many people would notice a shooter, his car, his direction of travel. Can you think of anyone who would want to kill you?"

He sounded like he was asking if she could think of the name of the teller at the bank. Kate swallowed a sudden tightness. She'd been a cop for thirty years and had only been shot at twice. And one of those times had been an accident. She had put plenty of people away, some pretty bad ones. Would any of them hold a grudge?

"I can't think of anyone, Bert. I need my notes." At home she kept all her old notebooks, including copies of files in cases where she'd had to testify. Maybe she would find something there. "I need to get back to Mendenhall. Can I borrow your truck until I can replace my Explorer?" Besides his Honda, Bert had a navy Ford Ranger that he used for hauling lumber or gardening supplies. It was old and none too pretty, but it was solid.

"No," he said.

Kate's attention returned to the phone with a start. "Pardon me?"

"No, Kate," said Bert patiently. "I don't want you driving anywhere without protection. This guy's already tried once to kill you. If he knows that he made a mistake, what's to keep him from trying again?"

The sun had reached the window in the door and was warming her bare feet, still up on the chair. Kate stared at her sunny toes and considered Bert's words. He was genuinely concerned for her safety. If she stepped outside of the situation and looked in as an outsider, she could see why. But she didn't feel like she was in danger.

"Bert, what if it was random?" she asked slowly, still trying to puzzle out her feelings. "What if the fact that it was McKell, or my car, means nothing? What if the shooter just happened to pick my car and wasn't actually waiting for it?"

There was a long silence at the other end. "You're thinking that being a cop had nothing to do with the shooting," he finally said. "That the shooter didn't care who he was shooting."

She shrugged. "I think it's worth considering. I mean, there are much easier ways of killing me than waiting on a half-built over-pass for me to drive by. And besides, doesn't it seem to you like this was a crime of opportunity? He saw that there were no construction workers on the overpass and took a chance?"

"And he was wandering around with a rifle, just in case such an opportunity presented itself?" She could almost see him shaking his head. "Until we know for sure, we have to behave like the shooter meant to kill you."

She shrugged again, in irritation this time. "Well, whatever the motive was, I still need to get back to Mendenhall."

"Then you'll have to wait until I get back and take you," he said firmly. She finally agreed, but only after he promised not to have unmarked units accompany them. Enough was enough.

* * *

They stopped by the hospital before heading out of town, and Bert dropped her off at the main entrance with firm orders to get inside right away and wait for him. Feeling a little foolish, Kate did. When he joined her, they both went to the surgical ward on the fourth floor. When they got off the elevator, a feeling of déjà vu washed over her once more. She was definitely spending too much time in hospitals lately.

This ward was busier than the intensive care unit back in Quebec. Two nurses sat at a nursing station at the head of the ward, typing on a keyboard and studying readouts. Another nurse stood next to a trolley containing various plastic cups, syringes, and bottles. She was standing in front of the open door to one of the dozen rooms along both sides of the hallway, writing on a clipboard.

The walls were painted a particularly offensive shade of green, partway between mint and olive. Between the rooms hung cheerful posters reminding staff about the importance of accreditation levels, whatever those were. One or two photos depicted rural farming scenes. The place smelled of medicine and disinfectant.

Another nurse was just emerging from a room at the end of the hall, carrying a plastic case for blood vials.

They didn't have to ask which room was McKell's. A uniformed police officer sat in a straight-backed metal chair next to a closed door. His cap rested on one knee and his arms were crossed over his chest. He looked around when they came out of the elevator and stood up suddenly, only catching his cap in time. He waited until she and Bert were closer before speaking.

"Sir," he said in a low voice, clearly mindful that he was in a hospital. He nodded politely to Kate and she nodded back. He was a young man, younger than Trepalli, with wavy black hair that would no doubt be curly if he allowed it to grow out. His cheeks were full, as if he still hadn't grown out of his baby fat.

"At ease, Constable," said Bert. It always impressed her that the Winnipeg Police Services officers recognized Bert even when he was out of uniform.

"How is he?" asked Bert, nodding at the closed door. The door had the number 4018 painted in bright white on the outside.

"Still out, from what I've been told," said the young constable. Manley, by his name tag.

"Has anyone tried to see him?" asked Kate.

"No, ma'am." Constable Manley shook his head for emphasis. "And I've been here since midnight."

"Good job, Manley," said Bert. "As you were."

As the boy resumed his seat, Kate and Bert pushed open the door to the room and walked in. Kate had to control an impulse to check over her shoulder. It was hard to shake the feeling that she needed an authority figure's approval, even when she *was* an authority figure.

The room held two beds, separated by a curtain, but only one was occupied. McKell lay in the high hospital bed, the sheets pulled up tautly over his chest, his arms over top of the sheets on either side. His left arm was in a cast and supported by a pillow. His right leg was propped up so that it formed a hillock under the otherwise smooth topography of the bed. A lump over his chest level revealed the position of the dressing covering the operation incision. His hands and forearm were swollen and bruised, but except for a red scrape along his left temple and cheek, he looked peaceful, as if he had fallen asleep.

"Are you okay?" asked Bert. She nodded without taking her gaze from McKell's still form.

The man had made her life hell when she first came on as chief of the Mendenhall Police Department. He had undermined her at every turn, defied her, challenged her... If she could have strangled him and gotten away with it, she would have been sorely tempted.

But once they worked out their differences, he'd turned out to be an excellent deputy chief. He was stubborn, proud, smart, intuitive... not an easy man, by any means, but a good man in every sense of the word. A wave of guilt threatened to engulf her. Was she responsible for his injuries? Had he almost gotten killed because of her? Was he perhaps going to lose the use of his legs because someone mistook him for her?

The sound of coughing just outside the door was all the warning they got. The door opened suddenly and an older woman in the ubiquitous print scrub uniform of nurses nowadays stood in the opening, frowning fiercely at them.

"Out," she said.

Kate glanced at Bert and caught the look of alarm on his face. That was a real "out," the kind that brooked no argument and promised severe retribution if they hesitated.

"Yes, ma'am," said Bert meekly, and led the way out.

The nurse stood aside as they emerged into the hallway. Kate caught the young constable's apologetic look before she turned to face the nurse in charge. You could always tell which one was in charge.

The woman's face was long, with stern gray eyes and a straight nose above a wide, thin-lipped mouth. Her gray hair was brushed straight back and caught in a thick braid that fell halfway down her back. Now that Kate was standing next to her, she could see that the nurse was barely taller than she was. She had seemed much bigger when they were in the room.

She wished she could do that.

"Could you tell me how he is?" she asked, trying for meekness but not quite succeeding.

"You'll have to ask the doctor," said the woman, closing the door firmly and glaring at the seated constable. The nurse with the trolley walked past them, carefully not looking at them.

"All right," said Kate reasonably. "Where is he?"

"Dr. Sturgess will be doing his rounds later this morning or in the early afternoon," said the nurse. To Kate's annoyance, she wore no name tag.

"Ma'am," said Bert politely, "isn't there anything you can tell us?"

The woman looked as if she would turn them away and on impulse, Kate laid a hand on her bare arm. She could feel corded muscle under the warm skin.

"Please," she said softly. "He's my deputy chief, and he may have been hurt because of me."

The nurse stared back at her for a moment, then something shifted in her gaze. She nodded sharply.

"The bullet missed his heart but did damage to his lung. It will heal. His incision is minimal and the surgeon retrieved all the fragments. It should also heal quickly. He is very fit for a man his age." She shook her head when Kate opened her mouth. "I don't know if he has lost the use of his legs or not. You will need to speak to Dr. Sturgess about that." Then she relented. "I can tell you that it's still too soon to know. The swelling will have to go down before we remove the blocking agent."

Then she gently removed Kate's hand and walked away.

* * *

There was a fair amount of traffic on the way out of Winnipeg, it being Saturday, but they still made good time. Fifteen minutes after leaving the hospital, Bert pulled over on the shoulder to show her where the shooting had taken place. Kate got out and walked the scene, noting the skid marks where McKell had tried to brake, and the twisted guardrail and broken glass where the Explorer had flipped. They clambered down into the ditch and up to the other side, working their way through the scrub brush to the beginning of the overpass. They walked past the red and white barriers and the flashing, battery-operated yellow lights and past the police tape to the middle of the overpass. A series of metal grilles were set up side by side against the fresh concrete side wall, held down by heavy sand bags. They were clearly there to keep equipment and sundry items from falling onto the traffic below.

She could see the cars coming toward her clearly. A man with a rifle, standing where she was standing, would have had a clear view of vehicles as they entered Winnipeg.

"Why wasn't anyone working on it yesterday?" she asked, looking down at the metal rods, buckets of paint, and streetlights laid out end to end. It was as if the workers had just walked away. She had to raise her voice to be heard above the sound of the cars driving by below.

"The crew was pulled off ten days ago to work on an emergency repair job downtown," said Bert. "They're scheduled to finish this starting next week."

Huh. So, did that mean that the shooter knew the construction crew's schedule? Did he work for the city? Did he live in the area?

The wind carried the stink of exhaust on it, and plucked at her hair and her jacket. While Bert stood watch, she studied the ditch beyond the grilles. It was filled with a foot of water. Beyond was a service road that had recently been patched, and beyond that, a hay field that had recently been harvested, judging by the huge cylinders of hay, wrapped in white plastic, that lay in parallel rows throughout the field. Past the hay field were big-box stores and warehouses, with the odd manufacturing plant. They were all too far from the highway to provide any likely witnesses.

"It could have been so much worse," said Bert.

She glanced at him and he explained. "It looks to me like he deliberately steered into the guardrail. Otherwise, he would have gone into the median, and probably hit cars coming the other way."

Kate nodded. Yes, McKell would have kept his head, even with someone shooting at him. She looked down the highway at the cars driving toward her. She could make out individual faces. Anyone standing where she was would have had a great vantage point.

"The investigators found tire tracks at the north end of the overpass, in the mud," said Bert, pointing across the way to where the overpass reached the ground. "It looks like a motorcycle tire print."

"What time did the attack happen?" she asked.

"About seven thirty," said Bert promptly.

So, the sun was just up. She glanced up to orient herself. The shooter would have had his back to the sun, and the drivers would have been driving into the sun.

"He had the visor down," she murmured.

"Pardon?"

"McKell. He would have had the visor down against the sun. He probably never even saw the shooter."

"Let's go," said Bert. "I feel like a sitting duck out here."

"Yeah," agreed Kate, unsettled. If McKell hadn't seen the shooter, the chances were pretty good that the shooter hadn't seen McKell's face, either, since the sun would have been reflecting off the windshield. So he might very well have shot at McKell thinking he was Kate.

Or the shooting might have been random.

CHAPTER 12

THEY GOT to Kate's house half an hour later, and the moment she turned the key in the lock and walked into her front entrance, she sighed with relief.

The windows had been closed for days but the house still smelled a little like fresh ground coffee beans and the tomato sauce she had used on her spaghetti three nights ago. Or was that four? There was a thin layer of dust on the maple floor of the living room and she had left the headphones plugged into the stereo. Her slippers were still by her black leather easy chair and she'd left a glass of water on a coaster on the small table next to the chair.

It was good to be back.

"I'm going to change," she told Bert over her shoulder. "I'll just be a minute."

Without waiting for his answer, she headed down the hallway to the far bedroom, where she dropped her tote bag on the braided rug by the bed and immediately stripped off her jeans, jacket, and tee-shirt. Ten minutes later, she emerged from the bedroom still buckling the belt on her uniform.

She found Bert in the kitchen, rummaging through her fridge. A funny smell was coming from the open door but he didn't seem to notice.

"You have nothing to eat," he said reproachfully, straightening up. When he saw her uniform, his eyebrow rose but he said nothing. Then he caught sight of the Glock in its holster on her belt and his mouth tightened.

She didn't know why he was reacting this way. She wore the damned thing every day at work. It was policy.

"Want to help me carry a few boxes out?" she asked.

"Sure," he said, but instead he walked up to her and took her in his arms. "But first you need to promise me you'll be careful."

Well, of course she would be careful. She didn't want to die. Why was he acting like this?

She smiled and pecked him on the cheek before disentangling herself.

"Come on," she said. "They're in the spare bedroom." Which had been Amanda's room for the few months she had lived with Kate.

"What's in the boxes?" asked Bert, following.

"Old files. Including all my cases that went to trial."

Unfortunately, they were mixed together and she would have to take all ten boxes with her.

"Wouldn't it be simpler to go through them here?" asked Bert, eyeing the stack in the closet.

Kate shrugged. "I want to go in."

He looked at her, and after a moment, nodded.

He went outside first, however, his own Glock hidden against the side of one of the boxes. The fact that he was carrying had surprised Kate, as he'd dressed in jeans and a sweatshirt that morning. But the pistol had been tucked into a flat holster at his back. It must have been uncomfortable driving like that.

He did a thorough scan of the neighborhood before heading for the truck. Kate fought off irritation and watched from the doorway until he gave her the nod. She knew he was worried about her but she didn't need a protection detail. She could take care of herself.

Carrying a heavy file box, she stepped out onto the cement front stoop and down the few steps to the walk and then looked up, only to pause. Despite everything, a part of her had expected to see her red Explorer sitting in the driveway, not Bert's blue pickup. It brought home to her the fact that her car was gone. For the first time, she felt a pang at its loss. She'd only had it for three years and had been fond of it.

At some point, she was going to have to call her insurance company and find something else to drive. Much as she loved Bert, she didn't want to be at the mercy of his schedule or his protectiveness much longer.

"You okay?" he asked as he passed her on the walk.

"Yep," she said. "I'll be right there."

Ten minutes later they finished loading the boxes into the back of the truck and Kate locked the door to the house. She stood a moment on her stoop, looking around at the neighborhood. Mrs. Emery, the retired economist across the way, was out in her front yard, watering the flower beds. Jack Steiner and his little sister, Evelyn, were practicing their skateboarding on the quiet street, helmets, elbow and knee pads safely in place. From the Drecker house near the end of the cul-de-sac came the sound of vacuuming.

Normal, everyday sounds and sights on a Saturday morning in Mendenhall.

It was hard to believe that some madman was out there shooting people.

But he wasn't, was he? If it was a crazed shooter, randomly shooting people, he would have found another victim by now, wouldn't he?

"Kate."

She looked around to see Bert frowning at her and knew what he was thinking. She was setting herself up as a target by standing in one spot, on display, for so long. With a sigh, she went down the steps and took her place in the passenger seat.

"I'm going to need a car," she told Bert as he started the engine and began to pull out. "And soon."

* * *

"Chief!"

Kate almost grinned at the look of surprise on Nick Martins' face. He'd been sitting at the duty desk, the phone in the crook of his neck, jotting down information. He dropped the phone when he straightened in surprise and then scrambled to pick it up.

"Sorry, ma'am," he said into the phone. His gaze followed Kate and Bert as they rounded the duty desk and headed for her office in the far corner. "So when did you notice the bicycle was missing?"

There was no one in the duty room, and Kate stacked her boxes on one of the common desks in the middle of the room. The detachment smelled like old burned coffee and freshly mown grass. She took a deep breath and exhaled with satisfaction.

It was good to be home.

Behind her, Bert cleared his throat and she hurried to open the door to her office. "Sorry," she said, making room for him as he passed her in the doorway. She tossed her billed cap on top of her desk.

"I'm beginning to feel like a pack animal," he complained. But there was a smile on his face and she knew better than to take him seriously. She turned to head back into the common room but he pulled her into the relative privacy of her office and pinned her against the wall with an arm on either side of her.

"Now, what are you going to do once I leave?"

She raised an eyebrow at him. "Invite the dancing boys and have myself a party?" She kept her voice low so Martins wouldn't hear them.

Bert scowled at her. "Is that what you do when I'm not around?" he whispered severely. His right hand lowered to her waist and crept around to her back, drawing her to him snugly. "Maybe you need reminding that we're a party of two."

Kate's heart started beating faster and she raised her lips to his. After a moment, he stepped back, smiling with satisfaction.

"I'll be back tonight," he promised. "You stay here, or you get a patrol car to take you home. Right?"

"Right," she said a little breathlessly.

"Good. I'll bring in the rest of the boxes."

When all the boxes were stacked in her office, he gave her cheek a caress and left. She stood staring at the boxes, wondering where she should start. She heard Bert say goodbye to Martins, and after a moment, the constable knocked at her door jamb. She turned to face him. He was half a foot taller than her five feet three, and was thin so that his uniform always looked like it needed taking in. He had crinkly auburn hair and light brown eyes and a dusting of freckles on his cheeks and nose that always made her smile.

"Busy?" she asked.

He shook his head and held up a wad of paper. "You have messages."

Her eyebrows rose. "Anything I need to deal with right now?"

He hesitated, flipping through the pages. There were at least a dozen.

Holy cow.

"They're mostly from reporters," he said.

"They can wait."

"And the mayor wants to talk to you." He grinned at her in sympathy.

She nodded. She would have to talk to the mayor. As for the media... She sighed. She really wasn't good with media. Maybe the mayor would talk to them. She'd never worked anywhere where the media wanted to talk to her.

"Who's on?" she asked.

"Friesen, Olinchuk, and Paterson. Trepalli's still on leave."

That much she knew. But it bothered her that she had lost track again. McKell was the one who handled scheduling and personnel matters. Keeping track of who was on and who was off, let alone who was on leave, was just not one of her strengths. She swallowed hard.

"How's the DC?" asked Martins.

She looked up at him and forced a smile.

"It's looking good," she said. "All things considered."

He looked down at her, unsmiling, the freckles standing out like blotches on his pale skin. She sighed.

"We won't know for a little while if he'll walk or not," she said. "We have to wait."

The phone rang in the duty room and he left to answer it. She stood in the middle of her office for long minutes, considering her next move. Get coffee? Call the mayor? Start looking through the boxes?

Finally she made her way around the boxes to her chair and sat down.

She picked up the phone and dialed directory assistance.

"What city, please?" asked the operator.

She hesitated a moment. Was the hospital technically in Longueuil, or was it still in Greenfield Park? "Greenfield Park in Quebec."

"One moment, please." The line was silent for a moment and then a different woman came on.

"Quelle ville, s'il vous plaît?"

Kate brought out her rusty French and asked for the phone number for Armand-Cadieux Hospital in Greenfield Park. When she had it, she thanked the woman and hung up, only to pick up the receiver again and punch in the number.

To her surprise, the hospital switchboard put her through directly to her mother's room. The phone rang once and was picked up.

"Hello?"

A level of tension she hadn't known she was carrying dropped from Kate's shoulders and she almost sagged with relief.

"Hi, Mom," she said. "How are you?"

"Katie!" said Mom, clearly delighted.

She sounded wonderful—cheerful, bright, happy. Maybe it

was the drugs.

"How's your deputy chief?" asked Mom.

Kate sighed. "We won't know for a few days," she said. "They operated on him yesterday and got the bullet out. There's damage to his lung and his spine."

"His spine."

The grave tone in her mother's voice told Kate what she needed to know. Mom was definitely not under the influence of drugs if she could grasp the severity of McKell's situation that quickly.

"I know," said Kate. "All we can do is wait."

"I'll pray for him," said her mother.

Kate's throat closed up a little and she could only manage a whisper. "Thanks, Mom." She cleared her throat. "Now, tell me what's happening with you."

Taking Kate's cue, her mother gave a little laugh. "Well, it looks like I'll be around for a while longer. My leg is in one of those plastic casts and I'm not to put any weight on it at all. Looks like I'll have to use a wheelchair for the next two months."

"Well, you certainly sound cheerful about it."

"No use being grumpy, dear."

Maybe not, but Kate could see some issues ahead for John and Rose. They practically lived in the sun room, and it was reached by a flight of stairs. As if guessing her thoughts, Hetty Williams continued.

"I'll be staying with Fred," she said firmly. "His condo has an elevator and he has a spare room. Besides, he's retired and has time to look after me."

"Rose won't like that."

"She'll get over it."

Kate pulled the phone away and stared at it, then brought it back to her ear.

"Who are you and what have you done with my mother?"

Mom laughed, then groaned. "Don't make me laugh, dear. Every muscle in my body hurts."

"All right," said Kate. "I'll check in with you tomorrow." Then she added impulsively, "Say hi to Fred for me."

"Will do, sweetheart. You go take care of your deputy."

The moment Kate hung up, the phone rang, startling her.

"Williams," she said into the receiver.

"Chief, it's Leonard Dabbs."

Kate stifled a sigh, then pasted a smile on her face. "Mayor Dabbs, how are you?"

"I'm fine," he said in a tone that held a hint of impatience. She glanced down at the display window on her telephone. He was calling from the mayor's office. On a Saturday. "More to the point, how's McKell?"

Kate hesitated a few seconds while marshaling her thoughts. There was no love lost between McKell and the mayor. In fact, the mayor had never admitted it, but she suspected that she had gotten the Chief of Police job instead of McKell because the DC had been in the process of divorcing the mayor's daughter.

It made for tricky relationships.

"Chief?" prompted the mayor. She figured he was a little younger than her, somewhere between forty-five and fifty, and nice enough to look at, with brown eyes and a full head of gray hair. He was tall and thin and always dressed in a suit and tie. At least, that was all Kate had ever seen him in. She always had the impression that he was "on." His wife, Elaine, was the warm one.

"He went through the operation with flying colors," said Kate finally. "He won't die of his injuries. We just don't know if he'll walk again."

There was a long silence at the other end as the mayor digested the information. There had been hard feelings between Leonard Dabbs and Rob McKell when McKell's marriage failed, but while the mayor hadn't promoted the DC, he hadn't fired him, either.

The mayor swore softly under his voice. "What about the shooter?" he finally asked. "Are we any closer to finding him?"

This time Kate's sigh was audible. She leaned back in her ergonomic chair and stared at the line where the ceiling tiles met the pale cream wall.

"No, sir. Not as of an hour ago, anyway."

Again a pause. "Chief?"

"Yes, sir?"

"Do what you need to do, okay?"

She sat up straight, not sure what he meant. "Sir?"

"I'll authorize any overtime you need, any expense. Is that clear?"

The photo of the queen stared back at her from the wall and Kate blinked. "Sir, the Winnipeg police are in charge of the investigation—"

"I know," he interrupted. "I also know that you often work closely with them. McKell is one of ours, Chief. We need to be involved."

"Yes, sir," said Kate finally because she couldn't think of anything else to say.

The mayor cleared his throat. "I heard about your mother," he said gruffly. "How is she?"

Kate blinked a few times. "Out of danger," she said. "She'll be home soon."

"Good," said the mayor. "I'll let you get on with things." And he hung up.

* * *

"Hi, Chief."

Kate looked up past the open box of files to find Ben Friesen grinning at her from her doorway.

"Constable," she said. She had opened the window to let air in, despite which her office smelled of dust, damp paper, and musty cardboard. She'd already sneezed a dozen times and this was only her second box.

"Can I help?" asked Friesen, nodding at the boxes stacked up under her window. She wondered where Martins was but didn't ask.

She blinked up at him. "Aren't you supposed to be on patrol?" she asked. She could hear someone typing in the duty room. With Trepalli still on leave, the team was short one. Friesen would be patroling solo.

"I'm replacing Martins on the duty desk while he takes lunch," said Friesen. "It's pretty quiet."

He was a solidly built guy, maybe five feet ten, with dark blond hair and crinkly blue eyes. He was single and took full advantage of that fact. He liked women, and they seemed to like him, too. She knew he and Trepalli used to go to Winnipeg on their days off, doing whatever it was young, single men did in a big city. Amanda's arrival had put a stop to all that.

"I wish you could help me," she said with a rueful smile. But he wouldn't know what to look for. Heck, *she* wasn't even sure what she was looking for. "I have to do this myself."

She glanced at her watch. Twelve fifteen. As if in realization, her stomach growled loudly and Friesen smiled.

"Right. Martins will bring you back a sandwich from the Wheatland Café."

"That Nick Martins is a good man," said Kate. Then her phone rang and Friesen left her to answer it.

She glanced down at the display before picking up. Bert.

"Hey," she said.

"Hey yourself," said Bert. "Any luck?"

"No." Kate rubbed her nose to circumvent a sneeze. "Any news at your end?"

"Ballistics says the bullet is too fragmented to be of any use, even if we find the weapon."

Kate stared at the file folder she held open on the desk. It was for a fifteen-year-old case in which she had arrested a man for forgery. Not a likely suspect. "Well, hell," she said.

"Yes," he said grimly.

Kate stood up to let the blood circulate in her legs and feet. "Can they tell what kind of bullet it was?"

"A 7.62 millimeter cartridge."

Kate remained silent for a moment, absorbing the information. "That's a big cartridge," she said finally. The thought of something that size exploding through McKell's chest...

"I know," said Bert. "The ballistics tech says it's the size of round used in a sniper rifle."

She swallowed. "Surely someone would have seen a guy riding a motorcycle with a rifle strapped to his back?"

"Most sniper rifles come apart," said Bert. "Easy to transport and quick to put together."

What the hell was going on? Did someone hire a sniper to kill McKell? Or her? None of this made sense.

"Anyway," said Bert. "Still no luck with witnesses. Our public affairs guy will be on the news hour broadcast tonight to ask for any witnesses to come forward. We've got it up on the website and the local radio stations are running the appeal, too. So far, no luck with the tip line."

Kate stared out the window at the empty parking lot of her police detachment. Across the street, the parking lot of the Church of the Nazarene also stood empty. Cars drove by, heading for downtown, and beyond the downtown area, the suburbs. The sun was lower in the sky than it had been a month ago and it was definitely cooler, but the sky was just as blue. A teenage girl rode by on a ten-speed, in shorts and a bright yellow tank top, all long legs and perky breasts.

"Wear a helmet," she muttered under her breath, watching the girl cycle by.

"What?" asked Bert.

"I have to go," she said, suddenly deciding. She wasn't accomplishing anything here. What she was looking for was in Winnipeg, not Mendenhall. "I'll call you later."

"Okay. Don't take any unnecessary chances," he warned.

She hung up before he could ask any questions. For the past few days, everything in her life had been out of her control. She'd been reactive from the moment she'd received Rose's call about Mom. And she'd been hurrying from one thing to another, looking for answers, only to bump up against a wall at every turn.

She was sick of it.

She found her cap, hiding under the lid of the box on her desk, and carried it into the duty room. Sunshine flooded the space from the window by Charlotte's desk and from the open hallway door that led to the compound. The linoleum tiles in their black and white checkerboard pattern were looking a little faded and there were scuff marks on a lot of the white ones. Couldn't be helped with so many booted feet tromping in and out.

Friesen was on the phone at the duty desk, his back to her. Michael Olinchuk sat at one of the common desks in the middle of the big room, hunting and pecking on the computer keyboard. He was a big guy, well over six feet, with features that seemed carved out of a cliff face. A Cree from Ontario, he had high cheekbones and dark hair and eyes, and the biggest hands Kate had ever seen. She took a moment to appreciate the absurd sight of those big hands on the keyboard.

He and his wife had just had a baby, a girl, and he spent a lot of time wandering around with a foolish grin.

Sensing her attention on him, he turned in his chair, making it creak ominously.

"Chief," he acknowledged.

"Constable," said Kate. "How would you like to give me a ride to the dealership?" There was only one dealership in town—the Ford dealership. If you wanted a different brand, you went to Brandon or to Winnipeg.

Olinchuk's big finger stabbed the "save" key and he stood up. She had never understood the attraction some women had for tall men. As far as she was concerned, all that height was wasted.

"Right now, ma'am?"

She nodded, just as Friesen finished his call. "Anything serious?" she asked him.

"No, ma'am. A fender bender on Main Street. Samantha is on it."

"Good." She hadn't even read the log book when she came in. She should probably do that before she left again, but her feet were itchy. And her people were capable. "Michael's taking me to the Ford dealership."

Friesen's eyebrows rose in surprise. "You're going to buy a new car right away?"

"No." Kate looked over her shoulder to see that Olinchuk was standing a few feet behind her, cap on his head, keys in his hand. Nobody that big had any business being that quiet. "I'm going to rent one."

* * *

It was almost two o'clock by the time she pulled into the Grace Hospital parking lot in Winnipeg. It was a big lot, easily capable of accommodating a hundred vehicles. Someone had given some thought to its layout, and the lot was separated by rows of mature trees into mini-lots of twenty spaces. She had found a spot next to a row of beech trees that provided some shade.

She noted with approval that there were dozens of lights. The parking lot would be well lit at night.

Her cell phone had rung a couple of times during the drive, but she'd ignored it, mostly because the Focus didn't have a hands-free contraption but also because she was pretty sure it was Bert calling her and she didn't want to tell him what she was up to.

She knew it was logical to assume she had been the target, but it just didn't *feel* right. She sat in the rental, missing her Explorer, and tried to work it out.

How would the shooter have known when the Explorer would be going by that particular spot? For Pete's sake—he couldn't just hang around the overpass all day waiting for the Explorer—her—to drive by. There was too much chance someone would see him.

Whoever it was knew when to be there. That was the only explanation. And whoever it was hadn't followed McKell, either, or he wouldn't have had time to get into position.

Her hands squeezed the steering wheel as the logical extension to the thought struck her. No, the shooter couldn't possibly have followed McKell and managed to be in position as McKell drove by. That meant that someone else had followed McKell and given the shooter advance notice to get into position.

Holy cow.

Someone had seen McKell get into her Explorer.

They weren't after her at all. McKell *was* the intended victim.

CHAPTER 13

"THEY LET you see him?" said Trepalli wonderingly. "They wouldn't let me near his room."

He had met her at Joe's Diner, one of Bert's favorite places to eat when he was too busy to cook. The place looked like it had fallen right out of the fifties: red plastic booths with Formica tables, round padded stools, rotating dessert display, and all. Kate didn't mind it, except that everything on the menu was Bad For Her.

She shrugged. "I'm on the list. And I'm in uniform." She hadn't bothered changing back into civilian clothes before leaving for Winnipeg. Besides, somimes a uniform was an asset.

"Was Charlotte there?" asked Trepalli.

Kate nodded. Yes, Charlotte had been there, sitting by the DC's bed, reading out loud from a *Guns & Ammo* magazine. She had looked around as Kate entered. Her pretty green eyes had been a little bloodshot and she'd had dark smudges under them. She was wearing jeans and sandals and a pink, sleeveless cotton blouse that buttoned up the front.

"Hello, Chief." She smiled a welcome.

Kate nodded in acknowledgement. She had taken her cap off and now couldn't seem to stop clutching it. She walked over to the empty chair next to Charlotte and dropped the cap before she damaged it.

"How's he doing?" she asked.

As near as Kate could tell, McKell looked exactly the same as the night before, except that his color was better and he had stubble on his face.

"I think he's doing better," said Charlotte staunchly. "His fingers have been twitching. The doctor says that doesn't necessarily mean anything," she added reluctantly.

Kate placed a hand on the girl's shoulder and squeezed. "Did you stay in town?"

Charlotte nodded and stood up, placing the magazine on her chair. "At Josh's."

Immediately, Kate felt better. Josh was a veterinarian based out of Winnipeg. He and Charlotte had been seeing each other for a few months. If she was staying with him, then it meant that she and Trepalli really were only friends.

It's none of your business, she reminded herself sharply.

"How's the investigation going?" asked Charlotte, running her hands through her glossy brown curls and succeeding in looking even more fetching.

Kate looked at her and shook her head.

"Oh," said Charlotte. They both turned to look at McKell.

Kate didn't know if he could hear them or not, but she didn't want to discuss her lack of progress on the investigation in front of him.

He might not mind that Charlotte was here—McKell thought of her as a daughter—but he would hate knowing that Kate had seen him this way—asleep, unshaven, unaware.

Vulnerable.

Her throat tightened on tears and she gave herself a mental shake. For Pete's sake—what good was she doing, moping over the guy? Finding whoever had done this to him would be a lot more useful.

"All right," she said firmly. "Give me a call if anything changes."

"Yes, ma'am," said Charlotte solemnly.

Kate had given the girl's shoulder another squeeze and left.

Only once she was back in the rental car did she remember to check her phone. Sure enough, Bert had called, but the other missed call had been from Trepalli. She had called the constable back and arranged to meet him at the diner.

"Was he awake?" asked Trepalli hopefully.

She shook her head. "No, he's still drugged up. But he looks better." She pushed her menu aside and looked around hopefully for the waitress. It was past three and she hadn't eaten all day. No wonder she had a headache.

"What did you find out?" she finally asked. The damned diner was empty. Maybe the waitress was on a break.

He shook his head. "Not much," he admitted. "The shooter is a ghost. No cameras anywhere in the vicinity. I walked the scene and found nothing. Whoever the shooter is, he knows enough to police his shells. None of my contacts have anything to report."

Well. That was disappointing, but not surprising.

"The bullet was a 7.62 millimeter," she told him. "Too fragmented."

Trepalli's eyebrows rose. "Big round." He thought for a moment. "The kind snipers use."

Kate nodded, but before she could say anything, the waitress emerged from the kitchen and looked startled to see them.

"Sorry, hon," she said, walking toward them. "I didn't hear you come in. Have you had a chance to look over the menu?" She had served Kate and Bert a few times but Kate couldn't remember her name.

The woman's hair was thick and dark, threaded with silver. It went down to her nape, twisted into an old-fashioned, low-hanging bun that kept it out of her face. She was a little taller than Kate, maybe in her early forties, and was very thin except for a little pot belly.

"Yes," said Kate firmly. "I'll have the scrambled eggs, sausages, hash browns, and whole wheat toast with jam."

Trepalli and the waitress blinked at her and she shrugged sheepishly. "I'm hungry."

The waitress didn't miss a beat. "How 'bout you, hon?"

"Just coffee, please," said Trepalli.

"Right. Back in a few minutes," she said.

Kate could hear the waitress talking to someone in the kitchen. She leaned in closer to her constable. "We may be coming at this from the wrong angle," she confided.

His eyebrows rose once again. "How do you mean?"

"I don't think they were after me."

"They?"

She nodded. "There had to be at least two of them." She told him her theory about someone following McKell and giving advance warning to the shooter.

The more she talked, the more sense it made to her. She paused when the waitress brought Trepalli his coffee and placed a glass of water in front of Kate.

When Kate finished, she sat back and looked at her constable. He stared back at her but he wasn't really looking at her. She could almost see the cogs whirring behind his eyes.

Finally he blinked and focused on her.

"It's kind of a stretch," he pointed out. "I mean, the simplest explanation is that the shooter thought he was shooting at you. It *was* your car, and there's nothing to say anyone was following the DC. There *might* have been two of them, but not necessarily." He took a cautious sip of his coffee, then a bigger one.

"There had to be two of them," she pointed out. "Nobody would hang around an overpass all day, waiting for the Explorer." Much too risky.

"Well, he wouldn't have to, would he?" said Trepalli. "What if he already knew you were going to drive in for the chiefs' meeting?"

"How would they have known?" she asked.

"Chief Stendel issued a news release," said Trepalli. "Didn't you know?"

Well, wasn't that typical Stendel. Nothing special about the meeting, but it was his turn to host and he never missed a chance to get his name in the papers.

Every six months, the police chiefs of southern Manitoba met for a full-day meeting where they talked procedure and collaboration and shared any news worth sharing. It was always a long day.

That was why she and McKell had decided to travel to Winnipeg separately.

"He was going to a parole hearing," she said softly. The smell of frying sausages barely registered as she tried to clear the muddle in her head.

"Pardon?" asked Trepalli.

Kate shook her head, trying to remember what McKell had said. "The chiefs' meeting was on the same day as the parole board hearing at Red Hill Correctional Center. McKell was going to testify against someone up for parole."

Trepalli looked completely lost.

"We have someone up for parole?"

"No. Not one of ours." If only she could remember. "It was from his army days, I think. When he was military police." Damn it—had he even told her the name?

"Quite the coincidence that the parole hearing was scheduled for the same day as the chiefs' meeting," said Trepalli.

"It was deliberate," said Kate. "The parole board meets in Winnipeg twice a year. It takes all day to go through the applications. When we meet in Winnipeg, we invite the members of the board for dinner that night." At least, that was what the agenda for the chiefs' meeting had read.

Trepalli looked confused. He sat forward.

"Hang on, Chief. Are you thinking the DC could have been targeted to keep him from testifying at a parole board hearing?"

She stared at him. It sounded so far-fetched when he put it like that. Nevertheless, she nodded.

"Yes, I think that's it exactly."

Trepalli shook his head. "It still doesn't work. How would they know when the DC would head into town?" he asked. "The hearings last all day—how would the shooter know when the DC was scheduled to testify?"

Kate shook her head. "They couldn't know. The agenda isn't public."

He stared at her with dawning comprehension. "But the chiefs' meeting was public, as was the location. There's only one logical route the DC would take from Mendenhall into Winnipeg to reach the Four Seasons Hotel. And if the DC had to get to Winnipeg in time for the chiefs' meeting..." He shrugged. "It wouldn't be hard to find out exactly what time the chiefs' meeting started," he said.

Kate nodded. A phone call to a secretary, that was all it would take.

Trepalli glanced at his watch. "He would have left Mendenhall at roughly eight o'clock. No, let's say seven thirty, because of traffic going into the city."

The waitress brought Kate's meal and refilled Trepalli's cup, all without saying a word. The woman could obviously read a room.

"But why bother shooting him?" asked Trepalli and Kate almost smiled. He was flip-flopping as much as she had. "I mean, if he's going to the chiefs' meeting, he can't go to the parole hearing, right?"

Kate shook her head. "Depends. He was scheduled to give our presentation first thing. If he had to appear in front of the parole board in the afternoon, he could easily have done it, then returned to the meeting."

"All right, then," said Trepalli. He swallowed more coffee. "So, let's say you're right and the shooter had a good sense of when the DC would be driving by. All he would need, to be certain, is someone to follow the DC and give the shooter the heads up as the DC approached the overpass."

Kate dug into the eggs while he mulled over the theory. They were fluffy and hot, and the sausages tasted like sin.

The door opened and an older man walked in, carrying a newspaper under his arm. He made a beeline for the table in the far corner and the waitress met him there with the pot of coffee.

"Chief..."

She looked up from her plate find Trepalli looking at her.

"It still doesn't make sense," he said gently. "The only way they could be sure the DC would take the meeting is if they were sure you..."

He swallowed suddenly and his face went pale.

She stared at him as the eggs turned into lumps of clay in her stomach.

The only reason she hadn't been at the meeting was because she had been called away. Because someone had hit her mother and fled the scene.

Dear God in heaven.

Trepalli was shaking his head slowly. "Ma'am... no... Nobody would..."

But it all fit, didn't it? Mom's accident. Leaving for Montreal. McKell automatically stepping up to take the chiefs' meeting...

She put her knife and fork down gently in her still full plate. She had lost her appetite.

CHAPTER 14

MORE COFFEE, hon?" asked the waitress. Doris, Kate suddenly remembered. Her name was Doris.

"Sure," said Kate, pushing her nearly empty cup closer to the woman.

Doris poured, then looked at Kate. "You just let me know if you need anything, hear?"

Kate smiled. Doris' middle name was apparently "Discretion." She hadn't said a word when Trepalli left and only asked if there was a problem with Kate's food. When Kate said she wasn't as hungry as she'd thought, Doris offered to bring her coffee.

"As a matter of fact," she said, "do you happen to have a southern Manitoba phone directory?"

"Let me check," said Doris. She went behind the long counter and rummaged around in a drawer before returning with a slim, bright yellow phone book.

"Here you go, hon."

"Thanks, Doris," said Kate.

The waitress patted her on the hand and left.

Kate had convinced Trepalli to return to Mendenhall by asking him to search McKell's office for any information on the identity of the person McKell wanted to keep behind bars. She could have called and gotten Martins to search, but Trepalli's frustration was almost palpable. Best to give him something to do. When she asked how he would get back, he told her his friend would drive him back.

Kate didn't ask if the friend was female. She didn't want to know.

She pulled the phone book toward her and flipped through it until she found the listings for Canadian Forces Base Shilo. Ten minutes later, she disconnected and set the phone down. Her coffee had grown cold as she talked, but Doris had wordlessly replaced the cup with a fresh one filled with hot coffee.

Kate sat looking out the window at the waning afternoon with its long, soft shadows. The duty officer had promised to get back to her as soon as he found the information she had requested. In the meantime, she was getting tired of sitting. But first, she had to face the music.

Taking a deep breath, she picked up the phone again and called Bert.

"Hey," he said, picking up on the first ring. "I tried calling you earlier. Everything all right?"

"I need to talk to you," she said. She had been tempted to do this over the phone, but that was the coward's way. "Where are you?"

"At the office. Is this urgent? I was planning to come to you in time for a late dinner."

Kate took a deep, silent breath. "I'm in town. I'll be at your office in twenty minutes."

There was a long silence at the other end of the line.

"Are you alone?" There was a dangerous note in his voice and Kate winced. She had known he would be mad.

"Watch for me," she said, and hung up.

* * *

The Winnipeg Police Services headquarters was a five-story building that sat on Princess Avenue like a toad on a kitchen counter—ugly and out of place. Every time she saw its long, narrow windows that looked like bars on a jail cell, she felt grateful for her own one-story, post-World-War-II-era station house. Mendenhall's detachment might be much smaller than this monstrosity, and it was certainly draftier in winter, but at least she didn't feel like she worked in a fortress. The only thing missing on this building was a sign over the front door that read "ABANDON HOPE ALL YE WHO ENTER HERE."

And it wasn't even the jail.

She had parked around the corner and studied the building as she walked toward it. It was going on dinnertime and the sun had started its descent, leaving the street below it cloaked in shade so that she shivered a little in her uniform jacket. She liked the Mendenhall police uniform, especially the bomber-style navy jacket. It had a lot of pockets, even on the inside, and it was flattering, even for women.

Bert was waiting for her in the lobby. The building was closed on weekends and there was no way of getting in without a key card.

He pushed open the door and let her in, allowing the door to click shut behind them. He had propped open the inside glass door and she went through to the lobby, heading for the elevator. The lobby was tiled in oversized red bricks, and potted trees lined the glass walls. It was empty except for one security guard, a young woman with thick, dark hair up in a bun, at the horseshoe-shaped desk. She wore an olive green uniform from the security company.

She looked up and nodded when Kate entered. Kate nodded back. She had seen the young woman a few times. It always struck her as funny that the police headquarters building would hire a security company to guard their building, but she'd never had the nerve to say anything to either Bert or to Chief Stendel.

Aware of the young security guard's presence, neither of them spoke as they waited for an elevator to arrive. Bert must have taken the stairs down from the third floor. Kate glanced sideways at him. His profile looked as unforgiving as a cliff. There were spots of color high on his cheeks and knobs of muscle at his jaw line, from clenching his teeth.

Hoo boy.

The elevator door opened and he allowed her to step in ahead of him, then pressed the button for the third floor. They rode up in silence, mindful of the camera in the corner of the ceiling, and during the brief ride, Kate's cautious amusement soured to resentment.

This was starting to get irritating.

The ding announced that they had arrived and the doors opened. She followed him down the hallway to the Employees Only door. He pulled his identification card out and swiped it through the reader, then pushed the door open.

They walked down the hallway, past the lunch room and into the vast room that she had dubbed Cubicle City the first time she'd seen it. She couldn't tell if the room was empty or if someone was beavering away, hidden by the cubicle walls. The room hummed with the white noise of machines that were always left on, but she didn't hear any clacking of keyboard keys. She estimated that there were at least twenty cubicles in the room—chances were that someone was in there. She followed Bert past the cubicles to the far corner office in silence.

The moment they were in his office, he closed the door and turned on her.

"What the hell were you thinking?" His voice was low and tight, and very, very angry.

Kate's chin lifted and she felt her ire lifting, too.

Keep your cool, she warned herself. *He's worried about you.*

Unlike her, he wore civvies—his favorite jeans and a pale blue plaid shirt that she'd never seen, with its sleeves rolled up to reveal his muscled forearms. Sunlight filled the room with easy warmth, gilding the reddish gold hair covering his arms.

She took a deep breath. "Bert, I think we got it wrong—"

"Did you have an officer accompany you, at least?" In spite of the soft light flooding his office, his copper-penny eyes looked hard and dark. She had never seen him like this.

"No. I—"

"Are you telling me you drove here *alone*?" His voice rose on the last word. He seemed to be vibrating, he was so angry.

The stress of the last few days coalesced into anger that washed over her and left her trembling. Just who did he think he was?

"I'm not your witness, Bert," she said. Her lips felt stiff and she had trouble forming the words. "I'm a police officer investigating an attempted murder."

Bert was past seeing the danger signs.

"Which part of 'you're being targeted' don't you understand?" he demanded, his voice rising.

"For Pete's sak—"

"I told you to wait for me. I could—"

"Just let me—"

"Are you *trying* to get kill—"

Without another word, Kate turned on her heel, opened the door, and left.

* * *

Kate glanced at the dashboard clock in the Focus. Six fifteen. She had driven until she found herself in front of the pond in King's Park. There she parked and turned off the engine, letting the clicking of the cooling engine calm her while dusk crept into the car through the open passenger window.

The ash trees were in full color and the smell of cut grass and wet leaves filled the car, overpowering the faint leather scent of the seats and the residual smell of gasoline. The parking lot was almost empty, and she could see a couple walking a dog down one of the walking paths.

She sighed and slowly unclenched her hands from the steering wheel. Anger had sustained her for the drive but now it was fading, leaving her drained and exhausted.

It was always like this when she was in a relationship. At first everything was rosy and sweet, and then the realities of her job started encroaching, inserting a wedge between her and her lover until it pried them apart. And it didn't seem to matter if the lover was another cop. That seemed to make it worse. Another cop understood exactly what kind of pressures and dangers she faced.

She had hoped it would be different with Bert. Her job in Mendenhall was mostly administrative, as was his in Winnipeg. Sure, there had been a few incidents in the last year and a bit, but that couldn't be helped. She was a *cop*.

She wasn't about to compromise the job because he was worried. If he couldn't handle that...

With a sigh, she pulled out her phone and called Trepalli. He answered on the first ring.

"Have you left yet?" she asked.

"Waiting for my friend to get back from work," he said. "Soon."

"Tell me where you are," she told him. "I'll pick you up."

When she had jotted down the address, she cleared the screen and called Mendenhall.

"Mendenhall Police," said Martins. "Chief," he added, obviously recognizing her number.

"Constable," said Kate. "Could you find me Chief Stendel's cell and home numbers, please?"

"Yes, ma'am," said Martins, with a hint of amusement in his voice.

She ignored it. She had yet to figure out how to set up a contacts list on this phone, let alone how to access the Internet and her email. Bert had added his numbers and Amanda's for her. She missed her old flip-up phone.

Martins came back with both numbers and she thanked him and then called Stendel. She found him at home.

"Chief Williams," he said with surprise after she had identified herself. "Is there a problem?"

Kate smiled tightly.

"I need your help," she said. She then spent the next ten minutes laying out her theory about McKell being the intended victim, and not her. When she finished, she gave him time to digest.

Finally, he sighed. "I don't know, Chief," he said. "It's pretty thin."

Yes, it *was* pretty thin, but the nagging little voice in the back of her mind was getting louder. "Chief," she said softly, "why do you have a guard posted outside McKell's door?"

This time, his silence was even longer. When he spoke again, he sounded resigned. "Just in case," he admitted.

Kate smiled. "Well, just in case I'm right, can you find out from the parole board which prisoners they were talking to?"

"Probably," he said, and she could hear the shrug in his voice. "It might not be until tomorrow morning, however."

"In the meantime," she said, "I'd like you to double the guard on McKell's room."

She had thought he would object, but to her surprise, he said, "Yes, of course. No sense taking chances."

* * *

She and Trepalli drove back to Mendenhall in the gloaming, that time of day that was neither day nor night and which taxed her eyesight the most. Trepalli offered to drive but the Ford was a rental and it was her name on the agreement. She reluctantly declined his offer.

They drove out of the city in silence, both lost in thought. Charlotte was staying on for a few days, to watch over McKell. She promised she would call Kate as soon as there was any change.

"Kia Soul," said Trepalli suddenly.

"Pardon me?" she asked, keeping her gaze on the road. They had left the last of the streetlights behind and were now on the straight stretch toward Mendenhall. The car seemed to be surrounded by shadows.

"Wasn't that the type of car that hit your mother?" He tapped the dashboard with one finger. "A four-door, dark green Kia Soul."

Out of the corner of her eye, she could see his face turned toward her.

"Yes," she replied, although honestly, she couldn't remember the details.

"So, if we're right, there's at least one more person involved," he continued. "The guy asking for parole, the shooter, the shooter's lookout, and the guy who hit your mother."

Kate winced at his list, but he was right. This was starting to look like a conspiracy.

"Who the hell did McKell put in jail?" she wondered out loud.

"Don't know," said Trepalli in the darkness of the interior. "But we'd better find out quick."

* * *

Jim O'Hara was on the duty desk by the time they arrived in Mendenhall, past shift change. Martins had stuck around until she arrived so that she could brief them both at the same time. Trepalli nodded at both of them but disappeared inside McKell's office without a word. Both men followed him with their eyes, then turned to look at Kate questioningly.

"Is there anything to eat?" she asked hopefully. The only thing she'd eaten all day was the scrambled egg and part of a sausage. Her stomach was beginning to hate her.

Martins turned and walked out of the duty room without a word. After a moment, they heard the fridge door open and things being shifted around. Kate took a deep breath and stretched her neck, first one side, then the other. Her shoulders were so tight they felt like they could break.

The detachment smelled of fresh air. She glanced at the door next to her office where they kept three cells. The lights were off and the door was closed—standard operating procedure when they had no "guests." No matter how they scrubbed the cell area down, it always smelled faintly of old vomit and bleach.

The phone rang and O'Hara swiveled to pick it up. A sweet scent of aftershave wafted over to her. "Mendenhall Police," he said. She noticed for the first time that he was wearing a long-sleeved uniform shirt. Jim O'Hara had decided it was time for the fall uniform. He was right; it was starting to get cool, especially on night shift. Especially for someone on the duty desk who didn't move around much.

She was about to join Trepalli in McKell's office when she heard Martins' measured tread returning. He entered the duty room and handed her a plastic resealable container and a fork. Kate opened the lid and a smell of garlic and chicken immediately made her mouth water. Pasta salad. Yum.

"I'll make it up to you," she promised.

His eyes crinkled up with laughter. "No worries."

Kate pulled the lid off and dug in. The salad was creamy and garlicky and filled with chunks of chicken and green peppers and celery and carrot. O'Hara watched her devour the food and a small smiled flitted across his face. The phone rang again. From McKell's office came the sound of drawers opening and closing as Trepalli carried on with the search.

"At the Bull Pen," said O'Hara into the phone. "Proceed with caution." He listened for a moment, then nodded. "Call in Holmes and Parker if you need them." He hung up and swiveled to face Kate and Martins. At the look on their faces, he explained. "A ruckus at the Bull Pen. Seems the crops are in before the rains and people are blowing off a little steam."

Kate nodded, and swallowed a mouthful of pasta. "All right," she said. "First, no change in the DC's condition. I've been rethinking yesterday's events, however." She proceeded to share her new theory with them. After she was done, Martins looked skeptical, but O'Hara only nodded.

"I can help search," Martins said, glancing in the direction of McKell's office.

Kate shook her head. "Go home," she said. "There are enough bodies here to search."

Martins hesitated and she patted his arm. "It's all right, Nick," she said gently. "Go get some rest."

He glanced at O'Hara, who nodded. One day, Jim O'Hara would make a fine sergeant. Right now, however, he was a little inexperienced. And he would have to learn to communicate with something more than nods and grunts.

"I'll see you tomorrow," Martins told O'Hara, startling Kate. She had though a new crew would be on days tomorrow. Damn. She was going to have to pull out the duty schedules and make sure they were set for the next few weeks. She almost made a face at the thought, but controlled herself. She *hated* setting schedules. That was McKell's strength, not hers.

"Goodnight," she said to Martins. The phone rang again and when O'Hara turned to answer it, she headed into the DC's office. Trepalli was standing at the filing cabinet, flicking through file folder after file folder. He looked up at her, his face set, and shook his head. With a sigh, Kate sat down at McKell's desk and pulled open the top drawer.

* * *

It was past ten o'clock by the time Kate got home. She put the kettle on and drew all the curtains in the house, feeling suddenly exposed. While the kettle heated, she changed out of her uniform and into her pajamas. Her feet especially approved of her removing her boots and she sat on the bed for a few minutes, rubbing them.

How was it possible that they had found nothing in McKell's office? He would have to have some kind of paper trail, wouldn't he?

A sudden thought stopped her in mid-massage.

He had implied that this wasn't the first hearing he'd attended for this prisoner. And yet, there had never been an attempt on McKell's life before. Was Bert right? Had she gotten it all wrong? Had she been the target all along?

But... she was sure she hadn't been under surveillance since she'd gotten home. And she'd driven into Winnipeg and back, with no problem.

So, if McKell was targeted to keep him from testifying, why the elaborate, convoluted plan to get him to the chiefs' meeting, instead of her? Why not just stake out the location of the parole board hearing and shoot McKell there?

Then again, the shooter could hardly loiter around Red Hill Correctional without being noticed.

The kettle whistled and she padded down the hardwood hallway into the linoleum tiled kitchen and made herself herbal tea. She looked at the tea packet she had pulled out of the box at random. Alpine berry. She sighed. What she really wanted was coffee, but she knew better than to drink it at this time of night.

She glanced at the clock over her sink. Ten forty-five. A part of her had expected Bert to show up, or to at least call. If she were to be honest with herself, she would admit to a little disappointment that he hadn't come. But most of her was relieved.

She didn't want to deal with him right now.

While the tea steeped, she went to the entrance hall, where she had left her laptop case, and brought it into the kitchen. She pulled the computer out and turned it on. She hadn't checked her email in days, not since Rose had called her to tell her about Mom's accident.

Rose.

Kate's shoulders slumped in fatigue as she considered her sister. Rose would still be upset. Probably still be angry with her.

She didn't want to have to deal with Rose, either.

She pulled the mug toward her and removed the saucer covering it, then pulled the tea bag out and set it on the saucer, where it bled red.

Tomorrow, she would start in on McKell's computer. She could have left O'Hara to search it, but that didn't feel right.

The laptop finally finished booting up and she punched in her password just as the doorbell rang, freezing her fingers on the keyboard.

Bert? He had his own key, but with things so strained between them...

Maybe it wasn't Bert.

She got up from the stool and glanced down at her cotton pajamas, with their yellow and pink flowers. She really wasn't dressed for receiving company, but it was almost eleven o'clock at night, for Pete's sake. Company had some bloody nerve coming this late.

She stalked over to the front door only to pause with her hand on the door knob. She had no peephole in her door. If Bert was right, a killer could be standing on the other side, waiting to shoot her. Of course, most killers didn't ring the doorbell.

They don't wait on overpasses, either, she reminded herself.

The doorbell rang again and on impulse she whipped open the door, hoping to startle whoever was on the other side.

Instead, Kate's mouth fell open in astonishment.

"Hello, Aunt Kate," said Amanda, with a tremulous smile. "Can I come in?"

CHAPTER 15

KATE GOT up early the next morning, put on her sweats and her running shoes, and went for a run in the chilly morning air. Her cul-de-sac was still drowsy with sleep and would be for a few more hours—it was Sunday, after all—and she had the road to herself. Normally she ran at night, after dinner. Often, she would run down to the detachment and check in with whoever was on duty. It was different in the morning, with the sun just coming up and the sky glorious with washed out blues and pinks and oranges.

Her feet landed on the concrete sidewalk with regular slaps and she concentrated on her breathing, trying to reach the Zen place where all her worries and stresses fell away from her shoulders, leaving her lighter, freer.

There wasn't even a breeze. She left the cul-de-sac and headed down the road toward downtown. It wasn't the prettiest route, what with its industrial area before she would hit downtown proper, but it was familiar, and right now she didn't want to spare any energy on an unfamiliar trail.

There was a break in the houses and through it she could see Mendenhall sprawling below her, slumbering. Soon there would be frost in the mornings and she would have to watch her footing. And more often than not, she would catch the hint of wood smoke from the farming valley beyond Mendenhall.

Her mind circled back to her house, and to the strange car parked behind her rental car. The last time Amanda had surprised Kate at the house, she had driven all the way from Montreal, in February. And here she was again, seven months later, having flown in from Montreal the previous night, rented a Kia, and driven in from Winnipeg.

Kate was in no mood to be charmed by her niece's impulsiveness. What the hell was the girl thinking? She knew McKell had been shot. She had to know that the entire detachment would be working on finding the shooter. What in God's name led her to believe it was appropriate to intrude at a time like this?

Trepalli at least had had an excuse—he'd had no idea Mom had been in an accident.

Her breathing grew ragged as she lost concentration, and finally she stopped, breathing hard. She hadn't run in days, and now she was paying the price. She walked for a while, hands on her hips, staring down at the sidewalk as she cooled down quickly.

Maybe she'd been a little harsh with the girl. But last night, the last thing she had wanted to do was listen to a long explanation about why Amanda had landed on her doorstep like a hair on soup. She had pulled a clean towel and facecloth out for the girl and told her she would see her in the morning.

She hadn't even gone back to her laptop to check her emails. All she had wanted to do was close the door to her bedroom and shut out the whole sorry day.

Instead, she had tossed and turned all night, getting only brief snatches of sleep until she finally rolled out of bed at five a.m. to go for a run.

With a sigh, she turned around and stared up the street to where it climbed back up to her cul-de-sac.

Whenever she was in the middle of an investigation, she hated weekends, especially Sundays. Weekends made it so much harder to get hold of people. In the case of McKell's shooting, weekends added to the risk. The longer the shooter was out there, the greater the risk he would try again.

Although, really, was that likely? Had the parole board come to a decision about whoever it was McKell was going to testify against? Did they even know about McKell's shooting? And if so, had they known before they heard the would-be parolee? Would it have made a difference?

She would have to check with Stendel, but she doubted the parole board would have known about McKell's shooting before Friday night, when they were due to meet the chiefs of police for dinner.

She had stopped in the middle of the sidewalk, lost in thought, and now she started walking again. She felt a little queasy. Nerves. Stress. Fear. Between Mom's accident and McKell's shooting, she hadn't had a decent night's sleep since Wednesday.

She was sick of not knowing the source of the danger and whether or not the danger was over. She was sick of wondering if her mother's accident was connected to McKell's shooting. She was sick of worrying about how Bert was going to react.

This needed to end. Now.

* * *

The smell of fresh coffee filled the house by the time Kate got back. She didn't bother taking her running shoes off but went straight to the kitchen, which was empty. Her French press sat on the counter, with a clean cup next to it, along with a creamer and sugar bowl. She never bothered with her mother's cream and sugar set, but for the few short months Amanda had lived with her, the set had been in use every day.

Kate sighed. She had missed the girl.

She fixed her coffee, treating herself to a bit of sugar to go with the cream, and then walked out the kitchen door to the deck. Amanda was sitting in one of the chairs at the round patio table, still in her pajamas but with a heavy sweatshirt and a blanket from her bed wrapped around her. Her legs were tucked up against her chest. She was facing the valley view, although from her angle she couldn't see much of Mendenhall proper, only the farmlands beyond. The sun was up, steaming the dew off the deck.

Kate walked over to the table, pulled out a chair, and sat down across from Amanda. Her butt immediately grew cold from the dampness of the vinyl cushion.

Amanda clearly knew she was there but she didn't look at Kate. Her shoulder-length, honey blond hair was tousled around her face and shoulders, and her profile was very still as she stared out at the view. They had sat like this often, enjoying the view and not feeling a need to talk.

Now, however, Kate sensed a tension in the girl. Her stillness did not come from peace. Oh, no. Something else had driven the girl to hop on a plane, earning her mother's anger in the process, if Kate was any judge. She sighed silently. Crap. She would have to call Rose, after all, if only to tell her that Amanda was safe.

"All right," Kate said finally. "Talk." Her tone contained none of the impatience and irritation she had been feeling. It was pretty clear that the girl was miserable. No need to add to it.

Amanda glanced at her, then looked away, leaving Kate with an impression of bloodshot blue eyes and a pale face. Finally, she took a deep breath and began to speak, still staring out at the vista.

"Aunt Kate, I think I screwed up."

Oh, God. She really didn't want to get involved in this. She had tried to discourage those two from seeing each other. Her niece and her constable. For Pete's sake, how could it possibly end well?

"He asked me to marry him. That's why I had to leave."

Kate gave her niece a sideways glance. Apparently she couldn't avoid participating in this conversation. "That doesn't make sense," she pointed out.

Amanda looked at her. "How could I stay? I would see him almost every day. It would break my heart."

"Not to mention his," said Kate.

Amanda hunched into her blanket as if at a sudden chill.

"I know," she said in a low voice. The cup next to her on the table steamed into the morning air, reminding Kate of her own coffee. She took a sip and it warmed her immediately.

"If you don't want to marry the boy," said Kate reasonably, "why are you here?"

Amanda turned to look at her full on. She looked much older than her twenty-five years. "Because I love him."

Oh, for Pete's sake.

Kate's impatience must have shown on her face because Amanda gave her a twisted smile. "Why have you never married, Aunt Kate?" she asked softly. "Mom says you had plenty of opportunities. Why didn't you?"

How the *hell* had this become about her?

"We're not talking about me, Amanda," said Kate quietly. "We're talking about why you came here."

"He's a cop," said Amanda simply. "In the seven months I lived here with you, he was involved in a shooting and in trying to catch a crazy criminal. Twice, he could have lost his life for this job. How can I live with that kind of worry?"

That was when Kate realized that Amanda was lost. Yes, Trepalli had been at risk in those two cases, but Amanda was the one who had gotten shot, and who had almost drowned, thanks to the escaped convict. And yet, all she saw was the risk to Trepalli.

"So, after turning him down and ignoring him at your parents' house only to give him a dressing down, you decided the best way to deal with the situation was to follow him here?"

Amanda stood up, tightening the blanket around her.

"I owe him an apology, and an explanation," she said quietly. "And I didn't want to do it over the phone. I'll be out of your hair as soon as I get a chance to talk to him."

And with as much dignity as a person wrapped in a blanket could muster, she padded to the kitchen door and went in.

* * *

Kate swung by the Tim Horton's on her way to the detachment

and picked up a dozen doughnuts and a large coffee. Downtown Mendenhall was quiet, with most businesses closed on a Sunday, let alone this early on a Sunday.

Samantha Paterson was walking into the detachment from the compound, notebook in hand, when Kate walked in through the front door. Paterson nodded at her, her gaze flitting over Kate's jeans in surprise.

Well, it *was* Sunday, after all.

"Ma'am." She finished writing something in her notebook, then looked up at Kate again. "How's your mother?" Paterson was the only other female constable in the department, and she didn't like Kate much. Kate didn't know why and she'd stopped worrying about it. Paterson was a good cop, thoughtful, always looking beyond the obvious. Kate couldn't remember for sure, but she figured Paterson was around forty. She had two kids under the age of ten and her husband had just landed a job as the chief administrative officer at the city. Whatever that was.

"She's going to be fine," she said. "How's Amy?" she asked, barely remembering in time that Paterson's daughter had fallen off her bike and broken her arm.

"She's fine," said Paterson. "Everything's healing well. She's getting all the kids in her class to sign the cast." She had nice green eyes that lit up whenever she talked about her kids.

Kate grinned. "Sounds about right."

"Mornin', Chief," called Martins. She looked around to see him peering at her through the opening to the duty desk.

"Good morning, Nick," said Kate. She glanced up at the clock on the wall next to him. Almost seven thirty. "Everything all right?"

"Yes, ma'am," said Martins. "According to O'Hara, it was pretty quiet for a Saturday night. No guests, despite the ruckus at the Bull Pen."

Kate smiled. He meant they had no one in the drunk tank. Always a relief not to have to clean up the following day.

She followed Paterson into the duty room and found Olinchuk,

Paterson's usual partner, sitting at one of the common desks, reading the log book. He looked up as she walked in.

"Chief." His normally impassive face softened into a barely perceptible smile. "Glad your mom is doing okay."

Kate nodded and swallowed, surprised by the tightening of her throat.

"So, are those all for you?" asked Martins innocently.

Kate stared at him uncomprehendingly, then followed his gaze to the box of doughnuts she was holding. She grinned.

"No. I'd have to run a marathon to work them off." She turned on her sneakered heel and went to the lunch room, leaving the doughnuts on the counter by the coffee machine before returning to the duty room.

"Anything I need to know?" she asked Martins, nodding at the log book in Olinchuk's hands. Her cardboard coffee cup was starting to burn her hand and she switched it to her left hand.

Martins shook his head. His light brown eyes looked darker this morning, but maybe it was because the overhead light cast his eyes in shadow. "Friesen is already on patrol. They," he nodded to Olinchuk and Paterson, "are just leaving."

"And that's a cue, if ever I heard one," said Paterson, taking the log book from Olinchuk's hands and bringing it to the end of the counter, where it usually lived. The scent of a light perfume trailed after her, surprising Kate and reminding her that Samantha Paterson was more than a cop, though she couldn't remember ever seeing her in anything but her uniform. Olinchuk nodded to Kate as he followed Patterson out the door into the compound, where the patrol cars were parked.

"Right. I'll be in my office," said Kate.

Martins nodded and pulled the duty book toward him before turning back to the computer at the duty desk. It was the day officer's job to transcribe the incidents written in the log book during the previous twenty-four hours into the computer log, assign reference numbers and search terms. McKell had instituted the system, and she had to admit that it worked pretty well. No more scrolling through screen after screen, trying to find the one incident they were looking for.

McKell was a fine cop, and an even better administrator. If she chose to retire, she would make damned sure the mayor didn't let his personal feelings for McKell get in the way of making him Chief of Police. If McKell still wanted the job. He was only a few years younger than her, after all.

And then she remembered that McKell was lying in a hospital bed, maybe paralyzed. Dear God.

The heat from the coffee finally registered and she made her way to her office, the rubber soles on her sneakers squeaking on the linoleum. She had opted for jeans and a long-sleeved tee-shirt under a zippered fleece jacket, and even then she had been chilled on her way to the detachment. Mornings were nippy and afternoons, while gloriously sunny, were definitely cooler than they had been.

She walked into her office and set the cup down on her desk before walking around the desk to sit down. It was time to put away the summer clothes. Should she send out an official notice to change from summer dress to winter? She glanced out the only window in her office. It gave onto the parking lot, such as it was, but when she was sitting down, all she could see were the tops of the maple trees across the street and above them, blue, blue sky.

Maybe she would wait a while. No sense making her constables sweat in their heavier uniforms if there were still warm days ahead. Besides, some were already shifting, at least in part. Let them decide for themselves during this transition time.

She sighed and leaned down to turn her computer tower on. Then she leaned back and sipped her coffee while the computer booted up. No matter how she hated to think about it, she had to prepare in case McKell didn't come back, or took a while to recuperate.

Stan Albertson would be the natural choice to replace McKell temporarily. He was older, calm, had a lot of experience. Her constables already turned to him when McKell wasn't around. Albertson's leadership style was different than McKell's. Instead of giving firm orders that left no room for interpretation, Stan Albertson used quiet humor and suggestions. Both men were respected and both men got the job done. The problem was that Albertson already knew how to lead. He could step into the deputy chief's job with no problem.

This was an opportunity to give one of the other constables the experience of being DC. A temporary acting position was the ideal chance to learn what the job entailed and whether or not it would interest him. Or her.

Kate considered Samantha Paterson. She was certainly smart enough. And she had some good experience. She had come to Mendenhall from Vancouver five years ago. But was she leadership material?

The computer finally finished its calisthenics and she reached for the mouse and clicked on the email icon. She hadn't checked her email since Wednesday. She was going to pay for that.

She sat drinking her coffee while the program came on line and then stared in dismay as the list of new messages grew. When it finally stopped, she had fifty-eight new messages.

Good grief.

The front door to the detachment slammed shut and she heard Martins talking to someone, then things grew quiet again. She scrolled through the messages, trying to figure out which ones were urgent. One popped out, marked as urgent. It was from Stendel and had been sent last night. She opened it. His note was brief:

Couldn't reach any of the parole board members as they were in transit back to Vancouver. Did speak to someone from their Vancouver office. She emailed me the list of prisoners who were scheduled to appear before the board this week. I've attached it. Unfortunately, we won't know the disposition of each of the hear-

ings until they report back. I'm waiting for a callback from Elda Symington-Jones, who sits on the board. As soon as I hear back, I'll let you know.

Kate clicked on the attachment and a page popped up on the screen. A title at the top of the page read: "Parole Application Hearings, September 20-22, Red Hill Correctional Center." On it was a table with a time in the left-hand box, the name of the prisoner in the next box, a reference number in the next one, and a box for notes. There were twenty-two names listed.

Kate read through the list, but none of the names popped out at her. This was useless without context. She was grateful to Stendel for getting her that much, however. She knew that she wouldn't have been able to get the list that quickly, certainly not on the weekend. She suspected that the "someone" Stendel knew in the Vancouver office was a Sweet Young Thing.

She sighed, reminding herself that she and Stendel were on the same side. McKell was well respected in Winnipeg.

Maybe she didn't have pull with the parole board, but she could try another avenue. She printed out the list of names and snatched up the pages from the printer before striding into the duty room. Martins looked up from the computer as she approached.

"Busy?" she asked.

He shook his head. "It's Sunday."

"I've got a job for you," she said. She stepped up to the platform where he sat on the swiveling stool and he shifted over a little so they wouldn't crowd each other. She set the pages on the desk.

"This is a list of the prisoners the parole board was supposed to meet with this past week at Red Hill," she explained. "I want you to look up their files and note what they are incarcerated for, how long they are in, and who the arresting officer was. Then I want you to call Red Hill and find out everything that isn't in their files."

The freckles on Martins' face seemed to stand out. "I'll pull Samantha off patrol to help," he said.

Kate nodded. It was a big job, but CPIC—the Canadian Police

Information Center—kept digital records in an online database. Besides, it was Sunday, and barring an accident on the highway, nothing much happened in Mendenhall on Sundays.

Martins was studying the list. "Do we know the disposition of each case?" he asked.

"Not yet," said Kate. "Chief Stendel is working on that part."

She went back to her office and to the email. A few minutes later, she heard the front door open and slam again and the tread of boots coming into the duty room. That would be Samantha Paterson. After fifteen minutes of answering the more urgent emails and deleting the junk, she came across one from a name that looked vaguely familiar: ptremblay.

She stared at the name for a full ten seconds, going through her memory banks, until the information finally clicked. Paul Tremblay, the Longueuil Police duty officer she had dealt with regarding her mother's accident.

She clicked on the name and the message opened up.

Chief Williams, it began, *I thought you would like to know that we have found the man who hit your mother. Please call me at 450-555-1224 at your earliest convenience. If I am not at that number, you can call me at my cell phone number of 450-555-5222.*

Kate's stomach clenched as adrenalin flooded her system. She had left him her phone number—why hadn't he called? Then she glanced down at the date and time on the message. It had been sent at dinner time last night, after she had turned her cell phone off. She hadn't wanted to talk to Bert. But her card also had the detachment's number. Why hadn't the man called and left a message for her?

She rummaged around her desk. Martins had placed the pile of messages under a rock paperweight on the side of her desk by the telephone. She took the rock off and started flipping through them. There were even more than yesterday. Finally she found the one from Tremblay. He had called yesterday at around four thirty.

Without consciously deciding to, she reached for the telephone on her desk and punched in the first number he had given her, only to learn that he was off duty. She punched in the second number and was rewarded with a male voice on the third ring.

"*Oui, allô?*"

"*J'aimerais parler avec* Sergeant Tremblay?" she said in her rusty French.

"Chief Williams?"

"Yes," said Kate with relief. "Is this Sergeant Tremblay?"

"Yes, it is," said the sergeant. "I expected your call much earlier."

Kate sighed. "I only just got the message, Sergeant. Thank you for giving me your home number."

"*Mon plaisir,*" he said automatically.

"All right," said Kate, taking a deep breath. "Tell me what you know."

"We have found the Impreza," he said. "It had been abandoned in an industrial park, at the back of a glove factory. We tried to find the..." he hesitated a moment, then clearly found the word he was looking for, "...the fingerprints, but there were none, not even from the owner."

Kate's heart sank. Damn it.

"I guess we shouldn't be surprised," she said. "We are dealing with a professional."

"Yes," agreed Tremblay. "However, we found some loose change in the crack of the driver's seat, upon which we found partial fingerprints that did not belong to the owner or his family."

The sly bugger. He was saving the best for last.

"And...?" she asked hopefully.

"They belong to Jean-Sébastien Chouinard, a small crook. He has been in prison for theft, especially of vehicles."

Kate was wondering what Chouinard's size had to do with anything when she suddenly realized Tremblay must mean small-*time* crook.

"We have not found him yet," continued Tremblay, "but I

thought you would like to know we are progressing."

"I appreciate that, Sergeant Tremblay," said Kate sincerely. "What about the witness? The boy?"

"Raymond Massicotte," said Tremblay. "Eleven years old, a student at École Gustave Bolton. He will remain under police protection until we have found Chouinard."

A weight she hadn't realized she was carrying lifted off Kate's shoulders.

"Thank you, Sergeant Tremblay. Will he testify?" Too often, witnesses were afraid of testifying in case of repercussions.

"I believe he will," said the officer drily. "Now that his parents know he was not at school, and there is no reason to hide what he saw, he seems most excited to go to court and denounce the man."

For the moment, Kate didn't care about a conviction. She wanted to talk to this Chouinard and find out why he had assaulted her mother. She needed to know his connection—if there was one—to the attack on McKell.

"What exactly *did* he see?" she asked.

"He was skateboarding down the middle of the street and stopped when your mother began crossing the street. He was a little distance away but saw the car coming up the street. He said it was a dark green Kia Soul and that it sped up as your mother began to cross. He says she never saw it coming."

"Good," said Kate. She had known that already, but it was reassuring to have corroboration. "But I'd feel better knowing Chouinard was in custody."

"So would we, Madame," Tremblay assured her.

Kate wondered if she should tell him that she suspected a connection between the assault on her mother and the attack on McKell, but in the end, she decided it was better to wait until she had more facts.

After promising to let her know as soon as they found Chouinard, Tremblay signed off. Kate sat staring at the desk phone for a few long minutes, trying to figure out what she was feeling. The whole thing was a tangled mess. Mom's accident. McKell's shooting. The parole board.

She was starting to get a glimmer of a path through the underbrush, but she was missing information. She sighed. The list she had given O'Hara was the key. She was sure of it.

Three people doing the research would get through it faster than two.

* * *

"Hello?"

"Hello, Mr. Stilwell," said Kate. "It's Kate Williams. How are you?"

"I'm very well, thank you, and it's Fred."

She grinned. "Fred. How is my mother doing?"

Kate was sitting at the rebuilt Wheatland Café, which had suffered a fire earlier in the summer, waiting for sandwiches to bring back to the detachment. Martins and Paterson were still working on the list, but she had needed to get up and move around, and had volunteered to fetch food for all three of them. While she waited for it to be ready, she figured she'd call Mom.

"Your mother is doing very well," said Fred. "I believe she is feeling housebound, but the doctors want to wait a bit before giving her a walking cast. Would you like to speak to her?"

"Yes, please." A walking cast was good news. Mom had expected to be stuck in her wheelchair for two months.

He brought the phone to her mother and Kate heard her shooing Fred out of the room. For the next few minutes, Kate heard about the indignities of bathing with a cast and the fact that the health center had sent a male nurse to check on her instead of a female nurse. By the time the sandwiches arrived in a large paper bag, Kate was grinning and feeling better than she had in days.

Just before she let her mother go, Kate remembered what she had wanted to ask her.

"So, do you remember anything more about the accident?"

Hetty Williams was silent for a moment. Finally she cleared her throat.

"Not really. I remember leaving Sophie's place. I remember thinking that the tea set she had given me would look nice on the hutch. Then I woke up in the hospital."

Kate wanted to ask her if she'd seen the driver of the car, but she knew better. If Mom had seen him, she would have said so.

"Did Amanda make it safely?"

Kate winced. She had forgotten to call Rose. "Yes. So you knew she was coming?"

"John drove her to the airport," said Mom. "Rose was not happy."

I'll bet, thought Kate. Was John *trying* to upset Rose?

"How's your friend?" asked Mom. Kate frowned, her mind momentarily blank. What friend? Oh. She meant McKell.

"It's too soon to tell," she said. "He'll live, but we don't know what damage was done to his spinal cord." God. It sounded so blunt.

"Oh," said Mom. "We'll pray for him, dear."

Kate paused before replying. Mom was thinking of herself and Fred Stilwell as "we."

"Thanks, Mom. He'll appreciate that."

They signed off after Kate promised to come see her as soon as she could. The little café was filling up with brunch goers and she was taking up a table for nothing. But still she sat, staring at the bulletin board on the wall in front of her. It featured announcements for upcoming concerts in Brandon and Winnipeg, musical instruments for sale, yoga classes at the community center.

Chouinard's record spoke of theft, not of violence. That could mean that he'd never been caught assaulting someone. Why would someone who'd only ever been a thief suddenly deliberately hit someone with a car?

Finally she grabbed the bag of sandwiches, then got up and left the café, walking back the four blocks to the station. The sun had warmed the breeze and she left her fleece jacket open while she walked. The fire hall's bay doors stood open, revealing the emergency response vehicle and the ladder truck, but no firefighters. Maybe they were at lunch.

She got back to the station to find Martins typing furiously and Paterson standing next to him, feeding him information from sheets in her hand.

"Go take a break," she told them. "I'll take the desk."

Martins looked uncomfortable at the thought, but she insisted and finally he and Paterson escaped to the lunch room. Kate started reading through the abbreviated notes they had made on the printout, but only twelve of the twenty-two inmates were filled out. She went to the computer file he had created with each prisoner's record. They were all male, and their offences ranged from aggravated sexual assault to murder. Working with the partially filled in chart, she found the prisoners still left to analyze and started going through their files.

She went through each file carefully, but didn't find what she had expected: McKell's name as the arresting officer. She sat back and stared at the computer screen with dislike. There had to be a connection, for crying out loud. There had to be a reason McKell had been shot.

Frowning, she went back to the first file and started reading it carefully. The phone rang and she answered it. Martins returned to the desk and Olinchuk picked up Paterson and they went back on patrol. Kate went back to her office, where she opened up the file on her computer and kept reading.

She finally found what she was looking for on the fourteenth file she checked, buried deep in the background information. The prisoner's name was Thomas Elliot Cassidy, arrested eleven years earlier for importing marijuana, for which he got fifteen years. The file didn't go into details, but it was his earlier background that caught her attention. He had been a military police officer in the Canadian Armed Forces, stationed at Shilo, where McKell had also served as an MP.

CHAPTER 16

H E'S AWAKE," said Charlotte, her voice tinny on the cell phone.

Kate closed her eyes, almost afraid to ask. Before she could, Charlotte rushed on.

"They gave him a shot that would keep him from moving," she said. "They don't want him to aggravate anything in there until they can give him an MRI."

Kate wasn't too sure what an MRI did, but she assumed it would help them know if his spine was irreparably damaged or not.

"How's he doing?" she asked.

"He is not happy," said Charlotte, "and he's in pain, although he won't admit it. But he's all there, Chief."

Kate smiled to herself. McKell had taken a nasty knock on the head, in spite of the air bags. She was willing to bet he had a heck of a headache. If Charlotte said he was all there, however, that meant that no matter what happened to McKell physically, at least he had all his faculties.

Please God, don't let him be paralyzed.

"Is there still an officer outside his door?" she asked.

"Yes, ma'am," said Charlotte promptly. "Two. Someone new comes on every two hours."

Good.

"All right," said Kate. "Tell McKell I'm coming down. I have some questions for him."

"Will do," said Charlotte.

"How about you?" asked Kate impulsively. "Are you still staying at Josh's?"

"Yes. But he's gone to Minnedosa today and tomorrow."

"All right. I'll see you when I get there."

* * *

The moment she saw the gray Focus in the detachment parking lot, her mouth twisted. She missed her Explorer, and she didn't have time to go shopping for another one. With a sigh, she unlocked the door and slid in. She started the engine and opened the window to let some fresh air in. Then she sat, staring at the steering wheel.

She felt scattered. Disorganized. Too much had happened, too quickly. She felt like she stood in the middle of a whirlwind, trying to see through the flying debris. It was time to take a deep breath and think, rather than react.

What did she know, really? She sorted through the facts, trying to place them in order.

On Wednesday, Chouinard, a petty criminal with a record for theft, had struck her mother down, forcing Kate to go to Quebec.

As a result, McKell had been forced to take her Friday chiefs of police meeting in Winnipeg. More than likely, he would still have been able to testify at the parole board hearing in spite of the change of plans.

The only connection she could find with the list of prisoners scheduled to be heard at the parole board hearing was this Thomas Cassidy. But she couldn't see what the connection was except that they had both been MPs at Shilo at approximately the same time.

McKell had borrowed her Explorer for the drive into Winnipeg, since his car was in the shop.

Someone had shot McKell as he drove her Explorer.

She leaned her forehead against the steering wheel. Dear Lord in heaven. All the pieces had to fit somehow. She just couldn't figure how.

A car pulled in next to hers and she straightened and turned to look. Trepalli was staring back at her from behind the wheel of his classic 1965 Mustang. He had spent months refurbishing it and she had to admit that, with its shiny silver paint and the double black stripes along the hood and roof, it looked pretty sharp.

They stared at each other for a moment, then Kate waved him over. He got out of his car and opened her passenger door to lean in and look at her.

"I'm going to Winnipeg," she said impulsively. "Wanna come?"

He hesitated, then glanced back at his car. He was wearing well-worn jeans and a gray cotton shirt with multiple pockets and long sleeves that he'd rolled up his forearms.

He ducked back down to look at her. "Let me grab my coat."

A minute later, he slipped into the passenger seat and tossed the leather coat into the back. He smelled of fresh air and sunshine and some scented soap that she couldn't place.

She pulled out of the parking lot and onto Mendenhall Drive.

"What were you doing at the detachment?" she asked.

He shrugged. "I was going to offer to help."

She glanced at him. His profile was set, his jaw clenched. The boy had good bone structure and a well-built, slim, muscular body. He and Amanda would make beautiful babies.

Oh, dear Lord. Did he know Amanda was here?

Traffic was light and she made it out of the downtown core easily and onto the on ramp for the Trans-Canada Highway East.

He couldn't know. He wouldn't look so calm if he knew Amanda was here. Would he?

She had invited him along impulsively, but now she wondered if deep down she was trying to keep those two apart.

Crap.

"Did you know that Amanda is in town?" she asked.

By his start and his sudden turn toward her, she decided that he hadn't known.

"Is she staying with you?" he asked.

She nodded. "She arrived late last night." And she probably wouldn't want Kate telling the boy why she was here. Kate sighed. "Do you want me to turn around?" She could take the next exit and be back at the detachment in ten minutes.

After a moment, he said, "No, thank you, ma'am."

Surprised, Kate glanced at him. He was studying her face.

"What?" She was starting to wish she had left him behind and driven in on her own.

"Why is she here?"

"You'll have to ask her that," said Kate. Thank goodness traffic was light. She was having trouble concentrating on the road. And with the sun beating down on the car, she was starting to get hot in her fleece jacket.

"Does she think this is a game?" asked Trepalli suddenly.

Startled, Kate looked at him again. His cheeks were red with emotion and his blue eyes looked dark with anger.

"Excuse me?" asked Kate. She'd never seen him this way. He was a calm man with a disposition that tended to the good-natured and carefree. The intensity emanating from him was a little disconcerting.

"She made it very clear how she felt," he continued in a low voice. His hands clenched on his knees and he turned to face front. "She refused to see me when I was down there and had time to see her. Now that I'm back, and dealing with the DC's shooting, she suddenly wants to see me?" His hands opened suddenly and did a quick chopping motion. "I've had it with this crap."

Kate found herself breathing shallowly and finally remembered to close her mouth. Holy cow.

Stay out of it, she warned herself sharply. *Just keep your mouth shut.*

She kept her gaze on the road and avoided looking at her young constable. She knew that beneath the anger was a deep hurt, and probably confusion and more than a little bruised ego.

After a moment, he cleared his throat lightly.

"Sorry, Chief," he said. "I know you're in a bad position."

She swallowed a sigh. Yes, she was.

They made the rest of the trip in silence and while there was some traffic in Winnipeg, it was light compared to week days. Without consciously deciding to, she avoided taking the route where McKell had been shot.

Kate finally roused herself from her thoughts as she headed for Grace Hospital.

"Could you call Martins?" she said. "Ask him if he's got anything on Cassidy."

"Who's Cassidy?" asked Trepalli, automatically fishing into his back jeans pocket for his cell phone.

So she filled him in on what she had learned that morning. By the time she drove into the hospital parking lot, he was finishing up with Martins.

"Nothing yet," he reported. "The warden at Red Hill isn't in. He's trying to reach the acting warden."

Kate nodded. Good. CPIC was a great resource, but it didn't tell you how an inmate got along with the others, who he hung out with in the institute, or if he was part of the black market of the institution. Every correctional center had one.

She finally found a parking spot in the far corner, under a mature maple tree with leaves starting to turn red.

It was a relief to get out of the car. Marco Trepalli had apologized for his outburst, but his anger was still palpable. Within the confines of the small car, she had felt it beating against her, even though she knew it wasn't directed at her.

The pavement smelled of burned oil and gasoline as they wound their way from one mini-parking lot to another, heading for the entrance.

Everybody in Winnipeg must have someone to visit in hospital, she thought. But at least the day had warmed up enough that she had left her fleece jacket behind in the car, along with Trepalli's leather one. He walked up the stairs to the front entrance beside her, slowing his pace in deference to her shorter legs.

Once inside the lobby, they stood blinking as their eyes adjusted to the relative darkness of the interior. Trepalli nodded to the elevator and she shook her head when she saw how many people were waiting for it. Without a word, they headed for the stairwell.

Trepalli's anger seemed to dissipate with movement and by the time they reached the fourth floor, he seemed much more relaxed. Kate, on the other hand, felt a little winded.

That's what happens when you avoid exercise, she told herself, nodding her thanks as Trepalli opened the door to the main medical ward. It gave Kate a measure of comfort to know McKell wasn't in intensive care anymore.

She looked up and down the hallway, a little disoriented from arriving by the stairwell rather than the elevator, and found the guard at McKell's door staring right at her. This one was a young woman with short, curly black hair and brown eyes that seemed to take up most of her face. She stood up as Kate and Trepalli approached. She was even shorter than Kate and looked as if her utility belt, with its cuffs and holstered weapon, weighed more than she did. She couldn't be older than twelve.

Then Kate got a good look at her eyes and revised her opinion. This one might be young, but she had experience. Her name tag read STARLING.

Kate pulled her identification from her pocket, grateful she had remembered to take it out of her jacket pocket. There was something in this young woman's face that said no ID, no entry.

"Chief Kate Williams, Mendenhall Police," she said crisply, showing the young officer her badge and card.

The constable took her card and studied it, then studied Kate's face before handing the card back with a nod.

"You're on the list," she said. Her voice was surprisingly deep.

"Where's the other guard?" asked Kate. Stendel had promised he would double the guard on McKell's room until they figured out what was going on.

Starling nodded to the end of the hallway, where another Winnipeg police officer stood staring at them, arms down by his side.

For easier access to his weapon, Kate realized. It made sense. Separate the guards. It would be harder to incapacitate both of them at the same time. The second officer was in his mid-thirties, and black. He was well over six feet tall and was built like a brick outhouse, as Dad used to say. Kate nodded at him and he nodded back, his eyes watchful.

Officer Starling turned to look at Trepalli, who handed her his own identification. She went through the same process. To Kate's surprise, there was none of the usual spark of interest that women showed for Marco Trepalli. Either she was immune to his charms, or he was past caring about charming other women.

Starling handed Trepalli back his identification and said, "You're not on the list. You'll have to wait outside."

Trepalli opened his mouth to object but Kate placed a hand on his arm. No argument would budge the woman. He closed his mouth and nodded.

"Tell him we're all thinking of him," he said.

"Of course," said Kate. She turned to Starling. "Is Charlotte still in there?" The last time she had been here, they were only letting visitors in one at a time.

"Miss Hrebien has gone to get coffee."

Kate smiled her thanks and pushed open the door to McKell's room. The closest bed was empty, its sheets and blanket tucked with military precision. The second bed, the once closest to the window, was partly screened by a dividing curtain on a rail. All she could see was the shape of a pair of legs under a yellow cotton blanket. She stared intently at the legs as she approached, desperately hoping to see movement. The window was cracked open, letting in fresh air and the sound of cars driving by on the street below.

"Hello?" croaked McKell from behind the curtain.

Kate pasted a smile on her face and said, "Hello, yourself," just as she stepped past the curtain and got a good look at her deputy chief.

Holy... "Geez, Rob. You look like something the cat dragged in and didn't have the heart to eat." As Mom would say.

McKell laughed then winced.

"Don't make me laugh," he said. "It hurts."

"I'll bet," she said. All she'd had was a bullet in the shoulder and it had hurt like hell. He'd had surgeons rummaging around in his chest, looking for a bullet fragment. Anger surged through her as a vision of McKell, trapped and bleeding in her Explorer, flashed through her imagination. At that moment, if she'd had the shooter within reach, she would have happily strangled him.

Kate studied McKell. He was lying flat, with the blanket pulled up to his waist, his left arm in a cast and sling, supported by a pillow. Long lines led from beneath his hospital gown to a machine next to his bed that had script and numbers scrolling across its screen. The pale blue, short-sleeved hospital gown washed out his features and emphasized the dark circles under his eyes. A thick pad of bandages made a lump on his chest. There was a smaller one on his shoulder.

She'd always thought that his blue eyes were his best feature, but now they were bloodshot and sat in their sockets as if they had shrunk. While his crew-cut hair was still mostly brown, with some gray, his stubble was coming in completely gray. His normally lean cheeks were now scored with lines of pain, aging him and making his cheekbones protrude alarmingly.

She had never seen him look so... haggard.

"I'm glad you're awake," she said finally. And she was. Hearing his laugh, even if it was laced with pain, had flooded her with relief. For all that he had been such a pain when she first came on as chief, he had become her ally and partner in running the detachment. They might not be friends, but they respected each other.

She really didn't want to lose him.

"I'm glad I'm awake, too," he said soberly. "What's happening with the investigation? No one's telling me anything."

Kate smiled. "First things first." She walked around the bed and pulled a chair closer to him before sitting in it. "Everyone at the detachment says hi. Trepalli's pacing the hallway outside the door. Apparently he's not on the list of people allowed to see you."

McKell frowned. "I know. It's a pretty limited list. Only you, Charlotte, Stendel, Bert, and my brother Sam are on it."

Kate's breath stopped for a minute. His brother Sam. "I'm so sorry, Rob," she said, her face flaming. "I completely forgot to notify your family."

He gave her a lopsided smile. "Charlotte let him know. He'll be here later tonight."

Kate couldn't believe she had forgotten to call McKell's next of kin. This was the kind of detail McKell *never* forgot. She took a deep breath.

"What's the deal with your injuries?" she asked bluntly.

His face cleared of all expression and his right hand lifted only to drop to his side. "They got the bullet fragments out," he said, as if he were reporting to her on an incident. "They did some minor damage along the way, but one fragment nicked the spine." He looked at her, clearly reading the question she didn't want to ask. He nodded to his legs. "They've given me something to keep me from moving from about here," he placed his hand just above his chest, "to my feet. I guess things are still swollen in there." Something dark moved behind his eyes. Fear? "They've pushed me through one machine after another, and they still don't know if I'll walk again."

Kate nodded and they sat in silence for a moment, both absorbing the implications. She wanted to yell at someone, force the doctors to let him know, one way or another, but it would take the time it took, and no amount of raging on her part would make any difference. In the meantime, she could put that fine mind of his to work.

"Has anyone from Winnipeg interviewed you?" she asked.

He shook his head. "No."

Kate was surprised. That Officer Starling would surely have informed her boss that McKell was awake. "Who is Thomas Cassidy?" she asked.

McKell's eyebrows shot up in surprise. "Cassidy? Is that bastard behind this?" Color briefly flushed his face, only to recede, leaving him paler than ever. Kate swallowed her alarm. He was much more fragile than he let on, she suddenly realized. There was a reason the nurses only allowed one person in at a time.

"I don't know," she said calmly. "We're trying to figure out what happened, and why."

McKell frowned. "I was driving your car," he pointed out.

"I know. And I don't know if that's important or not. What do you remember?"

He scowled at the blue sky outside the window. The light deepened the harsh lines on his face, making him look much older than fifty-one.

Pain will do that.

"I left Mendenhall early," he said. "I wanted to beat the traffic and I wanted to get to the meeting early to set up the presentation." He turned to look at her. "I guess the laptop is toast?"

Kate shrugged. "It's still in the Winnipeg evidence lock-up."

He nodded. "I was coming up to that new overpass they're building on Portage. It's got some kind of fencing all over it. The sun was in my eyes and I was just reaching up to turn the visor down when I saw sunlight glinting on something metal on the overpass. I thought it was just the scaffolding, but then the windshield exploded. After that, I don't remember anything."

Kate swallowed and looked down at her lap. Holy cow.

"You managed to steer away from oncoming traffic," she said softly. "You hit the ditch on your side of the highway and rolled." She looked up at him. "If you hadn't, you would have caused a massive accident, with loss of life and multiple injuries."

He nodded slowly. "Well, that's good, then." He cleared his throat. "So, you think Cassidy is behind this?" he asked again.

He was starting to look even worse. She was tiring him out. But she had to get answers before she let him go.

"What's your connection to him?" she asked.

He started to take a deep breath, then stopped, obviously in pain. She wondered if he was taking the full allotment of pain killers. She knew he would hate to lose control of his faculties. In that way, Rob McKell was a lot like her.

"He was a military policeman. Served with me in Shilo," he began. "This was about twelve, thirteen years ago. He was a bad apple. We all knew it, but we could never pin anything on him. One day, on patrol, I found a young private, female, passed out on the firing range. She'd been drugged and raped. I took her into the base hospital and they did a rape kit, but there was no trace evidence. I suspected Cassidy had done it. There'd been rumors of someone using Rohypnol on women, but we could never get the women to come forward, even though some of them suspected Cassidy. They were afraid of him. The base commander refused to do anything about Cassidy without proof. All the private could remember was sitting in the mess hall at the same table as Cassidy, but there were others there, too, and he left the mess hall before she did."

He stopped to catch his breath. His face was expressionless, but there were two splotches of color high on his cheeks, making him look feverish.

"She was convinced it was him. He'd been following her, she said, but she couldn't prove it. She wasn't the most popular girl on base. None of them were. That was how he operated. He picked the girls who had no support network—no friends, no family in the area. That was why they were all so reluctant to pursue any investigation. But this private..."

He trailed off and Kate let him collect his thoughts. A car door slammed somewhere down on the street and laughter floated up to the room, and still McKell remained silent. Finally he looked up.

"Her name was Jessica Stutkovich. She was a communications specialist. She was only twenty. She tried for three months to get Cassidy arrested. I was the one who told her we were no longer pursuing him because of lack of evidence. The next morning she didn't turn up for work. We found her hanging in her bathroom."

Kate closed her eyes. Crap.

Then she remembered.

"He was never arrested for sexual assault," she said. "His file says he was arrested in Winnipeg for importing marijuana."

McKell nodded. "He was finally "persuaded" to leave the Forces. He stuck around Brandon for a while, but too many people knew him in the area. So he moved to Winnipeg. The cops here suspected he had set up a network of dealers and was importing pot from Afghanistan, so they contacted us in Shilo and we worked with them on a sting operation." He sighed. "It took a while, but we got the bastard. He got fifteen years. And I'm going to make sure he serves every one of those years."

Kate nodded. "By attending his parole board hearing and providing testimony against him."

McKell smiled tightly. "He only became eligible to apply for parole last year."

The door opened suddenly and a nurse walked in. She was a big woman, close to five feet ten inches, Kate judged, with dark hair in a thick braid down her back.

"Mr. McKell needs to rest now," she said firmly. She stopped by the machines next to McKell's bed and pushed a couple of buttons. "You haven't been taking your pain meds," she stated, looking at McKell.

He smiled at her. "Don't need them yet."

One dark eyebrow rose. "You're stressing yourself out needlessly," she said matter-of-factly. "Take the pain killers, get the rest you need. You'll heal faster. You." She pointed at Kate. "Time to go."

Kate glanced at McKell and saw a smile hovering on his lips. This drill sergeant routine must be familiar to him, she thought. She got up and replaced the chair.

"Chief."

Kate looked at him.

"You going to talk to him?"

Kate gave him her best shark grin. "You bet."

A look of frustration crossed McKell's face and he didn't need to say a word for her to know he desperately wanted to be there when she did.

The nurse gave her a warning look and Kate nodded. "I'll check in on you later," she said to her deputy chief. "Listen to your nurse. I need you back sooner rather than later."

Her throat tightened on the last words and she left without waiting for his response. Starling was still at the door.

"Thank you, Constable," said Kate.

Starling nodded. "Just doing my job, ma'am."

Kate smiled at her. "And it's a great comfort to me." Now, where was Trepalli? She looked around and saw him talking to the big officer at the other end of the hallway. Nurses walked in and out of rooms, carrying trays or pushing carts. A patient in a bathrobe and fuzzy slippers shuffled down the hallway, pushing an IV drip. A speaker overhead asked Dr. Steinberg to please dial 4115. Had it been this busy when she first came up the stairs? She had been so focused on seeing McKell that she hadn't noticed.

She stood still for a moment, trying to absorb what McKell had told her. The only thing she knew for sure was that she had to talk to this Cassidy.

But first she needed to talk to Stendel and find out how the investigation was going. She sighed. And eventually she would have to talk to Bert. Part of her was relieved that he had stopped trying to tell her what to do, but she had to admit to feeling a little hurt that he hadn't tried contacting her.

You are such a princess.

With a small nod to Starling, she started down the hallway toward Trepalli. She didn't know why she had invited him to come with her. Now she was going to have to drag him with her to the correctional center, or drop him off somewhere. Maybe she had just needed the company.

The elevator doors opened, disgorging three people, including Charlotte, who carried a cardboard tray with three paper cups. The two other people headed for the nursing station near the elevator. Charlotte saw Trepalli and she smiled at him. Then her face crumpled up and she began to cry. Trepalli took the cardboard tray from her and handed it to the officer, who discreetly stepped away from them. Charlotte clung to Trepalli and he patted her back while she cried.

Kate hesitated. She didn't want to interrupt what was clearly a very emotional moment. At that instant, she caught a movement out of the corner of her eye and turned to see the door to the stairwell open. To her amazement, Amanda emerged and stood looking around. Her gaze fell on Officer Starling, then on Kate, and then, as if drawn by a magnet, on Trepalli and Charlotte, holding each other at the far end of the hallway.

Kate watched the next few moments unfold with fatalistic fascination. She glanced from Amanda's stricken face to Trepalli, who had his back to her. Charlotte, however, saw Amanda and immediately pulled out of Trepalli's embrace. She said something to him that Kate couldn't hear and he turned around and saw Amanda.

Kate turned back to Amanda in time to see her niece whirl and head back down the stairs, almost bowling over Bert, who had come up the stairs behind her. Kate glimpsed his surprised face and saw Amanda flee down the stairwell. Before she could react, Trepalli barreled through the door right behind her, almost knocking Bert over again.

Instinctively, Kate rushed through the doorway, too, only to be stopped by Bert's hand on her arm.

"Let them work it out for themselves," he said grimly. "We have our own working out to do."

CHAPTER 17

GRACE Hospital's cafeteria was three times the size of the hospital cafeteria in Mendenhall, but it seemed to serve the same chicken noodle soup and tuna salad sandwiches. Something was cooking in the kitchen—a roast maybe?—and it smelled wonderful, but Kate settled for coffee, even knowing she would regret it later. Between the drive, the stress of seeing McKell, and the emotional upheaval she had just witnessed, she felt as if she had been hung up wet and left out overnight. She needed caffeine to get her through this.

The cafeteria had a wall of windows, with doors that opened onto an empty, leafy, flagstone courtyard with picnic tables and bright yellow and green molded plastic chairs. Without a word, Kate and Bert headed for it, settling at the picnic table.

"I've emailed you the parole board decision on all the prisoners they saw at Red Hill," said Bert without preamble. "Stendel said you were looking for it."

"Thank you," said Kate. She swallowed coffee to ease her suddenly dry throat. He was being very polite. Very formal.

He must still be angry.

"Do you have access to the disposition of the case for Thomas Cassidy?" she asked.

His eyebrow rose and she thought she saw a flicker of a smile before his expression smoothed over.

"You're eventually going to have to learn to work your phone," he said.

She grinned sheepishly. "I know."

He pulled out his phone and began punching buttons. After a while, he read out loud. "Thomas Elliot Cassidy. His parole request was approved."

Kate's heart beat a little faster. So. McKell hadn't testified and Cassidy would soon be released on parole.

"Who's this Cassidy?" asked Bert. "Why is he so important?" Under the natural sunlight, his gray-threaded red hair looked almost strawberry blonde and his freckles stood out.

"I think he's the one behind McKell's attack," she said. Carefully, she laid out her theory. The last time she had tried to explain it to him, he had lost his temper and then she had lost her temper and walked out. This time, he watched her, studying her face as if he wanted to memorize her features.

"It's thin," he said finally. He took a sip of coffee and winced. Kate agreed. The coffee was awful.

"It is, a little," she conceded. "But it's the only connection that makes sense." She wrapped her hands around the porcelain mug, suddenly realizing that they were cold. "That's why I want to interview him."

Bert's mouth tightened. Then he said, "You could be wrong, Kate."

Kate took a deep breath. "Yes." Yes, she could be wrong. But she didn't think she was.

He nodded. "But you're still willing to risk your life on you being right."

Her eyebrows rose in surprise. That wasn't exactly the way she saw it. McKell had been shot on Friday morning. She had arrived in Winnipeg that same day. In the two days since, no one had attacked her. She'd seen no one acting suspiciously around her. All her instincts told her she wasn't the target. McKell was.

She didn't know how to respond to him, so she remained silent. He studied her for a while longer, then gave her a sad smile.

"I can't do this anymore, Katie," he said softly, and her heart fell. "I worry about you all the time. You place yourself in danger without giving a thought to the ones who love you."

She stared at him, shocked beyond words. He was a *cop*, for the love of God! He knew what the job was all about.

"You knew this when you met me," she pointed out. "You knew I was a cop."

Bert shook his head. "No, Kate. I knew you were the chief of police. You don't see Stendel running around getting himself shot. A chief's job is administrative. Only that's not what you want, is it? You want to be in the thick of it all the time."

Kate felt the blood leaving her face and the coffee turn to acid in her belly.

"Clearly, you've never worked for a small force," she said carefully. She put up a hand to forestall him when he opened his mouth to speak. "It's all right," she continued. "I can see where this is going. I just wish you had thought of this before we started seeing each other."

Before I grew to love you.

She pushed her mug away and swung her legs over the bench of the picnic table before standing up. Bert stayed where he was, looking at her with a grim expression on his face.

There really wasn't anything left to say. She turned and walked away.

* * *

Trepalli wasn't at the car. She opened the car door to let the afternoon heat escape, then stood for a minute next to the rental, trying to get her emotions under control.

She couldn't believe that they had just broken up. Just like that. He must have been thinking about it for a while. She'd gotten shot a year ago, *before* they had started seeing each other. He knew what he was getting into. Why was he suddenly so upset with her?

It's something else, she told herself. *You know that.*

It was true. In her experience, whatever argument was put forward to explain a break-up usually hid a deeper reason beneath it. Maybe he had met someone else. Maybe he had realized that he didn't love her after all.

Whatever.

She had gotten along fine without him. She would be fine again.

Unfortunately, her heart was too busy breaking to listen to her head.

In the shade of the maple tree, she leaned her forehead against the door frame and squeezed her eyes shut against the threat of tears. This wasn't the first time a relationship had ended for her. They had been seeing each other for seven months, and that was about four months longer than any other relationship she'd had. She liked Bert. Liked him a lot. But not enough to quit being a cop.

"Chief?"

She straightened with a jerk. Trepalli was standing on the other side of the Focus, looking at her over the roof. They studied each other for a long moment. His usually generous mouth was compressed into a thin line and there were lines of pain around his eyes. So. Things hadn't gone well for him, either. She swallowed her questions. He probably didn't feel like talking, either.

"Wanna go for a ride?" she asked him.

He was standing in the sunlight and squinted at her, obviously trying to interpret the question.

"What did you have in mind?" he asked cautiously.

"I need to interview Thomas Cassidy. He's at Red Hill." Red Hill Correctional Center was half an hour north of Winnipeg. Normal procedure would have her call whoever was in charge and advise them that she needed to speak with a prisoner. The warden would then advise her what time was best. But she didn't want to risk being told that tomorrow would be better or that the warden wasn't in and she would have to wait to speak to him. She didn't know when

Cassidy would be formally released.

It would be harder to turn her away in person.

"You haven't heard from Martins?" asked Trepalli. He folded his bare forearms over the roof, his muscles moving sleekly under his skin.

Kate shook her head. "It's Sunday. Red Hill is probably reluctant to call the acting warden. They probably think it's best to wait until tomorrow."

Trepalli's mouth quirked up on one side. "And you're not the patient type, are you, Chief?"

She waggled her eyebrows at him and finally slid in behind the steering wheel.

* * *

The road to Red Hill was bordered by a tall chain-link fence topped with strands of barbed wire. Inside the fence was another tall fence with a roll of barbed wire across the top. Between the two fences was a twenty-foot no man's land of weeds and stubby grass. The access road ended at a parking lot, beyond which was a sprawling, low, red-brick building with three floors of narrow windows. Peeking up over the building was an older building of quarried stone with a squat central tower, like an air traffic controller's tower.

"That is one butt-ugly building," said Trepalli in wonder.

Crude, but accurate, thought Kate. She parked in one of the visitor spots. There weren't many available. She glanced at her watch. Almost four o'clock. Maybe it was visiting time.

They followed the sidewalk to the main door, aware that cameras were following their movements. The main door opened automatically at their approach and they entered to find themselves in a small vestibule with a solid-looking gun-metal gray door in front of them, with a keypad lock and a thick but narrow glass insert through which one could peer. Presumably it led to the jail proper, or to the administrative wing. A sliding window in the right-hand wall revealed a small room with stacked cube lockers against the wall. A bench sat beneath the window. On their left was a matching small room, but the bullet-proof glass on the window did not slide. A guard sat at the counter on the other side of the window, hands poised on a computer keyboard, watching them. He was a grizzled veteran with crew-cut white hair and sunbaked wrinkles around his mouth and eyes.

Kate pulled out her identification and put it up to the window.

"Chief Kate Williams, Mendenhall Police Department," she said crisply. "This is Constable Marco Trepalli." She gave Trepalli time to flip open his wallet and show his identification. "I'd like to see one of your prisoners."

The guard studied them for a moment. His short-sleeved uniform revealed ropy white scars on both arms. Kate found it hard to keep from staring at them.

"We usually get the courtesy of an advance warning," he said mildly, his voice sounding tinny through the small speaker embedded in the glass.

Kate nodded her agreement. "Yes." She knew better than to browbeat this one. Instead she looked him in the eye. Finally he allowed himself a small smile.

"Have a seat," he said. "I'll have to call the acting warden." He nodded to the bench crammed against the opposite wall of the small vestibule. "Who's the prisoner?"

"Thomas Cassidy," said Kate. She followed Trepalli to the bench and sat down, prepared to wait as long as it took. She could see the guard, whose name she hadn't seen, talking on the phone although she couldn't hear what he was saying.

So the acting warden was already here. Why hadn't he called Martins back?

Trepalli was looking around the vestibule. Above their heads was the sliding glass window to the locker room. Were they in uniform, they would have had to turn in their handcuffs, weapons, bags, wallets, and pocket contents to the duty officer, who would lock them into a locker. Kate always hated turning in her weapon, even when she understood the importance of it. Finding herself in a jail full of hardened criminals without a weapon always left her feeling vulnerable.

She could feel the tension rolling off Trepalli in waves.

"What is it?" she asked him in a low voice, aware that they were probably being recorded.

"I don't like enclosed spaces," he muttered, looking around the ten-by-ten vestibule. "Especially when they're in a jail."

Well, she could certainly understand that, although it wasn't the enclosed spaces that got to her. It was the oppressiveness.

At that moment, the inside door opened, startling them both. She got to her feet a moment before Trepalli, just as a man in his mid-forties entered the vestibule, looking around as if there was room to lose someone in there.

"Chief Williams?" he said, automatically sticking his hand out. He was a tall, thin man with a prominent Adam's apple and thinning dark hair that was freshly cut. Intelligent brown eyes barely distracted from the truly magnificent nose that protruded from his face.

"Yes," said Kate, taking his hand. Like the rest of him, his hand was big and bony, but his shake was firm without trying to crush her hand.

"And this is Constable Marco Trepalli," added Kate.

The two men shook, then the man turned to Kate.

"I'm Acting Warden John Porter. Milo tells me you want to see Thomas Cassidy?"

Milo? She slid a glance over to the guard behind the bulletproof glass but he was busy at his computer.

"That's right," she said. "His name has come up as part of an investigation and I'd like to ask him a few questions."

"I'm sorry, Chief," said Porter regretfully. "If you had called, I could have saved you the trip. Cassidy was paroled."

Kate rocked back on her heels.

"He's out already?" she asked in surprise. "The parole board only met Friday."

Porter nodded. "Special circumstances. His mother is dying."

A cold finger of fear slid down Kate's spine. Was McKell safe? She needed to warn Stendel. She glanced at Trepalli, saw the same frown on his face.

She looked down at the industrial gray linoleum and tried to think. It had never occurred to her that Cassidy would be out. That changed everything.

"I'm going to need an address for him," she said slowly. "And for his mother."

"Ma'am?" said Trepalli.

She turned to look at him.

"It would be useful to know who's been visiting him," he said.

Yes, it would. She turned to look at Porter, raising her eyebrows inquiringly.

"Come with me to the office," he said. "I'll get you the information."

* * *

"He has permission to leave the province," said Stendel, at the other end of the line. His tone was somewhere between outrage and disbelief.

"Yes," said Kate in disgust. "He has to return in a week to a half-way house, but his parole officer gave him permission to travel to Toronto." She was sitting alone in the deserted Grace Hospital cafeteria, drinking a truly terrible cup of machine-dispensed coffee and juggling her cell phone. "His mother is dying."

The kitchen part of the large room was closed off by a metal grille, but apparently the dining room stayed open for the night staff to eat their lunches. Or dinners. The dimmed lights reflected off the many windows. She kept her back to the courtyard.

"That should make it easier to find him," said Stendel. "A parole officer will put him on the bus and another one will pick him up in Toronto. But even if we do locate him, no judge is going to sign a warrant. There's no evidence to indicate his involvement in McKell's shooting."

Kate had to agree with his assessment. Cassidy had been clever. He could certainly not be accused of shooting McKell himself—he had been incarcerated at the time.

"I know," said Kate. "We have to figure out what the link is between him and the shooting. I'm betting it's in the visitors' log."

"I've got officers doing background checks of the visitors," said Stendel in her ear, "but there weren't more than six or seven over the entire time he's been incarcerated. And none in the past two."

"I know," said Kate again. "But it's all we've got."

She heard the discouragement in her voice and frowned. Now wasn't the time to lose hope. McKell was lying helpless in a hospital bed because of this Cassidy. She was damned if she was going to let a raping, drug-dealing, would-be murderer get away with it.

Even now, Trepalli was upstairs talking to the officers guarding McKell. She would join him as soon as she finished talking with Stendel.

"Kate," said Stendel gently.

Hearing her first name coming from him still shocked her. It implied a closeness they didn't have.

"Yes?" she asked cautiously.

"We have to be mindful that you could be wrong," he pointed out. "Or if you're right, there's no point to attacking McKell now. Cassidy got what he wanted. He's free."

"Yes," she said. It was possible that she was wrong, but every instinct screamed at her to get this Cassidy before he got another chance at McKell. She just didn't know how to get him. In the eleven years Cassidy had been incarcerated, he had never made a phone call from the correctional center. He had written letters—hand written them, to be precise. Letters were confidential but telephone conversations were recorded. In fact, he had received exactly one phone call in the last decade, and that was three weeks ago, from someone telling him his mother was dying of cancer.

It was probably true. A parole officer would have done an assessment when Cassidy applied for parole. Still, she had asked

Martins to contact the Toronto police to verify that the address Cassidy had given the parole officer was indeed his mother's. It was an hour later in Toronto—that would make it almost nine o'clock there. Still early enough to knock on someone's door.

"It's getting late," said Stendel. "Get some sleep. I'll find out who the Toronto parole officer is and talk to him. Or her. If I learn anything, I'll call you. We can pick this up in the morning."

Kate hesitated. She didn't want to sleep. She wanted to find Cassidy and lock him up permanently. But Stendel was right. She would do McKell no good if her thinking was fuzzy from lack of sleep.

"All right, John." She sighed. "We'll talk in the morning."

They hung up and she sat staring at her still full cardboard cup. Who was she kidding? She wasn't going to get any sleep tonight. She wasn't even going to leave the hospital.

She pushed herself up from the table and turned away. As she did, she caught a movement out of the corner of her eye and turned to see her reflection staring back at her from the wall-to-ceiling courtyard windows. She could almost see her shadowy self sitting across from Bert at the picnic table.

Her eyes closed against the sudden tears.

* * *

She was on her way back up the stairs when her cell phone rang. Only when disappointment stabbed through her at the sight of the unfamiliar number did she realize she had been hoping it was Bert.

But it wasn't, of course. The number had an 819 prefix and she tried to remember which part of the country that represented. Ontario?

"Chief Williams," she answered finally.

"This is Captain Albert Millwater, retired," said an unfamiliar man's voice. "I'm told you've been trying to reach me."

Kate stared at the landing in front of her, her mind a complete blank. Then she remembered the call she had made to the military police detachment in Shilo.

"Thank you for calling, Captain Millwater," she said. "I take it you were Rob McKell's commanding officer?"

"I was," replied the man crisply. "And a finer MP you couldn't ask for. I'm told he's been injured?"

"Yes, sir," said Kate. She told him what had happened and he listened in silence until she finished. When she did, he waited a beat or two before speaking.

"Do you know who did it?"

Kate took a deep breath. "We have some leads."

"And you think I can help you with them," said Millwater. "A good cop always makes enemies. What do you want to know, Chief Williams?"

"Does the name Thomas Cassidy ring any bells?"

His short bark of laughter startled her. "It's not a name I'm likely to forget. He was a sociopath, maybe even a psychopath. And he was my problem. He came to my detachment about fifteen years ago. We suspected him of a series of rapes on base, but could never prove anything."

She knew this already. But then he continued.

"Then drugs started appearing on base. Lots of them. McKell was sure Cassidy was behind it but the bastard was smart. Nothing ever led back to him."

"What was his relationship to McKell?"

The man at the other end sighed heavily. "I think it would be fair to say they hated each other. Hell, we all hated Cassidy, but McKell just wouldn't quit. He hounded Cassidy. Always watching him, always making sure Cassidy knew he was watching. The base commander finally convinced Cassidy that it was in his best interest to quit the Forces, but even then McKell kept an eye on him in Winnipeg, every chance he got. He's the one who tipped off the RCMP about Cassidy receiving shipments of marijuana. He's the one who provided photos and witnesses. Hell, he was the Crown's main witness." He paused to catch his breath and Kate suddenly wondered how old he was. "Rob's the reason that freak is in jail."

Well. It seemed McKell had left quite a bit out of the story.

"Are you saying Cassidy is responsible for McKell's shooting?" asked Millwater. "I thought he was at Red Hill."

"Not anymore," said Kate grimly. "He's been paroled."

"*Paroled?*" Millwater's voice sounded strangled. "Didn't the board know...?"

"Apparently not," said Kate. Because McKell wasn't there to tell them.

CHAPTER 18

McKELL SNORED.

Kate lay on the mat on the floor between his hospital bed and the window and listened to the decidedly untuneful sounds emanating from her deputy chief. Even if she had been inclined to sleep, she couldn't have.

My God, he sounds like a bear.

He had been given a sedative earlier in the evening and didn't even know she was there. She planned to be out before he woke up. This whole thing of watching over him felt uncomfortably intimate and she knew he would hate it.

But she wasn't leaving him unprotected, especially not after that conversation with Captain Millwater. During the day, between the comings and goings of the doctors, nursing staff, and the Winnipeg police officers Stendel had provided, he should be safe. But at night… Night time felt risky.

She flipped over on her side and tucked a hand under her ear. It was almost two in the morning. The nurses had been very reluctant to allow her to sleep in the room with McKell, but Kate had made it very clear that his life might be in danger. The fact that two guards already stood outside his door helped her argument. In the end, the duty nurse pulled out a narrow, self-inflating mat and handed it over to Kate, along with a pillow that she took from a locked closet.

There was a perfectly good bed standing empty in the room, but nobody even considered it. Kate didn't *want* to be comfortable. She wanted to be awake.

To Trepalli's frustration, he still wasn't allowed into the DC's room, so he contented himself with the visitor's lounge at the end of the hallway. Every hour or so, Kate got up and silently left the room to check out the hallway. It was always quiet. The most activity she'd seen so far was when one of the nurses came in to physically check on McKell.

Kate heard a noise outside McKell's door and stiffened. It was too soon for the nurse to return. She desperately wished she was wearing her uniform. At least she'd be armed.

She stood up, glad she had kept her shoes on. She went to the door and listened. She could hear voices talking softly. Unlikely to be a killer, then. Still, she opened the door and stepped out.

The young man who had been guarding McKell's door was standing, talking to an older female officer, whose lines around the eyes proclaimed her to be close to Kate's age.

The young officer glanced over his shoulder as Kate softly closed the door behind her.

"Here she is now," said the young man. "Chief Williams, this is Constable Standish. She'll be replacing me."

Kate nodded to the woman. "Have you been briefed?" she asked.

Officer Standish nodded. "Potential danger to DC McKell. Only personnel with identification get in, plus those on the list." She had dark hair liberally threaded with silver. It was gathered into a neat French braid at the back of her head that showed off great cheekbones and cool grey eyes.

Kate nodded and glanced down the deserted hallway. A light glowed faintly at the nursing station and she could see movement in the shadows as the duty nurse moved beyond the light. As she watched, another nurse stepped out of a room further down the hallway and glanced in their direction. She nodded at them and

Kate nodded back.

By the elevators, two men stood, heads leaning in, talking. Kate recognized Trepalli's grey shirt and jeans.

"Jones won't be replaced for another two hours," said Officer Standish, following her glance. "Staggered shifts."

Good. That meant that there was always someone on who knew what had taken place before the arrival of the new guard.

Trepalli slapped the guard by the elevator on the shoulder and headed toward Kate. Officer Standish sat down and pulled out her notebook as the young man she had replaced headed toward the elevator. Trepalli introduced himself to Standish, who stood up to shake hands with him.

"You're not on the list," she said.

A smile tugged at Kate's lips as a pained expression crossed Trepalli's face.

"I know," he said. He turned toward Kate. "How are you doing, Chief?"

"Fine," said Kate. "I'm going back in." She could see by his face that he desperately wanted to be inside with her, making sure that the DC was safe. But there were four people guarding the man. Nothing would happen to him tonight.

"Try to get some sleep," she ordered. "We have work to do in the morning."

She pushed open the door and re-entered McKell's room, but once the door had closed behind her, she stood in the middle of the room and stared at the curtained window. McKell's snores had moderated a little but still sounded like he had swallowed a snarling wolverine.

The room smelled... stale. She wished she could open the window, but she didn't want McKell to get cold. She looked down at her wrinkled, long-sleeved white tee-shirt, noting a couple of dried coffee drops on the front.

She should check in with Mendenhall. Guilt washed over her at the thought. She was being derelict in her duties. With McKell out of commission, her people needed her there, not babysitting McKell. Stendel was looking out for her DC, much better than she could. Really, the best use of her time would be to return to Mendenhall and resume her duties. And what about Trepalli? When was he due back on shift?

She sighed. She didn't know, and she should know. No matter what happened with McKell, she promised herself that she would pay more attention to the duty roster from now on. At least carry a copy on her phone. Once she figured out how to use email on the phone.

After the Amanda incident, Charlotte had returned to Mendenhall. She had called Kate from the detachment to tell her that the mayor had been calling, wanting an update. Charlotte had taken it upon herself to brief him on McKell's status and on the little she knew about the investigation, explaining that Kate was too busy to call him right now.

Kate was grateful for the girl's intervention, but the truth was she wouldn't be of any use to anyone until Cassidy was found and she figured out one way or the other if he was behind the attack on McKell. Right now she felt like she had one duty and one duty alone: to keep McKell safe.

Her people were well trained and they were smart. They would carry on without her.

She should still call in.

With another sigh, she turned back to the door and opened it. Standish looked up from the notebook in which she was writing with a raised eyebrow. Kate shook her head to indicate that there was no problem.

"I'm going to find a private space to make a phone call," she told the woman. "Back in a few minutes."

Standish nodded and went back to her notebook.

Kate took the stairs down to the cafeteria only to find half a dozen workers sharing a table and eating their lunches. Or dinners. Someone had turned a radio on and a salsa tune played in the background. A few of the diners looked around in curiosity as she entered, then went back to their food.

She made her way to the corner farthest from them and punched in the detachment's number.

"Mendenhall Police," said Jim O'Hara. Then, recognizing her number, "Chief. Is everything all right?" There was a tightness in his voice, a control that spoke to the level of worry in him. Her guilt spiked.

"Yes, Jim," she said. "The DC is sleeping well. I'm just checking in."

O'Hara sighed softly. "Everything here is under control. It's good to have Charlotte back."

Kate smiled at the wall. O'Hara was being positively chatty. She could understand his relief. Most days, she wished she had two like Charlotte.

"Chief?" The hesitation in O'Hara's voice straightened Kate's spine.

"Yes, Constable?"

"Tourmeline, Boychuk, Fallon, Oppenheimer, and Albertson will be taking shifts over the next few days. We'll rotate as we come off shift. For as long as it takes."

Kate blinked at the wall, aware that the salsa tune behind her had been replaced by some kind of country and western song. Shania Twain? She didn't know much about country and western.

Finally, and inelegantly, she said, "What?" What was he talking about?

"Have you had any sleep, Chief?" asked O'Hara gently. She could almost imagine his serious grey eyes frowning. Before she could answer, he continued. "They've just come off days. They're each going to take a shift watching over the DC, until we catch the bastard who tried to kill him."

Kate's eyes suddenly filled with tears and she moved the phone away from her constricting throat so he wouldn't hear her swallowing back the tears. Finally she brought it back to her ear.

"I'm sure the hospital will appreciate that." She was trying for dry, but it came out too gently.

O'Hara cleared his throat but said nothing.

After she hung up, Kate stood with her hands on her hips, trying to regain control of her emotions. She was turning into a basket case, weepy and emotional all the time.

She wished Bert were here.

The traitorous thought hit her like a blow to the gut and she wrapped her arms around herself, trying to contain the pain. Finally she took a deep breath and turned toward the cafeteria door. Bert wasn't here. He had made his choice, and so had she. Now she would have to live with it.

She glanced at the clock on her way out. Two-thirty. She should warn the guards and Trepalli to expect some of her officers to arrive. They wouldn't be on the list, either, but it was a comfort to her to know there would be more eyes watching out for Rob.

Now that the first wave of emotion was past, she found herself smiling as she started up the wide staircase. She should have expected it. All her constables liked and respected McKell, but it was more than that. When you worked closely with someone, day in and day out, especially in a job like theirs, colleagues became family. Closer than family, thanks to shared danger and hardship. It was no surprise that they would step up to help McKell. He was one of theirs.

She stopped suddenly between the first and second floors, eyes staring blindly at nothing.

He had gone through a lot with them. He was family.

And family did for each other.

She grabbed the railing and began to run up the stairs as quickly as she could.

CHAPTER 19

KATE ARRIVED on the fourth floor and burst through the door into the hallway, only to find Constable Standish waiting next to the door, weapon drawn but pointing at the floor. The officer stared at Kate with reproach in her eyes. At the other end, by the elevator, the other officer stood, legs apart, his weapon in hand, too.

"Sorry," said Kate, breathing hard. "I wasn't thinking."

"Good way to get yourself shot," said Standish, holstering her weapon and resuming her seat by McKell's door. "Everything all right?"

"Yes," said Kate, but she didn't elaborate, heading instead for the lounge where Trepalli slept. The officer by the elevator—what the hell was his name, anyway?—had resumed his own seat, tucked away by the corner where someone coming off the elevator wouldn't see him right away. He gave Kate a sour look.

Kate pushed open the door to the lounge. It was dimly lit by the flickering images on the television set bolted to the ceiling in the corner. Trepalli was slouched in an upholstered chair, his head back, mouth open, snoring softly.

At the sight, Kate came to her senses. What was she doing?

Ordinarily, she would have run her theory by McKell, but she often discussed her work with Bert, too. She suddenly felt untethered. She hadn't realized how much she depended on both men. Now, neither one was available to her and she suddenly felt very alone. She had been about to wake up her constable, but only because she needed to talk to someone—not because she could do anything tonight.

She had better get a grip, and soon, because McKell's life might depend on it.

She turned around. Enough of this flailing about. She would figure out exactly what she needed to do first. Let the boy sleep.

"Chief?"

Trepalli's groggy voice paused her hand on the door handle. She turned around.

He was sitting up and trying to rub the sleep from his eyes. She wondered if they felt as gritty as hers did. She caught a whiff of herself and almost winced. She needed a shower and a change of clothes. And her weapon.

"What's going on?" asked Trepalli, pushing himself to standing. His gray shirt was untucked and wrinkled, and his dark hair tousled. A day's worth of beard shadowed his chin and lean cheeks. He looked like he belonged in a black leather jacket and on a motorcycle. Amanda never stood a chance.

Kate took a deep breath. All right. She was hardly clear-headed and Trepalli hadn't had much more sleep than she'd had in the past few days. But maybe between the two of them, they could work this out.

"We've had no luck with the visitors' list, right?" she asked without preamble.

He blinked at her, clearly trying to wrap his mind around her question. Finally he scrubbed his face with the palms of his hands and shook his head.

"No," he said. "Chief Stendel said there were only six visitors in all. The last one was years ago."

Kate nodded. "We're looking in the wrong place. We should be looking at family."

"But his family is in Ontario," said Trepalli. He yawned suddenly and Kate heard his jaw crack. "He's only got one sister and his mother, who's dying."

She shook her head. "Not that kind family."

Trepalli fixed her with a frown. Lights played off the side of his face and Kate blinked away the disorienting effect. Unlike McKell's room, this one smelled fresh. The curtains billowed gently at the far end of the bank of windows.

Then the frown cleared away. "Other prisoners," he said softly. "Maybe a cell mate."

Kate nodded. Yes, indeed. A cell mate or a prison mate. Someone Cassidy had befriended while in jail.

"We need to contact the warden." Oh, for Pete's sake—what was the man's name again?

"Acting Warden John Porter," said Trepalli. He glanced at his watch, a big thing with hands that glowed in the dark. "It's way too early to call..."

"We've wasted enough time," said Kate grimly. "Find a home number for him," she said, pulling out her phone.

"Who are you calling?" asked Trepalli, pulling out his own.

"O'Hara," said Kate. "I want someone to bring me my uniform and weapon."

* * *

Porter walked into the Red Hill Correctional Center just as they pulled into the visitor parking spot.

It was shortly past five o'clock and the sky in her rear view mirror had begun to blush with dawn by the time she and Trepalli arrived. She got out of the Ford, feeling ten years older than she had the day before. But at least she was in uniform, and her utility belt, including her weapon, was snugly around her waist.

Stan Albertson had been the first one to show up at the hospital from Mendenhall. He had brought Kate's and Trepalli's uniforms and a small overnight kit from each of their lockers. Their weapons, however, he would have had to get from their homes.

Kate had given O'Hara permission to release two weapons from the weapons locker at the detachment.

Trepalli's kit must have included a razor. He looked almost fresh in his uniform. The dawn chill worked its way through her light bomber-style uniform jacket and she shivered as she walked up to the front door.

John Porter was also in uniform—white shirt, black tie, and gray slacks. He had removed his own suit jacket and rolled up his sleeves, as though preparing to work. He nodded at them when they walked into the vestibule and silently handed them each a Tim Hortons coffee from a cardboard tray he held in one hand.

"Bless you," murmured Kate.

Porter grinned at them both and handed a fourth cup to the duty officer, who had walked around to open the door. He wasn't the same man they had met yesterday. He silently toasted his boss before returning to his little cubicle.

Kate and Trepalli followed the warden down the deserted hallway of the administration wing, their boots thumping in unison on the industrial linoleum. After a few more locked doors, they reached the secure elevator that took them up to the third floor.

Porter led them to his office, where he waved them to chairs as he rounded his desk. He set his coffee down and turned his computer on, then sat in silence, drinking his coffee as he waited for the computer to boot up.

He had informed them earlier that the warden was on medical leave following hernia surgery. Porter seemed like an able administrator, completely unflappable. He hadn't argued with her when she asked him to open up his records to her, only told her he would meet her at Red Hill as soon as he could get there.

Like every other window in the facility, Porter's office windows were long and narrow. And though two of them opened, they were too narrow to allow a man through. The office was unabashedly utilitarian, with painted cinder block outside walls, a plain wooden desk that had had a few too many hot drinks left on its surface, a gray metal desk lamp, and the ubiquitous orange plastic In and Out trays. Besides the Canadian flag next to the bank of locked, gray metal filing cabinets against the inside wall, the only other adornment was a picture of the Queen.

Except for the shiny, brand new computer on his desk, Porter's office could have stepped straight out of the seventies, complete with green metal waste basket.

What a depressing place to work.

Porter leaned forward and pulled the keyboard toward him, beginning to type.

Trepalli sat back in the hard wooden chair, sipping his coffee, apparently lost in thought. Kate wondered if any of those thoughts involved Amanda.

She should give Rose a call. And Mom. A huge yawn caught her by surprise and she almost spilled coffee on herself in an effort to cover her mouth.

"Sorry," she said as both men grinned at her.

"Here we go," said Porter. He clicked a few times and a printer began to whir somewhere in the office. Only when he bent down did Kate realize the printer was under his desk. He sat up and put several sheets of paper down on the desk in front of him.

"He's had five cell mates over the years," said Porter, reading from the pages. "One died three years ago of cancer while incarcerated. Another was transferred to Kent Institution in 2009 on compassionate grounds. One is still here, and the other two have been released."

Two possibilities, then. Kate accepted the sheets from Porter and began to scan them.

"Do we know for sure that Aucoin is still at Kent?" she asked.

Porter jotted something down in a black, hard-covered notebook on his desk. "Easy enough to find out," he said equably. "I'll check the system."

Kate nodded. "Thanks."

He turned back to the computer, and she said, "Oh, before

you do that..." He turned to her, eyebrows raised in question. His nose truly was remarkable. "Can you pull up the records for..." She glanced down at the names on the pages. "Trent Hombert and Jacob Turcotte."

He nodded and typed for a moment, then turned the screen toward them. "Hombert. Turcotte's file is also open. Just click on the tab next to Hombert's."

Kate and Trepalli leaned forward and began reading Trent Hombert's file while Porter picked up the phone. While he talked, she took notes on a foolscap pad he pushed toward her.

Hombert was a local boy, out of the North Main district of Winnipeg. He was thirty-six, single, and had served his full sentence of six years for aggravated assault during a robbery. Turcotte also was from the area—St. Boniface, although he had started his penitentiary career in Vancouver. He had raped his girlfriend and beaten her half to death. He, too, had served his full sentence, fifteen years, the last eighteen months in Red Hill. He'd been out one month, and Hombert five months.

She would have to get... who was on the duty desk this morning? She shook her head in despair at her failings. She would get whoever was on the desk in Mendenhall to dig a little deeper into Hombert and Turcotte.

"Nice guys," murmured Trepalli as he read.

"Hmm," said Kate. The notes at the end of each file said that the two men had been close to Cassidy.

Porter hung up and turned to them.

"Mr. Aucoin is still at Kent," he reported.

Kate smiled her thanks. "Any chance you have addresses for Turcotte and Hombert?" she asked hopefully.

Porter shook his head regretfully. "Beyond our purview, I'm afraid. Both men served their full sentence, and have paid their debt to society. We have no right to keep track of them."

"What about a last known address?" asked Trepalli.

"It would be on the first page," said Porter, indicating the screen.

Kate scrolled up, looking for the information, and jotted it down. The addresses were old, but maybe family still lived there and would know where to find the men.

Even as she thought it, she knew it was a long shot. Still. She pulled up each man's picture and printed it out.

* * *

Her phone rang as she was unlocking the rental. She fished the phone out of her pocket.

"Williams."

"It's Stendel. I just got a call from Toronto."

Kate glanced at her watch. Almost six o'clock. That made it seven o'clock in Toronto. Someone was on the job early. Trepalli leaned his forearms on the top of the car and watched her in silence. She put the phone on speaker so he could hear, too.

"Parole officer?" she asked.

"Police." His voice sounded grim. "Cassidy's in the wind. The parole officer picked him up at the bus station and brought him to the mother's house. What the parole officer didn't know is that the mother died soon after. He left Cassidy at the house, and that's the last he saw of him."

"Damn," said Kate. Where the hell was he? Back in Winnipeg?

Be honest, she told herself. *The guy could be anywhere by now. If he's smart, he's nowhere near here.*

But he was here. She could feel it in her bones. She and Cassidy had one thing in common. They both knew that McKell would go after him as soon as he was able to. If Cassidy hoped to disappear, he would have to get rid of McKell.

And she wasn't going to allow that.

"I think that's enough to get a warrant," she said slowly. "Don't you?"

Stendel laughed humorlessly. "You bet. And I'll put a national BOLO out on him."

Red Hill Correctional Center sat in the middle of miles of shorn fields, broken only by lines of trees acting as windbreaks. The trees leaned in the wind as the sun broke the horizon's hold, releasing a golden light that softened the prickliness of the fields. It was a cool wind, and it carried a hint of wood smoke.

Kate shook her head, even though he couldn't see her. A national Be On the Look Out for Cassidy would be a waste of time. "He'll be around Winnipeg," she said slowly. "We need to concentrate on last known addresses, known associates, anyone who came to visit him."

"What makes you so sure he's still in town?" asked Stendel.

"McKell is here," said Kate grimly. She was about to hang up when she remembered Hombert and Turcotte. She briefed Stendel on what she had learned at Red Hill.

"I can get someone on that," he said when she finished.

"That's all right," said Kate. "You concentrate on Cassidy. We'll search for these two." She suddenly remembered whose jurisdiction she was in. "If you don't mind, that is."

"I do mind, Kate." From the sound of his voice, he was scowling. "You're not going without back-up. You wait until they're in place before you approach. What are the addresses?"

Kate only had last-known addresses for Hombert and Turcotte, and those were old. The chances of them returning there were pretty slim. Still, his turf, his rules. She gave him the addresses.

* * *

"My stomach thinks my throat's been cut," said Trepalli plaintively as they drove back to Winnipeg.

In spite of everything, Kate grinned. She was hungry, too. And she was getting a headache.

"We'll find a drive-through," she promised and just then, as if called up by her words, she saw the golden arches of a McDonald's.

"Thank God," said Trepalli as she took the nearest exit and headed for the restaurant. They ordered more coffee and food and then got back onto the highway. It didn't take long for Kate to realize that she would have trouble driving and eating at the same time, and Trepalli was almost useless at navigating the map while scarfing down an egg sandwich.

She pulled over into a used car dealership and they ate in blissful silence. The traffic on the highway was getting heavier. The sun's rays glanced off the roofs of the cars in an almost hypnotic rhythm. She finally finished her breakfast sandwich and plucked the map from Trepalli's lap. He had a second breakfast sandwich to finish before his hands would be free.

She studied the map for a while, sipping her coffee. Hombert's last known address was off Main Street, a rough section of town. She studied the route she would take, familiarizing herself with the street names and turns. She knew Portage and she knew Main. Everything else was taking a chance.

"Done," said Trepalli, scrunching up the paper the sandwich had come in. "Ready?"

"Ready," said Kate. She handed him back the map and placed her cup in the holder between the two seats.

Just as she pulled out of the car lot, her phone rang again. She plucked the phone out of her jacket pocket and handed it to Trepalli to answer.

"Chief Williams' phone," he said cheerfully. Clearly the boy did better on a full stomach. "She's driving, sir. Hang on, I'll put you on speaker." He quickly found the icon and pressed on it. It had taken her a week to figure out how to do that. She accelerated to merge with traffic.

"Go ahead, sir," said Trepalli.

"Chief Williams," said Stendel, back to being formal. "My men are in place at Hombert's address. What's your ETA?"

Kate and Trepalli glanced at each other guiltily. Trepalli cleared his throat. "We're on McPhillips, Chief," he said. "And the traffic is increasing. Maybe ten minutes."

They both heard the man sigh. "All right. I'll get them to keep an eye on the place. What's taking you so long?"

Kate shrugged. "I'm not all that familiar with this part of town." Which was true.

"Look for the patrol car when you get there," said Stendel before signing off.

It took closer to fifteen minutes until Kate pulled up in front
of a dilapidated apartment building on Jacobsen Street. It was one
of a series of ten- and twelve-story buildings on both sides, with
barely a patch of grass in front or in between. Even the sidewalks
were crumbling and the brick pathway that led to the door was
missing well over a third of its brick pavers. Still, the front stoop
was swept clean and more than a few of the balconies had flower
boxes hanging from their railings, with flowers doing their best to
brighten the drab gray façade of the building.

"There's the patrol car," said Trepalli as they got out. Kate
looked around and saw it half a block over, on the same side of the
street.

The uniformed officers had been watching for them and came
to join them. To Kate's surprise, Stendel's "men" were both women.
While she was used to seeing women in uniform, she couldn't remember ever seeing two as partners. There just weren't enough of
them. The older one's name tag read Speiss and the younger one's
read Ursich.

"Ma'am," said Speiss. "We're to accompany you." She was a
tall woman, broad-shouldered and a little thick through the middle. Kate figured she was around forty. The younger officer, Ursich,
was barely Kate's height and a stiff wind would blow her away. Like
Constable Starling, she looked about twelve.

Kate nodded. "Thank you, Constable Speiss." She noted that
the officers wore their vests. "Kate Williams and this is Marco
Trepalli."

Trepalli nodded to both women, his face carefully neutral. But
when they turned toward the door, he glanced at Kate, one eyebrow raised. Kate shrugged. Just because Constable Ursich looked
young didn't mean she was untrained.

She hoped.

The building's small entryway barely fit all four of them. An old-fashioned wall mailbox system was on their left, with a buzzer above each box, and an apartment number, but no name. Kate was about to press on the buzzer for 307 when Trepalli tried the inside door. To everyone's surprise, it opened.

"Great security," murmured Speiss as she led the way inside.

The hallway was lined with dark wood and the floor was yellowing white marble. To the right was a door with a sign on it that read "MANAGER," and on the left was another door with no markings. Probably a utility room. They walked past the manager's door without stopping.

Like the outside of the building, the hallway was impeccably clean. It even smelled of furniture polish. They headed for the stairwell at the far end. There was probably an elevator close by—it was, after all, a ten-story building—but they chose the stairs. The banister was oak, curved and carved, well polished, and the marble steps were wide enough to accommodate three people abreast. The building resonated of a genteel past.

Hardly the kind of place she would expect to find an ex-con.

She and Speiss went up the steps side by side, and by the time they reached the third floor, Kate was a little winded. Speiss, however, still breathed evenly.

Unlike the main floor, the third floor hallway was carpeted in gray and blue. The walls were made of drywall and painted a soft white. A small brass plaque on the wall in front of the stairwell pointed the direction for apartments 301 to 310, to the right, and 311 to 320, to the left.

Without a word, they turned right. The carpet muffled the sound of their boots and they arrived at 307 in silence. Like all the other doors they had passed, this one was painted the same blue as the carpet.

Speiss waited until Kate and Trepalli were to one side of the door, with Ursich between them and Speiss, her hand on her holster. Then Speiss knocked.

"Winnipeg Police," she called in a strong voice. "Open up,

please." Then she, too, moved to the side of the door.

Kate tensed as they waited. She hated this part. She never knew what to expect. Was Hombert waiting on the other side of the door with a weapon? She strained to hear what was going on inside the apartment but the heavy wooden door was an effective sound barrier.

Then they heard the sound of a chain being slid off and dead-bolt sliding and they all drew back slightly. But when the door opened, it was to reveal a tiny woman with a rounded back, thin white hair in a bun, and pale, wrinkled skin. The hand clutching the heavy cream sweater closed was veined and arthritic.

"Yes?" she said, eyeing them. "What can I do for you, officers?"

Kate had studied the photos of Hombert and Turcotte, and she thought she detected a resemblance to Hombert in the woman's cheekbones and slanted eyes. Maybe this was his last known address because it was his mother's address. She decided to take a chance.

"Mrs. Hombert?" she said, stepping forward. "We're looking for Trent. Is he here?"

The woman's eyes were so dark they looked almost black. She turned that dark gaze on Kate and Kate felt a shiver course down her back.

"My son isn't here," said the old woman.

Kate nodded. "Can you tell us where to find him?" she asked politely, refusing to be spooked by the woman, who was, after all, even shorter she was. A glance over Mrs. Hombert's head revealed a living room with a settee and chairs with matching gold and blue upholstery set around a round glass coffee table over wall-to-wall royal blue carpeting. The woman had probably whipped the plastic covers off the furniture just before opening the door.

"Why do you want to know?" asked Mrs. Hombert suspicious-ly. "He's paid his debt. He doesn't owe you anything anymore." Her voice rose on the last words and Kate almost stepped back.

Get a grip, Kate.

She forced a smile. "He *has* paid his debt, ma'am," she said reassuringly. "We just have a few questions for him. Can you tell us when he'll be home?"

Mrs. Hombert studied Kate's face for a moment, then her gaze traveled to the others. Trepalli and Ursich stepped back under its onslaught but Speiss stood firm. Finally the old woman's gaze came back to Kate.

"You'll have to wait until he gets out of the hospital," she said stiffly.

Well now.

"Has he been injured?" asked Kate.

"His appendix burst," said the old woman. "He would have died if I hadn't come home early."

Kate blinked. "When did this happen?" she asked.

"Tuesday night," replied Mrs. Hombert. "Bingo night."

Kate controlled an urge to glance at Trepalli in surprise. Bingo. She could not imagine this woman sitting in a bingo hall. Standing in front of a cauldron, maybe.

"He should be coming home today," continued Mrs. Hombert. "His blood got infected." Her face softened and for the first time, Kate caught a hint of concern behind the woman's fierceness.

"I'm very sorry," said Kate gently. "What hospital is he in?"

"St. Jude's," said the woman. "But he's being released today. Come back tonight and ask your questions."

Without another word, she closed the door in their faces.

Ursich and Trepalli exchanged meaningful glances but Kate led the way back downstairs before they could say anything. She was pretty sure the old woman would be standing by the door, trying to hear what they were saying through the thick wood.

Once they reached the street, they all walked toward the patrol car. While Speiss called St. Jude's to verify Hombert's alibi, Ursich pulled the map out of the glove box and she and Trepalli pored over it, trying to figure out the best way to St. Boniface, Turcotte's last known address. In deference to Ursich's stature, Trepalli moved the map from the roof of the car to the hood.

Hombert had served six years for aggravated assault while committing a robbery. He'd had other small charges, mostly theft. And here he was, in his mid-thirties, having to start all over again, living with his mother.

She hadn't even met the guy and she felt sorry for him.

Kate leaned against the patrol car and took a moment to just breathe. She tried to clear her mind of worries and questions, and concentrated on taking deep breaths and expelling them.

In spite of the flawlessly blue sky, there was a bit of a breeze and it had bite to it. She could feel her cheeks blooming in the cool and wondered what the temperature was. The scent of freshly mown lawn floated to her, reminiscent of freshly cut watermelon. Despite the distant sound of traffic, this street was quiet. There were no cars driving by, no children playing, no sounds of a radio floating down from an open window.

Of course, it was a Monday morning in September. Most adults would be at work and most kids would be in school. And it could be that mostly older people lived in this neighborhood. Neighborhoods sometimes aged along with their inhabitants.

Speiss pulled herself out of the car and straightened.

"It checks out," she told Kate. "He was rushed to St. Jude's Tuesday night around eleven-thirty at night. The nurse said he came close to dying from septicemia. He's just been discharged. Still want to talk to him?"

Kate shook her head. "It's moot now. Let's go see if we can find Mr. Turcotte."

"Lynn," called Speiss to her partner. "Got a route?"

"Yes," said Ursich, walking to her and leaving Trepalli to fold the map. "It's not that far from here."

"You're good?" Kate asked Trepalli as he handed the map to Ursich.

"Yes, ma'am," he said. "We'll meet you there," he told the constables.

Speiss nodded. "Wait for us before approaching."

"Will do," Kate promised.

She let Trepalli drive. The boy clearly had a better sense of direction than she did and frankly, she no longer cared if the rental company objected. It took him twenty minutes to find the place, a small single-family home in the French district of the city. They were the first to arrive and parked a block up, in front of a small park with a swing set and monkey bars. Two mothers sat on benches and chatted while three children played. One woman rocked a baby carriage back and forth with her foot.

Speiss pulled up behind them and they all got out, causing the mothers in the park to stare at them. Kate nodded politely, then led the way to the house. It was two stories, with an A-line roof, and painted a pale green with a dark green front door. Judging by the small casement windows, there was some kind of basement, but she doubted a full grown man could stand up in it.

Just as they approached the front steps, the side door opened and a man came out, keeping his back turned to them while he locked the door. When he finished, he closed the screen door firmly and turned toward the street, only to stop when he caught sight of them. His eyebrows rose in surprise.

Kate's own eyebrows rose, too. The man carried a baby on his chest, in one of those complicated bags with zippers and padded shoulder straps that left his hands free. He couldn't be older than twenty-five or thirty. Turcotte was fifty, and scarred on the cheek.

"Can I help you?" he asked, pocketing his keys as he walked toward them.

Kate smiled. "Kate Williams, Mendenhall Police. Are you the owner?"

He nodded. "Ted Bicudo," he said. Then he waited.

"Mr. Bicudo, we're looking for Jacob Turcotte. Does he live here?"

By the blank look on Bicudo's face, he didn't.

He shook his head. "No. Only my wife and I live here."

Trepalli came to stand next to Kate. "When did you buy the place?" he asked conversationally. He leaned forward to peek at the baby and Bicudo obligingly turned so Trepalli could get a better view. Immediately Ursich approached to stare down at the baby.

"We bought it three years ago," said Bicudo, grinning at Ursich.

Kate and Officer Speiss exchanged a glance that threatened to turn into a roll of the eyes. Kate cleared her throat meaningfully and both younger officers started guiltily, then moved back.

"Who did you buy the house from?" asked Kate.

Bicudo shrugged, a movement constrained by the baby carrier. There was a movement inside the fabric bag.

"I don't remember their names," said the young man. "They were an older couple, in their seventies, and they were moving back east to be closer to their children."

In their seventies. They could be old enough to be Turcotte's parents. Then again, maybe they weren't. She'd have to do some digging in property records to figure out their names. Another dead end, at least for now.

Thanking the young man, she turned and led the way back to their cars while he headed for the park.

Damn it all. They were getting nowhere.

A wave of weariness threatened to swamp her and she glanced at her watch. Only nine twenty. It was going to be a long day.

"I need more coffee," she said to herself.

"Amen to that," agreed Trepalli.

Kate turned to Speiss and Ursich.

"Thank you for your help, Constables. We appreciate it."

Ursich nodded, but Speiss wasn't quite ready to be dismissed.

"I'll follow up with the property rolls," she said, nodding at the house. "I can call you when I find out more."

Kate smiled her gratitude. "Thanks. That'll be very helpful." She dug through her pockets for a business card, but couldn't find one. Finally, Trepalli handed her one of his. She took it and scribbled her name and cell phone number on the back, then gave the card to Speiss. The constables got back in the patrol car and waved as they left.

"Coffee?" asked Trepalli hopefully as he headed for the driver's side.

"In a minute," said Kate. "First I want to talk to some of the neighbors. Maybe they knew Turcotte when he lived here."

Trepalli nodded. "I'll take across the street."

Half an hour later, they met back at the car.

"Any luck?" she asked as she slid into the passenger seat. The car smelled of eggs and coffee.

Trepalli closed the door and placed the key in the ignition but didn't start the car. "The woman in the white house with the green trim said she knew Turcotte when she was younger. They both grew up on this street, but he was about ten years older than her. She said he was always in trouble with the law. She said she and her friends avoided him because he was "scary." She hasn't seen him in almost twenty years."

"Did she know if the old couple were his parents?"

He shook his head. "She said his parents moved away about fifteen years ago. Whoever the old couple was that Bicudo bought the house from, it wasn't the Turcottes."

Still, it was worth letting Speiss verify the information in city records. Just in case.

"All right," she said finally. "Coffee."

CHAPTER 20

THEY FOUND a small coffee shop in St. Boniface where the menu was in English and in French. Trepalli ordered something to eat but Kate wasn't hungry. She settled for what turned out to be very good coffee.

They sat in silence in the quiet café, each lost in thought. Trepalli added sugar to his coffee and then stirred it until Kate gave him a sharp look.

"Sorry," he murmured, taking the spoon from the mug and laying on a paper napkin.

Kate took her jacket off, then wondered if she should have. It was warmer inside than out, but she was still wearing her short-sleeved uniform shirt and goose bumps were thinking of breaking out on her arms.

She felt light, as if whatever usually anchored her to the ground had let go and now she was adrift, untethered. Rose hadn't even tried contacting her. Neither had John. She sighed. She should call home. Brave the beast.

But if she called, Rose would want to know what was happening with Amanda.

Where *was* Amanda, anyway? Had she flown back to Montreal? Was she at Kate's house in Mendenhall? Did she even know anyone in Winnipeg where she could stay?

Kate glanced at Trepalli guiltily. Maybe Bert was right. Maybe she was obsessive about her job. She hadn't given her niece a thought since yesterday.

Trepalli was idly rocking the spoon on its concave base, lost in thought. By the tightness around his mouth, he was probably thinking about Amanda, too.

How on earth had those two let things get so complicated? They clearly loved each other. What could possibly be keeping them apart? Location? Trepalli was a fine young officer. He would have no trouble getting a job in St. Lambert or in Montreal, although he might have to learn French. That gave her pause. For all she knew, he might already speak French.

As for Amanda, she had already proven that she could make a success of a catering business. She could even open a restaurant if she chose. If Mendenhall was too small for her, then Brandon or Winnipeg. Of course, with her talent, she could open a restaurant in Mendenhall and patrons would come from all over the region to eat there.

But Kate knew it wasn't location, or lack of love. It was fear. Amanda was afraid of getting deeply involved with Trepalli only to see him die in the line of duty. It was the same fear Bert had expressed.

But Bert had no excuse. None. He was a cop, had been one for as long as she had. Why had he even courted her? And he had. He had come after her with the persistence and gentleness of a stream, cutting through her defenses, changing the course of her feelings.

Only to break her heart.

It's someone else, she told herself firmly. *He's met someone else and he doesn't have the guts to tell you.*

But he never shied away from the hard things. He was one of the bravest men she knew.

Maybe that courage didn't translate to affairs of the heart.

Dear God, she thought as tears pricked at her eyes. How had

she let her life become such a mess?

She pulled her cell phone out of the pocket of her jacket, which she had thrown over the seat of the chair next to hers. As Trepalli watched, she punched in Stendel's cell phone number.

"Stendel—oh, hi Kate," said Stendel.

"John," said Kate. For a moment, her mind went blank. Then she remembered why she was calling him. "Hombert was in hospital at the time of McKell's attack. We struck out at Turcotte's last known address. The house has changed hands at least twice since he last lived there. Constable Speiss is following up with property rolls to see if we can track previous owners."

"Sounds like a dead end," said Stendel. She heard a squeak at the other end and imagined him sitting back in a swivel chair. She had never been in Stendel's office. Come to think of it, he'd never been in hers, either.

They were silent for a moment and Kate watched the sun's rays glance off the rooftops of the vehicles traveling the main drag of St. Boniface. Across the way, a couple of grocers were filling their outside displays with baskets full of apples and rows of squash, onions, and bushels of potatoes. Both grocers wore jackets over their aprons.

The man who had taken Trepalli's order returned carrying a coffeepot and a plate of pancakes, with a small metal container that looked like a creamer but which was full of what she assumed was maple syrup. The boy had a hollow leg.

"What about Cassidy?" she finally asked.

Trepalli murmured his thanks to the man, who nodded and refilled their cups.

"Still no news," said Stendel. "Don't worry. If he's in Winnipeg, we'll find him. It's just a question of time."

Kate watched Trepalli dig into the stack of pancakes and didn't answer.

* * *

When Trepalli was through eating, they headed back outside into the brilliant sunshine. Kate quickly zipped up her jacket against the cool wind. She headed for the driver's door and glanced at Trepalli. He sighed and tossed her the keys.

"Why don't you check in at the hospital?" she suggested as they both got in. She placed her cap on the dashboard and watched Trepalli do the same. Those caps looked silly with the bomber jacket uniform, but the mayor and council had vetoed her suggestion of using ball caps, instead.

"Good idea," said Trepalli. "I think Abrams is there now."

"How do you know?" she asked, starting the car.

"Martins emailed the rotation list," he replied. "Didn't you get it?"

"Probably."

"Chief," said Trepalli gently after a moment. "I can show you how to work your email on the phone."

Kate sighed again. "All right. But not today."

She caught his grin before he turned away. Cheeky bugger.

She tried to listen to his side of the conversation but her attention was taken up with trying to find her way out of St. Boniface. She didn't know why she'd asked Trepalli to check in at the hospital when she was going there anyway.

It wasn't like she could go over to Bert's office. Or his home.

She would have to get his keys back to him, somehow. Her breath hitched a little and she concentrated on her driving.

"No change," said Trepalli, breaking through her thoughts. He slipped the phone into his breast pocket and continued. "But the DC's brother finally made it. He checked into a hotel."

Kate blinked. She had forgotten all about McKell's brother. What was his name again?

"Why did it take so long?" she asked.

"He's been traveling," said Trepalli. "He was in Peru somewhere. Took a while to get hold of him."

Peru. What she wouldn't give to be in Peru right now, and away from all this mess.

Oh, be honest, she told herself. *You know damn well that you'd only have to get on a plane and come see for yourself what was happening.*

She sighed again.

At that moment, her cell phone rumbled against her belly, immediately followed by a ring. She jumped and cursed.

She pulled the phone out and handed it to Trepalli.

"Chief William's phone," he announced. "Oh. Just a minute." He placed his thumb over the microphone and turned to look at her. "It's Sergeant Tremblay, from St. Lambert. Says he has an update."

Without a word, Kate pulled into the right-hand lane and found a parking spot outside a second-hand women's clothing store. She took the phone from Trepalli.

"Chief Williams here," she said.

"*Bonjour,* Chief Williams," came the sergeant's voice. "I thought you might like to know that we have found Chouinard."

"Who?" she blurted.

"Jean-Sébastien Chouinard," said the sergeant patiently. "The man who hurt your mother."

* * *

"Where are we going?" asked Trepalli when she turned the car around and headed back the way they had come.

"Back to Hombert's," she said. "He should be back from the hospital."

"Did Tremblay tell you something about him?" asked Trepalli, clearly baffled.

"No."

She could feel his stare but didn't elaborate. She didn't have anything concrete to tell him, anyway. All she had was a feeling.

The sergeant had said that, so far, they had found no connection between the man they had captured, Jean-Sébastien Chouinard, and McKell. Only then did she realize that she hadn't informed her Quebec colleague of what she had learned at her end since she returned from St. Lambert. So she asked him to look for a link between Chouinard and Cassidy, Hombert, or Turcotte.

After they hung up, she realized she had made a mistake. Even if Hombert couldn't have attacked McKell, he might still know something that could help her.

Sloppy work, Williams.

Fifteen minutes later, she parked in almost the exact spot she had used earlier.

The front door was still unlocked, but this time the manager's door was ajar, as if someone had just stepped in to fetch something. Without a word, she and Trepalli walked quietly past the door and to the marble stairs. Their footsteps echoed as they walked up. By the time they reached the third floor, Kate was breathing faster, but struggling to hide it from Trepalli.

The wear and tear of the last few days was starting to show.

Then they were at 307 and Kate knocked on the heavy wooden door. After twenty seconds, she knocked again and this time the door opened immediately. Mrs. Hombert stood in the doorway. Her wispy hair was pulled back in a tight bun at the base of her skull. She was wearing a black dress with a white lace collar and small pearl buttons down the front. It hung on her slight frame, as if she had lost weight since she bought it. Was that what she had been wearing earlier? She'd had a sweater over top, Kate finally remembered.

"What do you want?" demanded Mrs. Hombert. Her teeth were perfectly even. Dentures.

Next to Kate, Trepalli swallowed audibly. It was her eyes, Kate decided. So dark it was as if they had no pupil.

"Ma'am," said Kate. "It turns out I will need to speak to Trent, after all."

Color bloomed in the woman's leathery cheeks, and for a moment, Kate wondered if her eyes would shoot lightning bolts at her.

"It's all right, Ma," called a man's voice from inside the apartment. Kate looked past the top of Mrs. Hombert's head. A man sat in a blue upholstered chair, holding a glass of water in his hands. There was a small pillow behind his head.

"Mr. Hombert," said Kate, nodding to him. Then she glanced down expectantly at the old woman, who hesitated a moment longer before reluctantly stepping back and allowing them in. Mrs. Hombert closed the door behind Trepalli, and Kate thought of jaws closing on prey. She took her cap off respectfully, as did Trepalli.

"My mother told me you'd been by," said Hombert. "What do you want?" There was no aggression behind the question, only curiosity. And why not? He'd been out five months already and he'd kept out of trouble. He was probably getting used to being free.

He was sitting down and so it was hard to gauge his height, but Kate figured he would only be a few inches taller than her five feet three inches. He wore gray sweatpants and a white, short-sleeved tee-shirt, and his arms were lean and corded with muscle, not to mention covered in tattoos. He had a full head of black hair, in a crew cut that was growing out, and brown eyes that weren't nearly as dark as his mother's.

"I need to ask you about one of your old cell mates," said Kate. She very carefully didn't look at Mrs. Hombert, but Trent's gaze flickered to his mother.

"Ma, I can take it from here," he said after a moment. "You should go to church, like you were planning."

Kate couldn't help it. Her eyebrows tried to climb off her forehead and she glanced at the old woman. That woman went to *church*?

"I don't think you should be alone with them," said Mrs. Hombert bluntly.

Trent shook his head and smiled at her. "I'll be fine, Ma. Go on."

To Kate's surprise, the woman nodded and went to the closet by the door. She pulled out a tan overcoat and a big handbag of black leather and slipped both over her arm. She glared at Kate and Trepalli and then left.

It was as if the room exhaled and Kate felt the tension leave her shoulders.

"Have a seat," said Trent, nodding to the settee across from his chair. Kate and Trepalli made their way around the glass coffee table and sat down. The settee was surprisingly comfortable. It probably didn't get used very much. Light flooded in from the large windows. Even the curtains matched the upholstery. It was light and airy in the room, now that the old woman was gone.

"I understand that you and Thomas Cassidy were cell mates," said Kate, jumping right in.

Trent Hombert went very still and his gaze fixed on Kate's face. She stared back at him, surprised by his total lack of reaction. Finally he placed his glass on the side table next to his chair.

"For a while. What about it?" His tone, like his face, gave nothing away.

Trepalli glanced at Kate but she wasn't sure how to proceed. What did his reaction—or lack of reaction—mean?

"We believe he's involved in arranging an attack on one of my colleagues," she said finally.

Trent's right eyebrow twitched. "Let me guess," he said slowly. "Deputy Chief Rob McKell."

Kate sat back, feeling as if the breath had just been knocked out of her.

"How do you know that?" asked Trepalli suddenly. His tone was unfriendly but Trent didn't seem to notice. He gave a short laugh that was more of a bark.

"I was Cassidy's cell mate for two months," he said. "All he could talk about was how McKell had screwed him over."

Kate took a deep breath. "Did he say how McKell screwed him over?"

Trent shrugged, then winced as the movement tugged at his abdominal stitches.

"He never went into detail. Something about McKell betraying him." He picked up his glass of water and took a drink, then kept it in his hands.

"Well, they both served as military police. Maybe Cassidy was upset that McKell turned him in."

Trent stared at her, mouth open. "You mean Cassidy was a *cop*?"

"Military cop," said Kate.

"You didn't know?" said Trepalli in disbelief.

Trent shook his head. "Hell, no. All we knew was that Cassidy had connections in Afghanistan and brought in dope. If we'd known he was a cop..." He went to shrug again, but thought better of it. "Cassidy was a total badass. If anybody had known he used to be a cop, someone would have shivved him for sure. He went through a bunch of cell mates while I was there. When he decided he wanted you, the previous bunkie had better get his ass out right away, or he'd end up like this." He set the glass down again and raised his tee-shirt.

At first, all Kate saw was the white bandage peeking out from under the right side of his waistband. It stood out against all the tattoos on the man's belly and chest. Then she looked closer. On Trent's left pectoral muscle, almost hidden among tattoos of spiderwebs and a jaguar, was a long, ragged, pink scar.

She heard Trepalli's quick intake of breath and looked up at Trent.

"Cassidy did that to you?"

He shook his head and his mouth twisted in a bitter parody of a smile. "Oh no. That's not Cassidy's style. He got someone else to do it for him."

"Who?" asked Trepalli.

"A real whack job. Name of Turcotte. He wanted to be Cassidy's cell mate, and slicing me was his way of announcing it."

"Did you report him?" asked Kate.

"And end up dead?" Trent shook his head. "I counted myself lucky to be still alive." He stared at Kate for a few seconds before adding, "If someone tried to kill your friend McKell, I would look to Turcotte first. He would do anything for Cassidy."

"He's out, you know," said Trepalli. "Turcotte, I mean. Finished his term about a month ago."

Trent nodded. "Yeah. I knew he was coming out soon. I'm not worried about him. It's Cassidy I worry about."

Kate and Trepalli glanced at each other.

"What?" said Trent, suddenly alert.

"Cassidy got parole," said Kate slowly. "He's out, too." She stared at Trent Hombert for a long moment. "Any idea where we could find him?"

Trent took a long, shuddery breath. "No. Probably the last place you'd expect to find the bastard. All I know is I hope I never see him again."

* * *

Once at Grace Hospital, she sent Trepalli on ahead while she sat in the car, thinking. She felt like she had as a kid when the puzzle was almost complete but she still couldn't see the whole thing because she was missing a few key pieces.

Well, she had all the pieces now, or at least all the pieces she needed, but she wasn't clever enough to figure out where they fit.

Jean-Sébastien Chouinard, the auto thief in St. Lambert who had mowed her mother down.

Trent Hombert, who had served six years for aggravated assault and shared a cell with Cassidy.

Jacob Turcotte, who had served fifteen years in federal penitentiaries, the last eighteen months in Red Hill.

And Thomas Elliot Cassidy, former military policeman turned drug dealer, out on parole after serving eleven years of his fifteen-year sentence.

She could discount Hombert. Not only had he been in hospital, recovering from an appendectomy at the time of the attack on McKell, but his fear of Cassidy was almost palpable.

Turcotte and Cassidy had been close, apparently. How close?

Had they formed an intimate relationship? And where did Chouinard fit in? Was he even connected to McKell's assault?

Was it possible that Mom's accident was a coincidence?

She leaned her forearms on the steering wheel and stared blindly out at the hospital parking lot.

There was coincidence, and then there was coincidence.

Sergeant Tremblay had called her as a courtesy, to tell her that they had apprehended Chouinard, but he wasn't involved in interrogating the man. She needed to speak to the detective who would interrogate him.

The inside of the car was getting warm from the sun beating in, but outside, the wind sent a volley of yellow leaves cartwheeling over the tops of the parked cars. Kate patted her pockets for her phone and finally found it on the passenger seat.

Time to ask Sergeant Tremblay for one last favor.

CHAPTER 21

S HE WAS just making her way through the sliding glass doors at the hospital entrance when the alarm went off. She jumped at the raucous noise and was almost bowled over by a woman trying to get out. Kate moved aside until the woman had passed but then another person came out, and another. She finally looked past them and saw that the lobby of the hospital was filling with people being herded ineffectually by one lone security guard.

Holy cow.

She could hear shouting but couldn't make out words over the cacophony of the alarm.

Instinctively, she raised her arms, locked her hands over opposing elbows and leaned into the steady push of bodies. They parted on either side of her, a stream to her boulder.

When she breached the doorway, she slid to one side and let the stream of humanity resume its course. She followed the wall, passing the empty security desk, until she reached the reception area, where she stopped and looked around. Dozens of people were emerging out of the stairwells at both ends of the long, rectangular lobby. More came out of the lab area and the cafeteria directly in front of her, heading further into the hospital where, presumably, there were other exits and few people clogging them.

Kate leaned against the desk and tried to think of the best way to get to McKell to make sure he was safely evacuated. The elevators were out. That left the stairwells, but she would be like a salmon trying to swim upstream.

"Ma'am," said a gruff male voice in her ear.

She turned to see a young man in a security guard uniform standing next to her.

"You have to leave," he said.

"What's the emergency?" she yelled over the alarm.

"Fire on the second floor," said the guard. "We're evacuating."

Kate nodded. "I can help," she shouted. "I'll go to the top floor and work my way down."

The guard hesitated, then looked around. He was the only show of authority on this floor. She knew he wanted her to stay and lend her uniform to the effort.

"These folks are making their own way out," she pointed out. "The ones upstairs can't."

He nodded reluctant agreement and plunged back into the fray, shouting at people to keep calm and move away from the building once they got outside.

Kate felt a little guilty at lying. Protocols would already have kicked in. Ambulances would be on their way to ferry patients to different hospitals even as nurses, doctors, and orderlies worked to get them down from the upper floors.

It was every hospital administrator's worst nightmare. All they could do was pray that the protocols would ensure that everyone got out safely.

She looked around the lobby, but all she could see were bodies moving fast. There was no panic. There were enough exits on this floor to ensure that everyone would get out quickly. The upper floors would be the problem, especially as the firefighters would be arriving soon, adding to the crush and confusion. And then it would be almost impossible to get to the fourth floor.

And she really, really wanted to get to McKell. Something

about this whole situation was just too... coincidental for her liking. Three emergencies in the last five days? It was too much to believe they weren't connected, somehow.

Bert would tell her she was being paranoid.

Well, Bert wasn't here right now.

She began to push her way through the crowd, propelled by a growing sense of dread. She couldn't smell smoke. She got to the south stairwell and shoved her way past two women who were blocking the doorway. People filled the staircase and someone cursed at her as she accidentally pushed them into the railing. She got to the second floor landing and found the fire door open and more people coming. A woman in a bathrobe and slippers and carrying an infant rushed through the open door, wincing in pain with every step. The maternity ward was on this level.

Kate hesitated, torn between helping the woman—and all the babies—and making her way up to the fourth floor. She stepped into the hallway of the second floor and took a deep breath. Baby powder. Disinfectant. Food.

No smoke.

She whirled back to the stairwell and forced her way past people trying to make their way downstairs. Partway up she encountered a man in a chair that was being pushed down the stairs by an orderly. The chair was on tracks and lurched from step to step, automatically braking at each step. The elderly man sitting in it was strapped at lap and chest. There was a stoicness to him, as if he was prepared for whatever would happen next.

The orderly shot an arm out as she passed him.

"Downstairs," he ordered. "We're evacuating."

"I can help," shouted Kate.

The orderly shook his head. "We've got it under control."

People were piling up behind his arm and now that she had stopped, she could see that many of them were patients, some with stands on wheels with their intravenous drips attached. Each one was accompanied by a nurse or an orderly.

"Move!" shouted the nurse behind the orderly and he tried to turn Kate around but the weight of the people behind him pushed him out of reach and she was able to make her way upstairs.

She got to the fourth floor landing at last and slipped past a nurse pushing a woman in a wheelchair. Kate had no idea how she planned to get the wheelchair down the stairs. She hesitated, almost turning to help, then forced herself to walk through the doorway and into the hallway.

At first, all she could see were men and women in scrubs and patients in robes, most in wheelchairs. Those were the partly am-bulatory ones. The bedridden ones would have to be transferred out on cots. The noise level was overwhelming, between the alarm and the voices raised to be heard above it.

She had expected chaos here, too, but the personnel did in-deed have everything under control. For a moment, Kate was re-minded of last February's emergency preparedness exercise with the mock train derailment. That had been organized chaos, too. Until they found the body.

Her eye finally stopped scanning the hallway and paused at the door to McKell's room. Unlike all the others, it was closed.

She blinked. Where was the guard? The chair was still there, but no guard. She glanced down the hallway to the elevator end, but didn't see the second guard either.

They must be inside, helping with McKell's evacuation.

Someone bumped into her and she looked around to see a nurse trying to help a patient through the doorway. As Kate moved away to clear the space, a shout down the hallway caused her to look around. At first all she could see were milling bodies. Then Trepalli's face came into focus and she waved at him to show she had seen him. Then she pointed at McKell's door and he nodded his understanding.

Pushing against the crowd without causing harm took more time and energy than she could afford, but she did it anyway. She didn't want to trip someone and cause a stampede.

Despite the greater distance, Trepalli reached the door moments before she did, thanks to his longer legs. And sharper elbows.

Kate beckoned him down to her level and said, "Where's Abrams?" Trepalli had said that Abrams was on first shift, supplementing the two guards already watching over McKell. But she couldn't see the Winnipeg officers, or her Mendenhall constable.

Trepalli shook his head, his expression grim. "I don't know where any of them are."

All right, then. Kate pushed at McKell's door, but it didn't open. Her heart lurched in trepidation. None of these doors locked. Someone had barred the door from the inside.

Trepalli pushed her aside and tried pushing the door himself, with no better luck.

"Careful," he warned, moving her even further out of the way. Then he moved away from the door, raised his foot, and kicked.

Something inside gave way with a screeching sound that carried over the alarm as the door burst open.

The first thing Kate saw was a chair turned over in front of the door. Then she saw a man in the Winnipeg Police Services uniform sprawled on the floor by the second bed. She couldn't tell if he was alive or dead. Without hesitation, she stepped over the poor man to reach the curtain shielding McKell's bed from casual view. As she pulled it open, she became aware of sharp grunting sounds from the other side, then Trepalli leapt past her and launched himself at the two struggling figures on the far side of McKell's bed.

It took a moment for her brain to make sense of what her eyes were seeing. The first thing that stood out was the blood on McKell's white sheets and on the beige wall behind him. Then she saw flailing limbs and the glint of a knife.

And then she saw Gerry Abrams's dark hair and she finally realized that he was struggling with another man, one who matched his six-foot-one height but outweighed him by at least forty pounds of muscle.

Then Trepalli was on the assailant, both hands clamped on the man's knife hand, trying to keep it away from Abrams. Abrams clamped one hand on the assailant's other hand, but despite their best efforts, they couldn't subdue him. The best they could do was a crab-like dance that brought all three closer to the foot of the bed.

Despite the clanging of the alarm, she could hear grunting noises coming from all three men.

Kate stepped back, grabbed a pillow from the empty bed next to McKell's, jerked the pillow out of its case, and turned back to the fight. The assailant still had his back to her. She sidled closer, looking for an opening. Then Trepalli saw her. With all his strength, he jerked on the man's knife hand and stepped away, clearing the way for her.

She stepped in and slipped the pillowcase over the man's head. He roared in fury and tried to twist away, but her constables kept him in position. Kate wrapped her fists in the pillowcase and jerked back. At the same time, her boot shot out and kicked the back of his knee.

He lost his balance, and unable to catch himself, fell back, hitting his head on the hard metal railing of the hospital bed. The knife went flying, to land on the windowsill.

A moment later, Trepalli flipped him over and pinned him down with a foot on his back while Abrams jumped on his butt and slapped the cuffs on him. Then they pulled him into a sitting position on the floor, his back against the footboard.

Once she was sure he was secure, Kate turned toward McKell, almost afraid of what she'd find. He lay still, his eyes closed as if he were sleeping. But no one could sleep through all that noise and commotion. Either he was unconscious, or he was dead.

CHAPTER 22

JAKE TURCOTTE was tall, and he was massive, with heavy shoulders and a deep chest. The green scrubs he had stolen in order to get into McKell's room strained over his chest and there was a rip under the armpit from the struggle. He had a short black beard, threaded with silver, and his short black hair was damp with blood from where he had hit the corner of the bed.

The injury didn't keep him from struggling against Trepalli as the constable hauled him to his feet and dragged him to the empty bed. Turcotte almost broke free before Trepalli kicked his feet out from under him, sending the man down on his rump, hard.

The man swore at Trepalli and tried to bite him.

Kate went over to the windowsill, took the knife, and walked over to where Turcotte was sitting on the floor. She grabbed his short hair and pulled his head back, revealing his vulnerable throat. The moment she placed the tip of the knife under his chin, he stopped struggling, but not cursing.

"Shut up," said Kate calmly. A trickle of blood appeared at the juncture of knife and skin. Turcotte's eyes rolled wildly but he shut up.

Trepalli gave her an uncertain glance but unlocked one of Turcotte's hands, then looped the handcuffs through the bed railing and hauled his free hand up to the empty cuff. A moment later, he and Kate stepped back. Turcotte resumed his cursing, but they ignored him. Let him try to drag the bed through the doorway.

Kate set the knife back on the windowsill and turned back to Abrams. She had forced him to sit down, even though he had insisted he was all right. Turcotte's knife had sliced into the muscle of his right biceps, narrowly missing the brachial artery, judging by the fact that the bleeding under the balled-up pillowcase was slowing down. And the fact that he was still alive.

There was a heavy smell in the room, partly the metallic stink of blood, but no doubt also the up-close smell of testosterone.

She had thought McKell was dead until she noticed the slow rise of his chest. She had flipped the sheet down to discover that he was unharmed—or at least, had no knife injury. Why he hadn't woken up was a mystery. She had run to the hallway only to find it deserted. There would be no help for now.

The alarm suddenly cut out, bringing blessed silence punctuated by Turcotte's swearing.

"Shut up," she said again, not even looking at him. He fell silent and she took a second to close her eyes in relief. "Trepalli," she said finally, turning to her constable. "There's got to be a supply room on this floor. Go find some bandages."

He nodded and turned to go, then stopped and looked at Turcotte.

"She stopped herself," he said in a low voice. "Make a move and I'll shoot you."

Kate's eyebrow rose and she watched the young constable leave the room. She glanced at Turcotte, but he was staring at the floor. When she looked at Abrams, she found him grinning.

"Who knew he had it in him?" he said. He was First Nation from up around Churchill, and had suffered a lot of scarring on his face from chicken pox when he was a kid. It gave him a forbidding look, until he smiled.

Kate knew what he meant. Trepalli was a fine young officer but he didn't tend to violence. She had never heard him utter a threat, but she fully believed this one.

"How are you feeling?" she asked Abrams. The whole right side of his pale blue tee-shirt and jeans was soaked in blood, but it wasn't a critical injury. His dark eyes looked even darker, his face gray, and his black hair was matted with sweat. Shock?

How ironic that they were in a hospital and she couldn't get any help for him. But as far as she could tell, the floor was now deserted. Maybe the entire hospital was deserted. Still, someone had turned the alarm off. The firefighters were here.

"Keep the pressure on," she ordered, and went to see to the Winnipeg officer.

She knelt on one knee by his side and felt for a pulse on his neck. She didn't dare turn him over, in case there was damage to his spine, but the pulse was faint and regular, and she couldn't see any blood. She ran her hand over his curly brown hair and found a lump by his ear.

Where was the second officer? She turned to Turcotte to ask him when a sound in the hallway stopped her. She stood up, her hand reaching for her weapon.

In the eerie silence, all she could hear was Turcotte's heavy breathing and the sound of footsteps coming down the hall, pausing regularly. Whoever was coming toward them was stopping at each room before moving on. Without thinking, she unsnapped her holster and pulled out her Glock. She heard a small movement from Abrams and waved him back into his chair.

Where was Trepalli?

Then the door pushed open and a figure appeared in the doorway. She had automatically assumed the two-handed stance that had been drilled into her at the academy, all those years ago.

Bert eyed the weapon, then looked around the room, one eyebrow lifted.

"Jesus, Kate," he said. "I can't leave you alone for two minutes, can I?"

* * *

The firefighters who swarmed the floor moments after Bert arrived tried to evacuate them but Kate refused. She knew they were only doing their job, but so was she, and she was not taking McKell into the chaos of an evacuation when there was no fire. Cassidy might be out there, just waiting for an opportunity. The firefighters glared at her but carried on with their sweep. Even they suspected there was no fire, or they would have forced the issue.

Bert stepped outside to call for reinforcements just as Trepalli returned with a man in tow. The man wore the ubiquitous green scrubs of just about every medical person in the hospital. By the look on both their faces, Trepalli had had to insist. Like Bert, the stranger stopped in the doorway and took in the situation.

"I'm Chief of Police Kate Williams, Mendenhall," she said. "You are?"

"Chief, this is Dr. Jarvis," said Trepalli. He carried a bulging, plain white plastic bag, the kind grocery stores used. "He's going to help."

It sounded vaguely threatening. Apparently the doctor thought so, too, because he bristled. Kate stepped in front of him to get his attention.

"Unconscious from a blow to the head," she said, pointing at the Winnipeg officer. "Pulse thready but regular." She pointed at Abrams. "Knife wound. It needs tending but the bleeding has slowed down."

The doctor nodded. He cast a professional eye on both men, then lingered over Turcotte, handcuffed to the bed, with a trickle of drying blood on his head. Finally he saw McKell in the bloody sheets and the blood spatter on the wall behind him. He took a step toward him. Kate put a hand on his arm. The room was starting to get very crowded.

"He wasn't injured in the attack," she explained. "The blood is all from Constable Abrams." Who was going to bleed to death if the doctor didn't do something soon. "I don't know why he's not conscious."

The doctor plucked the clipboard from its plastic stand at the foot of the bed and scanned the pages. "Sedated," he stated. He walked over to the head of the bed and checked McKell's wrist. He nodded with satisfaction. "All right," he said finally, looking at all of them. "Out." He pointed to Turcotte. "Take him with you."

When Trepalli headed for Turcotte, Dr. Jarvis shook his head. "Not you, smart boy. You're going to help me."

Trepalli's face blanched and Abrams chuckled. The doctor pulled out a cell phone and made a few calls in between ordering Trepalli to remove Abrams's tee-shirt and pull out some cotton swabs and disinfectant from the plastic bag.

Kate looked down at the Winnipeg officer, wondering if she should do something about him before dealing with Turcotte. The doctor saw her and shook his head.

"Leave him. We've just received the all clear. My colleagues will be here to help in a minute."

Kate nodded, then walked over to McKell. She stared down at him, while behind her, the doctor ordered Trepalli around in a clipped tone.

McKell still looked asleep, as if he were home in bed. She brushed a hand over his forehead. "Don't you worry, Rob," she whispered. "I won't let the bastard get you."

A noise at the door attracted her attention. Bert was standing in the doorway, staring at her. "I'll have a crew here soon," he said. For the first time, she noticed that he was in uniform, but wearing the short-sleeved shirt with the patch and the insignia on his shoulder tabs. "We'll take custody of your friend here and search the hospital."

Did that mean he planned to search for Cassidy or the missing officer? Both?

She nodded and almost staggered as a wave of fatigue rolled over her. The adrenaline had worn off. Before she could take a step, Bert was next to her and holding her arm.

"Come on," he said gently. "Let's find you a chair."

* * *

The Winnipeg Police Services building had four interrogation rooms, each one with its own viewing room, although these were rarely used anymore. A few years back, a federal government grant had paid for the wiring of each of the rooms and now interrogations could be watched from either the small communication room or from a computer screen on any computer with the right access code.

Bert had brought her and Trepalli into the communications room to watch the interrogation, which apparently was going to be short lived. Turcotte wouldn't talk. At all.

"Did he ask for a lawyer?" asked Trepalli.

Bert shook his head. He placed a wrapped sandwich in Kate's hands and handed one to Trepalli, who accepted it eagerly.

"No," said Bert. "He hasn't asked for anything or anyone. He's just not talking."

On the screen, Turcotte sat across from the detective questioning him. The camera faced Turcotte, and all she could see of the detective was a broad back in a white shirt, rolled up sleeves, and a balding head. Turcotte had a bandage taped to his forehead, from where he had struck his head on the bed. He was still in the green hospital scrubs, and the short sleeves revealed hairy, tattooed arms, impressively muscled. Despite his size, there was no fat on the man. She couldn't remember from his rap sheet how old he was but he looked to be about fifty. He, too, was balding, leaving a deep widow's peak in his thick, black hair. An old scar left a white track down his right temple and halfway down his cheek.

Kate unwrapped the sandwich and ate it, not because she was hungry but because she knew she had to keep up her strength. She was so tired she was light-headed. The adrenaline rush had subsided, leaving her spent and cranky. She ate mechanically, not really tasting the ham sandwich, and watched the detective futilely trying to get a response from Turcotte.

The firefighters sweeping the fourth floor had found the missing Winnipeg police officer unconscious in the bathroom of the small waiting room. He had a concussion but otherwise was all right. Thank God.

The first one, the one they had almost stumbled on in McKell's room, would also be all right, or so the doctors thought.

She had tried to send Trepalli home with Abrams, but Trepalli had balked and really, she could understand. Everything was still hanging. She felt like she was waiting for the second shoe to drop. So she had waited until four Winnipeg police officers arrived, two to stand watch inside the room with McKell, two to stand watch outside, before agreeing to go to Winnipeg police headquarters with Bert.

She felt like death warmed over.

It didn't help that Bert stood so close to her she could feel the heat of his body through the thin cotton of her shirt.

"What were you doing at the hospital?" she asked.

Bert glanced up at her from the screen. "When I heard there was a fire alarm at the hospital, I knew something was wrong." He shrugged. "I came as fast as I could."

Kate nodded and continued watching the interrogation. This was getting them nowhere. Turcotte knew he was going back to jail. He clearly saw no reason to cooperate with the police in getting him there. And the man had been close to Cassidy in jail. That close a bond would be hard to break. Even Hombert had said there wasn't much Turcotte wouldn't do for Cassidy. Family, of a sort.

She chewed slowly, studying the guy. He held himself straight-backed, as if he were sitting at attention.

She stopped suddenly, the sandwich halfway to her mouth.

"What?" said Trepalli.

"How far back did we check him out?" she asked slowly. She turned to look at her constable. "Doesn't he look like former military to you?"

Trepalli's eyebrows rose slowly. Then he pulled his phone out.

CHAPTER 23

THE DETECTIVE, George Stravinski, was much taller and younger than Kate would have expected from staring at the back of his balding head. He had fine, sandy hair and warm brown eyes and so few lines that the term "Baby Face" came to mind, but Kate knew he wouldn't have made detective if he didn't have the experience and the intelligence.

"Ma'am, I really don't think you should go in there alone," said Stravinski outside the interrogation room. A burly police constable stood on one side of the doorway, pretending he wasn't listening.

The interrogation rooms were in the basement of the building, along a wide hallway painted a stark white, with nothing but a series of brown doors labeled "1" through "4" to relieve the tedium. Industrial grade linoleum lined the floor in gray. A faint smell of sewer gas completed the appealing package.

"He did time for raping his girlfriend and beating her senseless," continued Stravinski, "but we suspect there were others." He moved the file folder he was holding to the other hand and glanced up at Bert, looking for support. "Everything on his sheet indicates a pathological hatred of women."

Well, it was nice to know he had so much in common with Cassidy.

"That's what I'm counting on," said Kate grimly. "Don't worry,

Detective. He's chained up and can't hurt me." *And I carry a weapon.*

Although she hadn't drawn her weapon when her constables were struggling to take the knife away from him. And neither had Trepalli. The close quarters had made it too risky.

Stravinski looked to Bert again and found no help there. Finally he sighed. "All right. The DC and I will be next door, watching. Your constable is already there. At the first sign of trouble, yell, and Donnelly and I will be in there." He nodded at the big man standing by the door.

The constable looked down at her and nodded solemnly. Kate tried not to smile. It wasn't funny. Not really. And she could understand Detective Stravinski's concern, but despite being tired and cranky, she knew she was the best person to interview Turcotte. She didn't want to waste time bringing Stravinski up to speed and coaching him on how to lead Turcotte to where she wanted him.

Bert placed a warm hand on her shoulder and squeezed, startling her. She glanced around but he was already walking to the viewing room next door. What kind of game was he playing? First he broke up with her, then there was no contact for days while she dealt with John Stendel instead, and now he was back, all solicitous and supportive?

She shook it off. This wasn't the time for distractions. She needed to deal with the problem behind this door.

Without another word, she took the file folder from Stravinski and pushed open the door.

The small room smelled rank with sweat, which was a good sign. Despite his mulish refusal to speak, Jake Turcotte was nervous.

He looked up at her entrance and a look flitted across his face, so fast that she only got an impression of something furtive. And ugly.

His hands were chained to a metal eye screwed into the heavy metal table, which in turn was bolted to the floor. His feet were chained to a similar eye on the floor.

He can't reach you, she reminded herself as she sat down in the wooden chair across from him.

"Mr. Turcotte," she said equably.

He fixed her with dark eyes filled with loathing but remained silent. The look unnerved her a little, but she didn't allow any of that to show on her face.

"May I call you Jake?" she asked sweetly.

"Fuck you, bitch," he said quietly but with venom.

Kate allowed one eyebrow to rise. "Oh, that's right. You don't like us. Women, I mean. That's how you ended up in jail, isn't it?" She leaned forward a little. "Because of a woman?"

He glared at her but didn't answer. She opened the file folder and spent a moment studying the information in it.

"Yes," she said softly, not looking up at him. "She was your girlfriend, wasn't she? She turned you in to the cops."

"Stupid bitch," muttered Turcotte under his breath.

Kate kept reading as if she hadn't heard him. "And she's not the only woman who's betrayed you. Didn't your mother call the cops on you when you were seventeen?" She kept reading and then looked up at him. "And nineteen?" She shook her head in regret. "You don't do so well with women, do you, Jake?"

"What the fuck do you want?" he demanded, rattling the chains on his hands in frustration.

Kate shrugged. "I'm just trying to figure you out. I'm trying to understand what would drive a man like you to become the bitch of a shit like Thomas Cassidy."

That caught his attention. He didn't look at her but grew very still.

Careful, now.

"You're bigger than he is," she continued softly. "You've got the street smarts. But you're the one doing all the dirty work. I guess he must be smarter than you."

A small smile formed on his face but he stubbornly refused to look at her.

"I'm nobody's bitch," he said calmly.

She shrugged again. "You asked to be transferred to his cell. You knifed Cassidy's previous cell mate. Sounds like true love to me."

"Trust a woman to get it wrong," said Turcotte with contempt.

"Okay," said Kate, "so how am I wrong?"

He shrugged, as if he were bored.

"So if you're not lovers," said Kate musingly, "you must be friends. Good friends, judging by the fact that you tried to kill Deputy Chief McKell for him."

He shrugged again. "I didn't try to kill anybody."

Kate cocked her head and stared at him. "I was there, Jake," she reminded him. "What did McKell ever do to you?"

"He's a cop!" said Turcotte, grinning in amusement. "Isn't that enough?"

Gotcha.

"But... Cassidy was a cop, too," she said, pretending confusion.

Turcotte grew very still but he didn't say anything. Kate studied him for a moment, her suspicion confirmed.

"You already knew that, didn't you?" she asked softly. "Probably because you served with him in Afghanistan."

Turcotte started then tried to cover it up with a shrug. "You're whistling in the wind, lady."

Kate laughed. "You know what I've learned about Afghanistan, Jake? Two things. One. I learned that Afghanistan is the world's largest producer of marijuana." She leaned forward. "You and Cassidy met over there, and you made connections, connections that allowed you to import world class marijuana into Canada. You and Cassidy were partners. At least until he got caught and you were sent away for beating your girlfriend. You have a bad temper, Jake."

She waited but he refused to look up at her.

"The other thing I've learned about Afghanistan is that Canadian soldiers distinguished themselves as snipers there. We're checking your records right now, Jake. I'm willing to bet that we'll find you were a sniper in Afghanistan." She paused. "Though you can't have been very good," she added softly, "since McKell is still alive."

His head jerked up. "If I'd wanted him dead, you stupid bitch, he'd be dead."

She watched him in silence for a few minutes, thinking. Finally she nodded.

"I believe you," she said. "McKell never did anything to you. I think Cassidy wanted you to kill him, but you just wanted to stop him from testifying in front of the parole board."

Turcotte opened his mouth as if to answer, then closed it and glanced away.

"Did he tell you why he hated McKell so much?" she asked. She waited a moment but he didn't look up, so she continued. "He and McKell were MPs together at Shilo. McKell suspected him of raping a bunch of girls but Cassidy left the military before anything could be proven. But then McKell found out that Cassidy had a nice little importing business in Winnipeg and helped take him down."

"The fucker should have left Tom alone," he muttered, still not looking at her.

Kate shrugged. "If there's one thing a good cop can't abide, it's a bad one. Heck, even inmates hate a bad cop."

Turcotte's cheeks were red and the smell of him almost made her gag, but she took shallow breaths and continued.

"Last year, McKell showed up at the parole board hearing and convinced the board not to let Cassidy out. When Cassidy found out that you were getting out just before this year's parole board hearing, he convinced you to keep McKell from messing with his application again. He told you that once he was out, you two could start up your little business again. Because he's the brains of the operation, isn't he?" she asked sympathetically. "He knew if he could only speak to the parole board without McKell there, they would let him out. After all, he kept his nose clean in prison by getting guys like you to do his dirty work for him. How many guys did you cut for him?"

Turcotte glanced up at her, uncertainty and wariness in his eyes.

"You're a lying bitch," he muttered. "Tom is my friend."

"Sure he is," said Kate sympathetically. "But has he contacted you since he got out? Even to say thanks? He got you to arrange McKell's accident, putting you at risk if you got caught. And you don't even know where he is, do you?"

He shook his head minutely and Kate sighed.

"Don't feel bad," she said gently. "That's what he does. He uses people up and then he throws them away."

She rolled her shoulders to try and relieve the tightness. She leaned forward. "Jake, you tried to kill a police officer. Twice. You're going back to jail. All that's left now is to cooperate for a reduced sentence... and to see if Cassidy will be going back in with you or not."

He was silent for a long time, and she gave him the time. He wasn't the brightest bulb in the pack. It might take a while for him to work it all out. Finally he looked at her. His eyes were no friend-lier, but at least he wasn't cursing her anymore.

"What do you want from me?"

"Tell me everything. From the beginning."

So he told her. He told her about Afghanistan and how he and Cassidy had gotten together in Winnipeg to import marijuana. He admitted that he had asked to be transferred to Red Hill, using for an excuse the fact that he had grown up there and that he wanted to stay there once his sentence was up. But in reality, he asked for the transfer because Cassidy asked him to. And once he arrived at Red Hill, he and Cassidy started planning to get rid of McKell.

"How did you know about the chiefs' meeting?" she asked

when he stopped.

He shrugged. "Tom told me."

Of course he did. Newspapers were available in the prisons.

"How did you know McKell would be driving my car?" she asked.

He looked at her, startled. "Your car?" He shrugged. "A guy I know owed me a favor. I got him to follow McKell and tell me when he was getting close. My guy described the car he was driving. All I had to do was wait on the overpass with binoculars."

"And shoot him," said Kate, much more calmly than she felt. This asshole was talking about how he had almost killed her DC. Her friend.

The fact that McKell had been driving her car was nothing more than a coincidence.

And then she remembered.

"How did you know when he would be coming into town?" she asked softly.

Turcotte's gaze flickered toward her but didn't actually meet hers. He looked down at his chained hands and didn't reply.

"How did you know, Jake?" asked Kate softly. Inside, rage began to build from the pit of her stomach to her chest, almost choking off the words.

"The parole board hearing was that day," he mumbled. "Tom told me he would be there."

Kate swallowed hard and took her hands off the table for fear they would tear his throat out. She placed them palm down on her thighs. They were trembling.

"But the parole board hearings are closed and you didn't know what time he had to be there. You couldn't wait around all day on that overpass, could you?" she asked. "Too much chance someone would see you. No, you had to narrow the window. Didn't you?"

He swallowed audibly but still refused to meet her gaze.

Breathe, she told herself. *Keep it together.*

"And then Tom told you about the chiefs' meeting. If McKell

went to that meeting, you would know almost exactly what time he would drive by the overpass. So you had to make sure he was the one going to the chiefs' meeting. And for that, you had to get me out of the way." She stopped and waited, breathing in and out. In and out. Watching him.

Finally, almost unwillingly, he looked up at her.

"So you hired someone to take my mother out. My seventy-eight-year-old mother."

His gaze remained fixed on her, as if he couldn't tear it away.

"It wasn't my idea," he said in a low voice.

Jesus Christ in a handbag.

"How much did you pay him?" she asked, her voice rising. "What's the going rate these days for knocking over a little old lady with a *car* and breaking her leg and her ribs, and giving her a concussion, and scraping her face *raw*?"

She was breathing fast now and her hands had balled into fists.

"Where do you find the piece of *shit* willing to do that?" She was shouting and suddenly she was on her feet. Turcotte looked up at her in alarm, his hands rising to protect himself automatically, only to stop short when the chain curbed the movement.

"It wasn't my idea!" he repeated urgently. "*Tom* told me who to call!"

Kate was already moving to go around the table when the door opened and Bert walked in, with Trepalli right behind him.

"Chief Williams," he said firmly. "Detective Stravinsky will take it from here."

* * *

Kate stood on the other side of the mirror, watching while Turcotte confessed to planning both attacks on McKell, under Cassidy's instructions. If he knew where Cassidy was, he wasn't telling. Kate suspected that he didn't know and that he was beginning to realize that Cassidy had set him up.

"It's going to be tough proving Cassidy's involvement," said Detective Stravinsky when he finally joined them in the small viewing room. "All we have is Turcotte's word that Cassidy put him up to it." On the other side of the one-way glass, the interrogation room was empty, Turcotte having been taken away.

Kate shook her head. "I think the circumstantial evidence is strong enough to link Cassidy to the attempts. After all, Turcotte had no reason to hurt McKell."

Bert looked at her in sympathy. "All that proves is that Cassidy told Turcotte about McKell. Not that he asked him to kill the guy."

Trepalli cleared his throat and they all turned to look at him.

"We can get a warrant to check Turcotte's financials," he suggested. "I'd be willing to bet a very large sum of money that he doesn't have the funds to pay for a lookout, or for someone in St. Lambert to take your mother out."

Bert looked at him and grinned, but all Kate wanted to do was throw up.

She picked up her jacket from the back of the only chair in the small room. "I need to get back to the hospital."

"I'm coming, too," said Trepalli, also straightening.

He looks tired, thought Kate. *He's been running on fumes, too.*

"You both need to go home," objected Bert. "You look like hell. We've got it covered at this end."

Kate looked at him. "You had it covered before, and look what happened."

Bert's ruddy face got even ruddier. "It's different now," he said.

Kate smiled thinly. "Yeah. Because now you believe me."

She walked out of the communications room, aware that Trepalli was right behind her. They made their way down the hall to the stairway in silence. When she glanced at the boy's face, she found it set on neutral and almost sighed.

That had been mean and they both knew it.

* * *

Kate and Trepalli walked out of the lobby of the Winnipeg Police Services building, joined by a stream of civilian workers leaving after the workday. Kate paused on the sidewalk outside the main doors. Cars passed slowly on their way to the main artery of Portage Avenue. Cars honked in the distance and the faint wail of an ambulance could be heard. It was past five o'clock. Rush hour.

"Maybe we should find a coffee shop and wait it out," suggested Trepalli, standing next to her.

"Good idea," she said.

But her work boots remained firmly planted on the sidewalk as she breathed in the exhaust from the passing cars, mingled with the smell of juniper planted in the long planters across the front of the building. She could smell wet earth, too. Someone had just watered the plants.

The sun was getting low in the sky, casting long shadows on the buildings across the street. Only the top floors of the tallest buildings still had sunlight falling on them. Already the day was cooling down. The maple trees in the planters along the sidewalk already had a pink tinge to their leaves.

Kate stood still, letting fatigue roll over her. Her sandwich rested at the bottom of her stomach like a rock. Should they go back to Mendenhall? An hour, maybe an hour and a half at this time of day, to Mendenhall. She could go to the detachment, make sure everything was all right, and get Trepalli back home. Then she could go through McKell's files. He had to have one on Cassidy somewhere—if not a paper file, then somewhere on his computer. There had to be a clue somewhere in there as to Cassidy's whereabouts. Someone he would turn to. Then she'd grab a few hours of sleep before heading back to Winnipeg.

But Trepalli had gone through McKell's files, and she had already gone through his computer. There hadn't been anything on Cassidy.

"Something wrong, Chief?" asked Trepalli.

She turned to look at him, ignoring the people streaming behind them. "You didn't find anything in McKell's files, did you?"

"No, ma'am." He uncrossed his arms and looked down at her.

Those deep blue eyes were now bloodshot and tired looking. "You searched his computer, right?"

She nodded. "But nobody searched his house."

Trepalli's eyebrows rose. "No, ma'am," he said slowly. "Nobody did."

Kate looked at the street again, the shadows deepening in doorways, the cars driving by in an effort to get home. She glanced up at the sky. Clouds were beginning to move in.

She swallowed hard as a cold feeling settled in the pit of her stomach.

"Chief? What is it?"

"Trepalli, where is the one place Cassidy would be certain no one would look for him?"

Marco Trepalli stared down at her for long seconds and then Kate saw the realization hit him.

"DC McKell's house," he said softly.

CHAPTER 24

WHEN THEY reached the rental car, which Kate had parked on her usual side street, they found a smiling Bert leaning against the driver's side door, arms crossed. He watched them approach, one eyebrow raised.

He must have used a side exit to get to the car without them seeing him. Clearly, she was predictable.

Kate frowned at him as they approached.

"How'd you beat us here?" asked Trepalli. He, like Kate, wasn't smiling.

Something about their mood finally penetrated Bert's good humor. He stopped smiling. "What's the matter?"

Kate pulled the car keys out of her pocket and clicked the button to unlock the doors. "Change of plans," she said grimly. "We're going to Mendenhall."

"Okay," he said after a moment. He straightened and waited for a man and a woman to walk by before asking, "Why?"

So she told him, expecting to see his face retreat to the careful neutrality he had been adopting lately, the expression that told her he wanted to humor her. But it didn't. Instead, he nodded.

"I'll drive."

Kate blinked. "You can't. The rental agreement—"*Hypocrite.*

He raised a hand to stop her. "Look at you two," he said, turning the movement into a kind of wave in their direction. "You both look like you haven't slept in two weeks. You're in no shape to drive."

"But the renta—"*A burning-in-hell hypocrite.*

"Kate, I've given you your options. If you or Trepalli get behind the wheel, I'm having you pulled over and the car towed."

Trepalli casually moved away, turning his back to them and studying the display window of a musical equipment rental shop.

Kate finally closed her mouth. Part of her wanted to say bad words, but the rational part of her realized he was right. She was physically, mentally, and emotionally exhausted. She would do no one any good if she drove them off the road.

"Fine," she said and tossed him the keys. "I have some phone calls to make anyway."

* * *

Kate strode into the detachment and despite everything, her spirits lifted. Someone had left the coffee on too long, as usual, and now it smelled burnt. She breathed in the old coffee smell and the lingering smell of shoe polish as she walked toward the duty room. The duty desk was empty when she passed it but she could see her constables getting ready in the duty room by the weapons locker.

Jim O'Hara looked around as she entered and nodded acknowledgement.

"We're ready, Chief," he said. "Your vest is in your office."

Kate examined her constables, making sure they each wore a vest. Kyle Holmes was helping Abrams with a recalcitrant strap, but otherwise they seemed prepared. She studied Gerry Abrams with a frown but he just shrugged. She couldn't deny him the right to participate, but she would have to make sure he kept to the periphery of the operation.

She considered her options. Each one had a service weapon, but she would like to have at least one or two rifles. She swallowed hard as she remembered that McKell was the best shot with a rifle.

Trepalli walked in behind her and threaded his way past his

colleagues, heading for the locker room where the vests were kept.

"And one for me, Trepalli," called Bert, walking in last.

Unlike her and Trepalli, Bert was still in his short-sleeved shirt. He hadn't taken the time to go back to his office to grab his jacket before they left Winnipeg. Kate suspected he hadn't trusted her to wait for him.

"Ma'am?" She looked around. O'Hara nodded her away from the others.

"What is it?" she asked when they were far enough away for discretion.

"Your niece was here today, looking for Trepalli."

Amanda. Holy cow, she had completely forgotten about Amanda. She glanced at Trepalli, but he was busy strapping his vest on.

Then St. Ives walked in, ready to start his shift. He stopped in surprise at the sight of all of them. So Kate provided a quick briefing.

"What do you want us to do?" he asked when she finished. His faint French accent seemed more pronounced tonight. He had been born in France but had moved to rural Quebec when he was five.

"You will take the desk and coordinate as needed," she told him. "We'll wait for the fresh shift to come on. Once we are in position, I want them to evacuate the neighboring houses until we have Cassidy in custody. If he's there."

St. Ives nodded his understanding. At that moment, Fallon walked in and stopped in his tracks when he saw them all gathered.

It took almost an hour, but eventually everyone was briefed and ready to roll out. Kate decided to keep her rental car. She and Bert would take point, since Cassidy wouldn't confuse the Ford for a police car.

McKell's house was in an older neighborhood of Mendenhall, one that had been built in the fifties to accommodate the influx of personnel at Canadian Forces Base Shilo after World War II. The houses were all small but they were well kept and sat on large lots. The entire neighborhood had mature trees and tailored lawns.

Night had descended on Mendenhall while they were getting ready, aided by the clouds that had rolled in from the north. Bert parked on McKell's street, three houses down, and waited in the car while she walked up to the house next to McKell's. Her jacket hid her vest, but Bert's vest would pop against his light-colored shirt the moment he stepped out of the car.

They had already determined that the house on the other side of McKell's was empty, and they had set up roadblocks at either end of McKell's street and the street behind his house to keep people from entering the area. Her constables were even now evacuating the houses across the alley from McKell's house. She had chosen to take the nearer houses. If anyone was going to get shot, it would be her, not one of her people.

Bert was keeping an eye on McKell's dark house, rifle ready. That gave her a certain amount of comfort. Not a lot, but some.

She had left her cap in the car and carried a clipboard, hoping that from a distance she would look like someone taking a survey. Now the wind brushed her cheeks with cold, bringing with it the smell of rain and mulch.

She could be wrong and all this was for nothing. But it made sense. McKell's house was the one place no one had thought to look for Cassidy, the one place he could be reasonably certain of finding empty. Even McKell's brother was staying in Winnipeg, at a hotel, to be closer to the hospital.

She reached the front door and knocked firmly. As her hand dropped to her side, she unsnapped her holster, just in case.

A young girl, no more than sixteen, opened the door. She wore the ubiquitous black yoga pants and a heavy gray sweatshirt with some band name stenciled on the front. It looked large enough to fit someone twice her size. Probably belonged to her boyfriend.

"Good evening, miss," she said with a smile. "Are your parents home?"

Before the girl could do more than notice her uniform, Kate stepped over the threshold, as if she had been invited.

"Hey—" protested the girl, but Kate closed the door.

"I'm Chief of Police Kate Williams," she said quickly, putting up a hand to forestall more objections. "We have an emergency situation and you have to evacuate right now. Is there anyone else in the house?"

The girl gulped and shook her head. "My folks are at a school board meeting and my brother is at the skateboard park."

"Good," said Kate. She took the girl by the arm and led her toward the kitchen at the back of the house. All the houses in the neighborhood had been built along the same layout. "Where's your back door?" she asked.

The girl pointed toward the kitchen with a shaky finger and Kate nodded. "All right. There's an officer waiting in the alley. I want you to go with him and do as he says. This will all be over soon."

"Wait!" The girl dug in her heels and tried to twist away. "My phone!"

Kate tightened her hold and shook her head. "No phones. No pads." The last thing she needed was for the girl to post something on social media before this operation was over.

A moment later, she was through the fence gate to the back alley, where Fallon waited.

"This is the last one," he whispered. "We're all in place, waiting for your signal."

Kate nodded and he took the girl from her and hurried her down the alley, away from McKell's house. Kate hurried back inside the house and to the front door, which she opened. She stepped out onto the front stoop and gave the door a little tug, then turned with a smile and a wave, as if she were saying goodbye, just before the door closed.

All right. She cast a furtive glance up and down the street but saw no one outside anywhere. Some of the houses had their front porch lights on, but some didn't, like McKell's. His house stood dark and silent, almost foreboding.

She looked down at her clipboard and pulled the pen out of her pocket, taking McKell's house key along with it. Like her, McKell kept a spare key to his house in his desk drawer. She pretended to scribble something on the clipboard, then pulled her telephone out of her pocket as if someone had called her. She turned away from McKell's house and quickly punched in O'Hara's number.

"Here, Chief," came his voice almost immediately.

"I'm approaching the house from the front," she said. "Get ready."

"We're in position," he said.

She tucked the phone away, and without looking at her car, headed for McKell's house. She heard the soft click of a car door opening and knew that Bert had slipped out. He would be using the house she had just left to cover his approach, but at one point, he would be fully exposed to anyone inside McKell's house looking out through the plate glass window. A movement on the far side of McKell's house caught her eye but she didn't look around. That would be Trepalli, approaching from the other side.

Her hands shook and she found herself breathing fast.

Keep calm, she ordered herself, just as another part of her realized that this was probably the dumbest plan she had ever concocted. What if Cassidy was on the other side of the front door, with a shotgun?

That was never his M.O., she reminded herself. *He gets other people to do his dirty work.*

Prison changes a man, her subversive self said.

Oh, shut up, she told herself. Then she was at the door and knocking with her left hand, while her right hand inserted the key in the deadbolt lock. A moment later, Trepalli was at her side, his weapon drawn, and she tossed the clipboard into the flower bed below the living room window. She pulled her Glock out of her jacket pocket.

Taking a deep breath, she finished twisting the key and heard the soft snick of the deadbolt being withdrawn. At least there was no window in the door itself. She glanced over her right shoulder to see Bert at the foot of the stairs, ready with the rifle. He nodded at her. She looked over at Trepalli and he nodded, too.

Glock in her right hand, she used her left hand to depress the handle. The heavy wooden door swung inward and she stepped in and to the right and felt more than saw Trepalli slide to the left. The first thing she noticed was the faint smell of gasoline. Then she noticed how cold it was, as if all the windows were open. Then she heard a scrabbling sound and her left hand scrambled to find the light switch. She found it and flicked it on just as she heard a crash at the back of the house.

"Mendenhall police!" came a voice from the backyard. "Come out with your hands up!"

She and Trepalli moved in unison toward the kitchen as a door slammed. Kate found the kitchen light switch and flicked it on. A man standing at the back door spun toward them, his hands out and empty.

His hair was bleached blond but there was no disguising those dead green eyes, or the tattoos peeking out from under his short-sleeved white tee-shirt.

"Thomas Cassidy," said Kate. "Step into the kitchen and get to your knees."

His glance flickered to the left and Kate smiled grimly.

"Make one move toward the steps, and I will shoot you."

"I would listen to her, Cassidy," said Bert calmly behind her. "And if she doesn't get you, you can bet I will."

Cassidy hesitated a moment longer. Then footsteps ran up the front porch and into the living room as her constables converged on the house, and a face appeared at the window of the back door—O'Hara, face lit from the light spilling out of the kitchen so that he looked like Death itself.

The fight went out of Cassidy. He stepped into the kitchen and went to his knees, lacing his hands behind his head.

CHAPTER 25

THOMAS Cassidy had filled red plastic jerry cans with gasoline and left one in each room of McKell's house, including the basement. Clearly, he had planned to torch the place when he was through with it. By the time they got through processing him and placing him in a cell, Kate was reeling with fatigue. Initial reports had been submitted and she'd sent everyone not on duty home.

St. Ives was busy on the phone with the RCMP detachment in Winnipeg. Mendenhall would transport Cassidy in the morning. In the meantime, he would spend the night in her cells.

"You have enough to hold him for breach of parole," said Bert, leaning against the door jamb of her office.

She nodded. "I'll want to talk to him before we take him back to Winnipeg." She could hear Fallon in the duty room, typing up his report. The other three, Frederickson, Black, and Jones, would continue patroling until he was done and could replace one of them.

Bert eyed her doubtfully. "Not tonight, I hope."

She shook her head. "I'm asleep on my feet," she admitted. "I need to get some rest first."

He studied her carefully. Then he stepped into the office and closed the door behind him. Kate watched him, too tired to even wonder.

"Katie," he began in a low voice, "about the other day..."

She put up a hand to stop him. "Don't," she said firmly. "I've been thinking about what you said, and you're right. For me, the job always comes first. Before you. Before Mom, even." She took a deep, trembling breath. "That's not going to change now." The overhead light gave Bert's face a yellow cast and hid his eyes in shadow. "A relationship only gets in the way of doing my job. I've always known that. It was unfair of me to start seeing you, and I'm very sorry."

Bert stood looking down at her, eyes hooded, arms crossed. In that moment, she remembered the warm man smell of him when he woke up, and the feel of his arms around her. It had been good. Very good. She would miss him for a long time.

Her heart squeezed a little but she kept her gaze steady on his. She knew that he'd had second thoughts about breaking up with her, so she had to be the strong one. He was a good man. He needed someone who would think enough of him to always place him first. She wasn't the one for him. And she didn't want to be constrained by his worry for her.

But God, she would miss him.

Finally he sighed. "All right, Katie," he said gently. "I'll be seeing you, then."

She nodded. "Yes. See you, Bert."

* * *

St. Ives took one look at her when she finally came out of her office and called one of the patrol cars to pick her up and take her home. When the car pulled up front of her house, she saw that the lights were on and a strange car was parked in front of it. Amanda.

"Thank you, Constables," she said as she got out of the patrol car.

"No worries, Chief," said Frederickson. "Give the detachment a call when you're ready in the morning and someone will come and get you."

She waved her thanks and trudged up the driveway. She was

going to have to start looking for a new car. A wave of exhaustion rolled over her, almost stopping her in her tracks. The clouds had thinned out and stars peeked through them, although there was no moon. She took a deep breath of the clean air. The roses were long gone, but sweet grass still perfumed the air.

On impulse, she followed the driveway to the back of the house and walked over to where the backyard fell away in an escarpment. Below her spread Mendenhall, all lit up and glowing in the dark. How had she come to love this little town so much? Wasn't she supposed to be a big city girl?

Beyond Mendenhall was a rolling darkness, interspersed every now and then with a dot of light that indicated a farmhouse.

This was a good place. It had taken her a while to see it, but now she couldn't imagine living anywhere else. Even alone. She had made friends here and belonged to the community. In a few years, she could retire here and fill her time with volunteering. If McKell recovered, she would recommend that he be hired as the new Chief of Police and would browbeat the mayor into accepting her recommendation, if need be.

And McKell would recover. He had to.

Her eyes closed against the sting of tears as grief welled up in her.

Get a grip, she finally told herself. *Amanda's inside, waiting, probably wondering what's going on.*

Finally she turned away from the calming view and faced the back of her house. Light spilled out from the kitchen door onto the deck, and there, silhouetted against the window, were Amanda and Trepalli, locked in an embrace.

* * *

Kate landed in Montreal the next day at dinner time. She still felt a little punchy with fatigue, but she had wanted to get back as soon as possible. She walked out of the terminal at the arrivals door and paused when she hit the wall of humidity. Holy cow. Much warmer here than in Manitoba.

"Chief Williams."

She looked around and saw Sergeant Tremblay standing next to a Longueuil police car parked at the curb. The setting sun gilded the side of his face, deepening the grooves on either side of his mouth. The attendant stationed at the door to prevent people from doing exactly what the sergeant was doing gave him a dirty look, which he ignored.

"Welcome back," said Sergeant Tremblay as she approached. He took her duffle bag.

"*Merci*," said Kate, watching as he put the bag in the back seat and opened the passenger door for her. She carefully avoided looking at the attendant. She was wearing jeans, a white shirt, and her heavy, red, Gore-Tex rain jacket. Hardly a police uniform.

She slid into the seat and closed the door, and seconds later, they were off. The sergeant had offered to pick her up at the airport when she called yesterday to let him know she was coming back. They could brief each other on what had been happening in their respective jurisdictions and he could give her a ride to Rose's.

"I appreciate this, Sergeant Tremblay," said Kate.

"My pleasure, Madame," he said gallantly. "Now, tell me what has been happening."

As she spoke, Kate watched the road as he navigated the underpasses and highways that lead away from Pierre Trudeau Airport. Billboards, high rises, hotels, box stores... how had this ever been home?

"Winnipeg has a forensic accountant," she said finally. "They're combing through Cassidy's financials. They've already found evidence in Turcotte's financials that he was paid a large sum of money. Once we connect the two, Cassidy will be charged with conspiracy to commit murder. Twice."

"Good," said Tremblay, accelerating to merge with traffic. Kate saw a sign indicating a turnoff for the Champlain Bridge up ahead. They were getting close.

"How about Chouinard?" she asked.

Tremblay shrugged. The sun was behind them, casting long, low shadows in front of them. To her surprise, traffic was moving along well, if slowly.

"Chouinard gave a statement. It was your Monsieur Turcotte who contacted him. Turcotte gave him instructions to injure your mother, but not kill her." He glanced at her to gauge her reaction but Kate turned away. She still had trouble controlling the killing fury she felt every time she thought about what Turcotte had done. And Chouinard. And Cassidy.

Bastards.

She cleared her throat. "Did you find the money trail?"

"*Oui,*" he confirmed as he took the turnoff. They were approaching the bridge. Now things would slow down. "We will liaise with Winnipeg. Do not worry. Chouinard is going away for a long time."

Kate nodded. Yes, indeed. So were Cassidy and Turcotte.

Let's see Cassidy try to talk his way out of this one.

It took half an hour, during which they filled in the details of their respective investigations, but Sergeant Tremblay finally stopped the patrol car in front of Rose's house. They sat in silence for a moment, then Sergeant Tremblay said, "*Madame,* I wish to apologize for not taking you seriously when you first approached us."

Kate looked at him and blinked. Finally she shrugged. "Let's face it, Sergeant, it was an unlikely story."

He grinned at her and for a moment, the resemblance to McKell was striking. Then he got out and walked around to the other side of the car to take her duffle bag out of the back passenger seat.

Kate let herself out and tried not to notice the twitching curtains in Rose's living room. At least Rose was home. If it had been John, he would have opened the front door to get a good look.

She turned to the sergeant and accepted the bag from him, then stuck her hand out. He shook it firmly.

"Perhaps you would like to have dinner with me before you leave."

Kate stared at him for a moment before his meaning sank in. "Sergeant, are you asking me out on a *date*?"

He shrugged. "Why not? You are attractive and we like each other, no?"

Her eyebrows rose and she felt the heat rising with them. "You are attractive, yes," she said. "But I am not interested in a long-distance relationship. They are very difficult."

He smiled at her gently.

"Nothing is perfect, Chief Williams."

"Goodbye, Sergeant Tremblay."

She watched him get back in the patrol car and drive away before turning back to the house. Rose was standing on the front stoop, arms crossed.

"About time you got back."

* * *

They stayed up late, talking about everything that had happened. Rose was upset that Amanda still hadn't come home, but John was very smug about the whole thing. Kate thought back to how she had found Amanda and Trepalli in her kitchen and decided that John probably had good reason to be smug. Amanda had decided to spend the night at Trepalli's and by the happiness in both their faces, they had clearly worked out their troubles.

She was happy for them, truly she was, but their happiness only highlighted her unhappiness. She had spent the flight thinking about Bert and how empty her future loomed without him.

At least Mom was doing better. She was back at her place and starting to get around with a walker. A nurse dropped in on her every day, and Mr. Stilwell—Fred—was there every time Rose went by. Kate called her mom and promised to come see her in the morning.

When she got up the next morning, John was gone.

"He had an errand," said Rose. "His classes only start at eleven."

After breakfast, Kate walked over to her mother's and spent a couple of hours telling her and Fred what had happened. When she finished, Fred took Hetty's hand and looked at Kate.

"How is your deputy chief doing?" he asked gravely.

"No change," she said, although she hadn't checked today. Come to think of it, she couldn't remember putting her phone in her coat pocket when she left Rose's.

"Is that good or bad?" asked Hetty. If anything, she looked even worse than when Kate left. The whole right side of her face was one glorious purple bruise and they had removed the bandage from her scalp, revealing the shaved area and the crusty stitches.

"I don't know," said Kate. "I just don't know."

She took her time getting back to Rose's, thinking through everything that had happened in the last week. She had the streets to herself, with kids in school and adults at work. Anybody still home was staying inside. To her surprise, the day had dawned clear and bright, but cold, and she walked with her hands tucked inside her coat pockets. Somewhere in the distance, a lawnmower provided an annoying backdrop to the quiet day.

She sighed. She would spend a couple of days here, mend bridges with Rose, and make sure Mom was set up. Then she'd go back and figure out what to do about McKell. Her hands inside her pockets automatically reached for her phone, but she must have left it on the charger in Rose's spare bedroom.

When she turned up Rose's street, she saw John's Forester in the driveway. She glanced at her watch. Ten-thirty. He was going to have to hurry to make it to the university on time.

She turned up the driveway, feeling obscurely sad. It was something about the nip of fall in the air, maybe. Or the letdown after so many days of high adrenalin. Maybe after everything was settled with McKell and Mom, she would take a vacation. Get away from everything and everyone for a while.

She opened the gate and entered the backyard, then closed the gate behind her. Even Rose's backyard was looking a little forlorn.

Leaves from the oak and maple trees were already starting to fall, their edges curled up as if against the cold.

With a sigh, she headed for the door to the sun room and as she opened it, she heard voices inside. She stood in the doorway blinking against the relative darkness inside and closed the door behind her. Then she became aware that the voices had grown still.

Rose and John sat in the loveseat, looking up at her expectantly. She blinked at them, wondering what they were doing. She opened her mouth to ask when she suddenly realized that there was someone else in the room. She turned her head and there, sitting in almost exactly the same spot as Trepalli had occupied, sat Bert.

She stared at him, her mouth slightly open, her mind completely blank.

Bert slowly rose and faced her.

"People have been trying to reach you," he said. "Did you lose your phone?"

A question. She could handle a question.

"I forgot it here. Why?" She found herself tense suddenly. Had he come to tell her something terrible about McKell? No, that didn't make sense.

Bert smiled at her.

"McKell woke up this morning."

Well, yes. She knew he was out of the coma—she'd talked to him. Then her breath caught. She cleared her throat. "And...?"

"And he moved his feet."

Kate sagged in relief, tears welling up. Thank God. Thank God. Thank God.

"Apparently he's complaining about the catheter," added Bert.

She grinned a great big, foolish grin, and she didn't care. McKell was going to be all right.

Then her grin turned to a puzzled smile. She glanced at Rose and John, and then at Bert. When no one offered an explanation, she asked the question.

"What are you doing here, Bert? Surely you didn't come to tell me about Rob?"

Bert took a couple of steps toward her, away from the coffee table and Rose and John.

"No, Katie. I only found out a couple of hours ago, when I landed."

She continued to stare at him, then turned her attention to John.

"You picked him up," she said. She didn't know what she was feeling, but there was a certain amount of outrage in the mix.

"Yep," agreed John, far from contrite. Rose, at least, had the grace to look chagrined.

She turned back to Bert. "Let's just skip over how you got Rose's phone number and circle back to why you're here."

Bert's face took on an expression she had never seen before. If she had to guess, she would hazard that it was something between fear and determination.

"I came to meet your family," he said. "I'm hoping that if they get to know me, they'll help me convince you."

This was making less sense, not more.

"Convince me to do what?" she asked patiently.

"To marry me, of course," said Bert.

Out of the corner of her eye, she saw John pump the air with his fist and Rose elbow him in the ribs, but really, she couldn't take her eyes off Bert's copper-penny eyes and the love she saw in them.

Without a word, she took him by the hand and led him outside, away from Rose and John. She stopped when they finally stood on the flagstone patio.

"We've already discussed why our relationship won't work," she said carefully.

"Shh, Katie," said Bert. He took both her hands and held them tightly. "Nothing is ever perfect, but anything worth having is worth fighting for. And Katie, you are worth having."

He released her hands and wrapped his sturdy arms securely around her in an unspoken promise. Her arms crept up around him to hold him one last time, even as she knew she would have to let him go.

THE END

NOVELS BY THE AUTHOR

Mendenhall Mysteries series:

The Shoeless Kid
The Tuxedoed Man
The Weeping Woman
The Untethered Woman

On Her Trail
Jilimar
Kirwan's Son
Obeah
Backli's Ford

ABOUT THE AUTHOR

Marcelle Dubé grew up near Montreal. After trying out a number of different provinces—not to mention Belgium—she settled in the Yukon, where people still outnumber carnivores, but not by much. Her short fiction has appeared in a number of magazines and anthologies. Learn more about her at www.marcellemdube.com.

www.ingramcontent.com/pod-product-compliance
Lightning Source LLC
Chambersburg PA
CBHW020610260626
47157CB00003B/939